The Secret Library

The Magian Series Book Two

MJ McGriff

ISBN: 978-1-7361622-1-7 (Softcover)
ISBN: 978-1-7361622-2-4 (Hardcover)

To my mom, my loving angel. I pray I made you proud.

CHAPTER 1

SERAPHINA

No one should ever set sail in such a storm. Fierce and furious clouds swallowed up the last bit of dusk. Thunder roared right into the heart of the most hardened pirate of the Pursuer.

Cold raindrops peppered Seraphina Davalos's olive skin as she checked the rigging on the secondary mast one last time. The lantern in her hand clattered as she held it up to the rope, hoping she was seeing shadows instead of a dozen frayed pieces.

By Macario's light, no such luck.

She didn't need to climb all the way up to see the cracks in the mizzenmast glaring at her with every bolt of lightning that streaked across the angry sky. The rigging ropes groaned as she made her way back to the deck, the wood screaming under her feet. Unfortunately, it wasn't the only thing under her feet. Seraphina could easily step on a loose nail or random shard of wood if she wasn't careful.

"Amrit, if you don't move your lanky ass, I will move it for you!"

Captain Mari Adlam charged down the upper deck steps, pushing a poor deckhand out of the way. Despite the lantern lights scattered about the decks, it was hard to see her sharp face and fierce green eyes underneath the shadow of her black tricorn hat.

Amrit, their new boatswain, shimmied down the rigging ropes from the crow's nest. He jumped down the last two rungs, landing square on his feet and into Mari's death stare.

He gave a pitiful bow. "You called, Captain?"

"Is this a joke to you?" Mari snarled.

"No. Just foolish. Might as well leave here in a rowboat."

Seraphina shuffled to the other side of the mizzenmast, where she'd left a sack of coconuts she'd brought aboard. *A rowboat may fare better.*

It had been a week since they slid the ship off the beach and into the sea. Poor Eduardo, the cabin boy, was still fishing water out of the hold, his hands always wet and shriveled. Not to mention that Seraphina wasn't the best seamstress. The patches she'd spent weeks sewing onto the sails would likely unravel at the shortest gust of wind.

But Mari would not hear of staying longer. Ever since she received word of Order ships patrolling the western coast of Bluegate, she was grumpier than usual. As if that were even possible.

"We set sail within the hour!" Mari's voice carried above the creaking of the *Pursuer*. Seraphina's right boot slipped out from under her. She grabbed the handle to the door that led to the lower deck. *By Macario's grace! The last thing I need is a twisted ankle on a shoddy pirate ship in the middle of a storm.* She clutched the railing as she walked down the narrow steps, the ship groaning as it swayed. The waves were getting angrier by the minute. Storms in the Majestic Isles always gave a warning.

Like the storms brought on by one nasty sea serpent.

She remembered the bodies of the drowned strewn about Aridia after the tidal wave in the harbor. The serpent's flames roaring through the Quarter, burning everyone in their path. Her sister, Samara, had finally put an end to that monster, yet Seraphina's chin quivered as those visceral images flashed across her mind.

Her boots hit the bottom step, bringing her back to where she was actually going. Hard thuds bounced off the narrow hallway that led to the cargo hold. It was wider than it was high, the former nun ducking under the splintery ceiling. The handful of wall lanterns swayed with the ship, casting eerie shadows about the vast and practically empty space. Brody, a gentle giant of a pirate, put down a barrel of water with a hard thud in a far corner.

"Dammit to hell!" He pulled at his scraggly strands of blonde hair.

"You all right, Brody?" Seraphina sprang to his side.

He swirled around, trying to smile. "Sorry, Sister."

Her first instinct would've been to spout ten prayers of forgiveness — five for Brody and five just for hearing such crass words. But alas, she was far removed from her life at the Santa Rosa convent.

"Oh, please, Brody. My ears have gotten used to all of your foul language." She handed him the satchel of coconuts in her arms and his thick fingers scrambled to open it.

"That's all I could round up before getting back on board," she said.

He closed the sack and looked up, shaking his head.

"Captain Blackwater wouldn't have us sailing back to Siren's Cove like this." He scowled.

Seraphina wasn't thrilled about Baz Blackwater, the former captain of the *Pursuer*, no matter how smitten her sister was with him. But at least he always had a plan. Whether he shared it—or it worked—was another matter. Nonetheless, the crew always had full confidence in him.

But Baz had his own role to play in the prophecy Macario foretold all those centuries ago. He'd chosen Samara to help save the world. She had to believe Macario also chose Mari to lead this crew to do His bidding. *Wouldn't have been my first choice, though, but who am I to say?*

"Blackwater chose Captain Mari Adlam for a reason," Seraphina said, patting him on the shoulder. "We have to trust in her like we did in him."

Brody nodded, gripping the satchel in his hand. "We'll need some of those prayers, Sister."

Seraphina glanced at the supplies stacked behind them, the barrels, crates, and satchels only taking up a quarter of the hold. *We'll need a miracle, my friend.*

She smiled and winked. "As soon as I heard we were leaving, I sneaked in a few extra ones."

A prayer for her sister, who'd left for the Griffin Vales to find the Spell Keeper.

Prayers for merciful seas, calm winds, and clear skies.

But when Seraphina went topside again, the rain fell sideways, stinging her cheeks. Men scurried about the deck, securing the last of the supplies. The night seemed even darker, the moon lost in the rain clouds. Waves crashed in the darkness, drowning out the commotion on deck.

A hand grabbed her arm and swung her around. Amrit's charcoal-lined eyes bored into hers, water dripping from his slick, black hair.

"Done slacking off?" he yelled over the grumbling ocean behind him.

"I was just—" Seraphina began, a clap of lightning scaring her mouth shut.

The boatswain looked up at the sky, shaking his head. "Get to your post." He stomped away, lightning ripping through the sky.

This is dangerous. They shouldn't leave port in this kind of squall. The same weather that had taken her father's life. *I can't die like that—like he did.*

Seraphina pushed loose strands of wet hair off her face, her long side braid heavy with water. She navigated to the captain's quarters at the back of the ship, ducking and dodging scared deckhands. Some watched her with wary eyes as she approached the door. Ignoring the dread in her stomach, she reached for the handle. The ship lurched and Seraphina fell through the door.

Mari looked up from her desk as Seraphina stumbled through the door, slamming it behind her. Empty ale mugs rolled along the mismatched wood-paneled floor as the ship rocked. Clothes and parchment were strewn across the bed.

"A word, Captain?" Seraphina squeaked as she straightened herself.

Mari removed her hat and tossed it on top of the papers sprawled across her desk.

"Sit."

Seraphina's boots sloshed as she walked across the room, taking care not to step on the pieces of parchment scattered about the wooden floor. She sat down in the only chair across from the captain, the water from her clothes already seeping into the faded green fabric.

"Spit it out," Mari commanded.

Should I just start with the fact that leaving right now is a horrible idea? Seraphina squirmed.

"Don't make me say it again."

Seraphina swallowed. "We cannot sail in this storm. Summer storms in

4

the Isles can always turn into a full-blown hurricane. The ship can barely take a regular storm."

She shifted in the hard-backed chair under Mari's cold glare. "I mean, I got the sails up in time and the rigging on the secondary mast is just minutes away from unraveling again. And supplies! You'll have enough to get to the mainland for sure. But if you plan to go the long way to avoid Order ships in Tradesman Harbor and then continue on to the Siren's Cove, the crew may starve before you clear the southern coasts of the Griffin Vales…"

Mari sat back in her chair.

"And I'm rambling, so I'll stop now." Seraphina folded her hands in her lap.

The Captain raised a brow. "You're right about the storm."

Seraphina sighed. *That's a relief.*

Her eyes darted away from Mari's intimidating stare and onto the map of the Majestic Isles laid out in front of her. They'd set the anchor on the eastern shore of Bluegate Island, the small strip of land at the southernmost edge of the realm. It was the place where she'd been born, spending her childhood running up and down its sandy beaches. The place she'd fled when her parents died, and her sister ran off with the same crew Seraphina now considered friends.

The island where Baz Blackwater battled Order seamen, took over their ship, and sailed it straight at Samara. Where they watched her twin sister master the magic of Macario's scepter and defeat the sea monster that almost burned the entire realm into ashes.

On the shores of Bluegate Seraphina had set her course away from the seminary where she'd thought she'd spend her life serving the Order, and to the place that held the answers she so desperately needed.

They'd defeated one monster. But more were coming.

"Whether or not I sail in this storm is my call," Mari said.

Seraphina's eyes found the floor. "I just wanted to voice my concerns, Captain."

"You're only concerned about finding that stupid library."

She scowled, biting the edge of her lip. *It's not a stupid library!* It was the

Oracle's Athenaeum, the place where the Ancient Order held their sacred teachings. There she would find the rest of the prophecy. Everything she needed to know about the monsters that the second coming of Bedros would release.

Samara needed to know how to use the scepter to defeat them. Summer storms would be the least of their concerns if Seraphina didn't get this information to her sister. Macario's magic had revealed the location of the ancient library in the book she'd found in the seminary back on the mainland. She hadn't labored on that beach mending ropes, sewing sails, and catching fish for an entire month to not find it.

"You can go." Mari rose from her chair, and Seraphina did the same. She turned on her heel and headed out the door.

Thunder rumbled in the distance, the rain relentless.

Macario, please help us all.

CHAPTER 2

MARI

Mari stared at the door long after Seraphina left. She wished she had another mug of ale to drown out the twinge of regret spreading across her chest. She'd promised the former nun she would take her to the mainland. But that couldn't happen.

Not now, anyway.

So why do I feel so crappy about it?

Mari was the captain. Making hard decisions was part of the job.

It was what she'd signed up for when she agreed to take over this ship, its crew, and its infamous legacy. That bastard, Baz, was so sure she could handle this ship and manage the crew. But this lot took the defeat of the sea serpent and Blackwater's departure as reasons to slack off. Piss away the time like those Order bastards weren't hunting them down.

The untimely death of the esteemed ruler of the Majestic Isles had bought them some time. A solid month, to be exact. *Plenty of time to suffer in whatever hell pit he made up.* Those people were serious about their religious traditions and she'd taken plenty advantage of it.

But it wasn't enough time.

Mari sank back into her chair. The map of the Majestic Isles slid to reveal the piece of parchment she'd received from Elsie a few days ago. The former Quarter girl had found a fresh place to offer her personal services along the west coast of Crystal Crest.

Brothel girls were so easy to sniff out. They all shared the same look of desperation behind that fake smile. They would take any extra coin if it brought them closer to getting out of that horrible life. She would know.

So it wasn't hard to make Elsie the eyes and ears Mari needed in that realm. Just when she thought she was paying way too much for way too little, Elsie handed Mari that blasted piece of parchment.

The sly girl had lifted an official order from a naval captain dated a week ago. Mari picked it up with her pale and callused hands, eyeing it as if she would see anything new. But the words still read the same.

"All Order naval officers are to report to Silver Key... The pirate ship *Pursuer* was spotted on Bluegate Island.... must apprehend its captain and crew dead or alive."

Silver Key was spitting distance away from Crystal Crest, the island just north of Bluegate. Those bastards were there right now, and from the looks of her ship, the *Pursuer* would be lucky to outrun a rowboat, let alone a fleet. They'd stayed in the Isles way too long. Blackwater had left her with a fine mess.

A boat beat up to hell. Half a crew. And a nun.

What a way to start a legacy.

She rubbed the back of her sweaty neck, her chest tighter than an Order man's pants. If Baz were captain, he'd have a plan to get them out of the Isles.

I'm not built for this shit. She tossed the parchment to the ground just as the door to her quarters swung open. A soaking wet Amrit stood in the doorway.

"You all right, Captain?" His charcoal-lined eyes weren't nearly so flippant as they'd been earlier, his gaze soft yet unwavering.

"Not now, Amrit."

He closed the door anyway, taking a seat opposite her. "There's no one else here. You don't have to be so cranky."

She rested her head in her hand, not meeting his brown eyes.

"Stop worrying. We'll make it to Siren's Cove." He cracked his knuckles. "Might have half a ship. But we'll arrive all the same."

If she'd had time to wait it out, she would have. But supplies were waiting for her on Crystal Crest. Supplies that would keep them from starving on the way to that Griffin Vale cove. No matter how many times she went over this plan in her head, she couldn't shake the nagging dread in the back of her head. Amrit sat back in the chair, crossing his arms as he always did before he cracked another stupid joke.

"I'm not drunk enough to enjoy your company."

He gave her a sly smile. "You love my company—sober or otherwise."

I don't need company. I need a guarantee this plan is going to work. She grabbed her hat off the desk, shaking the water off it. "I would love it if you left me alone."

"I wouldn't be a great crewman if I didn't support my fearless leader."

Mari slammed the hat down. He didn't even flinch. "Last time I checked, I was the captain of this vessel. I'm all the damn support I need." Never mind the fact that she was nowhere near ready to be anyone's captain. She was a navigator. Master of the compass. Tell her where to go and she would sail it, even if it was to the end of the world. It didn't require being the one everyone turned to for all the answers.

"Do you need to talk through the plan again?"

"No!"

"We can always take our chances in Azulis Key–"

"What part of No don't you understand, boatswain?"

His muscular shoulders remained relaxed, eyes trained on her. This time she maintained her glare, swallowing back the lump of doubt in her throat.

"Aye, Captain," he conceded.

"Is it your life's mission to annoy me, boatswain?"

"Yes. The grumpier you are, the better you sail." Thunder shook the cabin door. "And we're going to need Adlam the navigator tonight."

Rain pattered on the deck above her. Instead of sulking and second-guessing her decisions, she should be sailing them halfway up the coast by now. Mari stood, putting on her hat. Amrit smiled, accentuating his sharp cheekbones and deep-set eyes on his narrow and perfect brown face.

"Raise the anchor," she said. "And tell Ghad to get his bloody hands off my helm."

Amrit nodded, jumping out of his chair, swaggering to the door.

"After you, *Captain*," he said, pulling it open.

She wouldn't dare look him in the eye. She needed her resolve.

So, she nodded instead, stepping back onto the deck of the ship. They'd finally stored away the supplies on deck. The shrouds weren't crawling with sailors trying to mend the frayed pieces of rope.

But to expect they were up to par was just wishful thinking. Everything looked better in the dark.

Deckhands jumped out of her way as she strode toward the quarterdeck. The Isles were slim pickings for finding new crewmen. These lads were wet behind the ears, tattered shirts hanging off their slender bodies. The longer the harbor on the main island was down and out, the less food trickled down to these poor folk on Bluegate. Yet the promise of gold and food was still a hard sell.

"Macario will provide," was the common answer among most of the fishermen that lived there.

Such crap.

In this world, a person provided for himself, because no one else would do it. She'd learned that lesson the hard way back in the brothels on the Enchanted Cape.

"Anchor up!" a sailor cried.

Mari quickened her steps, climbing up the deck steps by two. Ghad was the only one up there, standing clear of the helm.

Smart man.

She walked right past him, not breathing until her fingers gripped the wooden spokes. Her heart pattered in her chest, part nerves and part excitement as her feet found their natural position. It was as if they had their own permanent marks on the deck.

Her hips settled. Back straight. Shoulders relaxed. The ship swayed with the angry waves, the rain lightening up. But she could still smell the storm in the air—a fresh, yet sweet scent that overpowered the salt of the sea.

We aren't out of the woods yet. The hard flapping of the sails in the turbulent wind was music to her ears.

"Anchor aweigh!"

Time to get the hell out of here.

The ship cut through the waves like a dull knife on a cold brick of butter as Mari steered the *Pursuer* out of port. The ocean tried its best to fight, splashing and spraying about the sides of the ship. She wished the moon would show itself, illuminate the shores that were dark and void of life.

It wasn't like she couldn't find her way out. She'd spent every moment on that island memorizing the juts and curves of the shore. But it would be easier with her eyes, instead of her mind. This would be difficult enough already.

How did Baz do it? How was he always so sure of himself all the time?

Fixing the ship was one thing. That was straightforward. But getting out of the Isles?

Setting sail through the realm like she planned was risky, but doable. The Order fleet was scattered around, cleaning up the mess the serpent left behind. It wouldn't be hard to leave Seraphina on the main island to chase after her dusty library.

How the tides changed.

Now taking this route was even worse, sailing right past Mazas, the place where pirates went to rot in jail cells. What if Elsie didn't come through? What if she didn't have enough time to secure the cove on Crystal Crest? They would starve before they ever reached the Griffin Vales.

I hate it when Seraphina's right.

Mari steered the ship further east before turning it north again. The sea was bloody stubborn, the swift wind blowing across her face. The ship creaked and groaned, but she was still afloat, gliding through the water despite its waves of protest.

"Ship's holding up pretty well, Captain."

Mari didn't dare take her eyes off the darkness in front of her to face Amrit. He had a dirty habit of sneaking up on her.

She rolled her eyes. "Don't you have something to hammer, boatswain?"

"There's always something to fix when *you're* steering the ship."

"Is that any way to speak to your captain?"

He walked past her and right into her line of sight, his smug smile on his face. He leaned on the railing.

"I thought you enjoyed my sense of humor."

"When you get one, I'll let you know."

He chuckled, and she darted her eyes away from his.

"Why are you here, Amrit?" She tightened her grip on the helm.

"Just wanted to enjoy the view." He turned to the sea. "To see this blasted island whizzing by us. This place has been nothing but trouble."

She wished she could, too. But there was an upside to sailing in the dead of night. They would reach the cove on Crystal Crest by dusk, giving them a bit of cover when they anchored. The wind whipped again, the sails flapping a bit too hard for her liking.

"Is it too early to remind you to name your first mate?" He raised his brows like a stupid little schoolboy.

"I'm not talking about that now."

"Well, you need to."

"No, I don't!"

The only person she needed by her side was Jules, the boatswain before Amrit. He'd helped her get away from life in the brothel. He'd been the father she'd always wished she had.

The only person who understood her.

Jules was supposed to be her first mate.

But he was dead.

Run through by a bastard traitor on that blasted island. She should've been the one to avenge his death. She should've been there to save him. And if she couldn't save him, at least say goodbye.

"When someone shows themselves worthy of it, I will name 'em," Mari said.

Amrit shook his head, another sea breeze twisting around them. It sent shivers through the leather of her waistcoat. Raindrops the size of gold coins started pelting her hat. The helm grew rigid, Mari's hands gripping the wheel so tight her fingers stung.

"Furl the sails, boatswain," she commanded.

"Captain are you sure?" Amrit began.

"Furl the damn sails!"

Amrit rushed off the deck. Lightning lit up the sky and the deckhands below yelled like scared children. They acted as if they hadn't sailed into a storm before. Which could be true.

At least there's no serpent to worry about.

Mari's hat blew away in the wind, the air whipping around her. She widened her stance to brace herself against the fierce gale all around her. A flash of lightning revealed the waves churning and swelling in front of her. She grunted as she turned the wheel, pointing the bow of the ship straight into the waves.

"Batten down the hatches!" Mari yelled out.

The first wave came off the starboard bow, the water heavy and cold as it washed over the ship. Salt filled Mari's mouth as water surrounded her, pulling her away from the helm, slamming her into the port side when it receded into the sea. Her waistcoat and leather pants heavy as she jumped to her feet.

She ran back to the helm, throwing her body against it as the second wave hit, veering the ship due west. Mari used the helm to pull herself to her feet, spinning the ship back east and away from shore.

We can't run aground!

Rain fell like sheets, mixing with the waves spilling over the ship. Roaring thunder drowned out the screams behind her. No need to focus on the chaos behind her. She couldn't afford to be rattled.

Just steer the damn ship.

She blinked away the water dripping off her hair into her eyes, using the spikes of lightning to guide her through the waves. One caught under the ship, lurching it forward so sharp and fast that she held onto the helm like it was a bucking horse. Wood cracked as the ship landed back in the sea.

Wind and rain slapped at her face and whipped through her dreads. She gripped the wheel tighter, every muscle in her body screaming as she leaned onto the helm. Any pirate worth his salt knew sailing straight into the teeth of a storm was the only way to survive. Hitting the wrong side of a storming ocean would cause all of their deaths, instead of a few.

Mari had survived the Cape.

Mari had survived the sea serpent.

She refused to let a pissy storm be the end of her.

An enormous crack sent a shiver down her spine. *Please don't let it be one of my masts.*

Then she saw it. A sliver of moonlight on the other side of the angry clouds. Her arms screamed as she turned the ship to that light.

"Amrit!" Mari strained to raise her voice. "Unfurl the mizzen sail!"

The wet wind screeched around her but no response from her boatswain. *If you fell over the side of this ship, I will drag you out of the sea and kill you myself.*

"Aye, Captain!" The wind tore his words away and Mari let out a breath.

Her hands trembled under the weight of the sea pushing against her ship. She heard the loud flap of the sail, and the *Pursuer* cut through the water like a sharp knife. It only made the ship fight harder, and Mari's knees buckled as she kept the ship sailing into the moonlight. The sail flapped so loud it must have been bursting at the ropes.

Dammit, we're going to make it.

The rain eased, the sea calmer, the helm gliding instead of fighting her grip. At last, the clouds parted, the light of the moon dancing on the ocean's surface. The dark shoreline of Bluegate lay far off to the west, a smudge on the horizon.

Open ocean to the east. Salty and damp air all around her. A familiar set of footsteps came up behind her. *Thank the stars he didn't get himself thrown overboard.*

"I expect a full report by dawn, Amrit," she said, her muscles relaxing.

"I don't need to wait until then to tell you that this ship can't take another storm."

"And there won't be one." Macario or not, she didn't need anything else to go wrong.

"But Captain–"

"If I wanted your opinion, I'd ask you for it!" It came out much sharper than she intended, but in the end, whether she liked it or not, she was the captain. What she said went.

"Aye, Captain." His voice trailed off in the post-storm breeze as he slowly walked away.

Mari blocked out the noise and chatter on the decks below. Finally, it was just her and the sea. With the way this voyage was starting out, there was no telling how long the calm would last.

CHAPTER 3

LUIS

Captain Luis Fozo leaned on the polished banister of his ship, the *Golden Rose*. Clouds passed over the quarter moon, casting eerie shadows on the islands on either side.

He'd finished his evening inspection of the ship an hour ago and should've retired for the night. Instead, he stood on the upper port-side deck, trying to quiet his mind.

The cliff-side city of Yaton loomed over them, the ship moving through the choppy water at a good clip. He'd spent many a day sitting on its rocky beaches as a little boy, watching the Order ships go by.

Wood sidings gleaming in the summer sun, their sails crisp and white as they caught the realm wind. The Order flag—an ocean-blue scepter set against a sea of pure white—waving above the crow's nest. But the ship with the mermaid statue draped in flowers on its bow was the biggest, with ten portholes for cannons on each side, instead of the standard six.

It never sailed alone, followed by at least three smaller, yet faster ships. Whenever it made its daily patrol around the main island, he used to point it out to his older brother, Guillermo.

"She will be my ship one day," he would say, and his brother would laugh. A high-pitched laugh that sounded ridiculous coming from a teenage boy. Then he would ruffle Luis's scraggly black hair.

"You can be whatever you set your mind to," he would say. "Say your prayers, never betray your values, and always do what's right."

Luis passed his hand along the smooth banister. He couldn't see the mermaid on the bow from where he stood, but it didn't make the ship any less majestic or any less his ship to command.

He slid his hand into his right trouser pocket, turning over the cool, bronze compass in his palm. How many trips had his brother taken down this sailing lane using this very compass? Had he looked at it when he sailed his ship to Bluegate that fateful night to put an end to the pirates wreaking havoc in their realm? Was this compass the Order soldiers recovered from Bluegate the last thing he'd held before those bastards killed him?

"Captain Fozo!"

Luis pulled his hand out of his pocket and stood up straight. First mate Jaime Ruiz approached him, the lantern he held casting shadows on his rich brown skin.

"We'll be at the rendezvous point within the hour," Jaime reported, looking up at him.

"And the storm?"

"Well to the west. Macario's blessings continue to cover us, Captain."

Was it a blessing or just sheer luck?

Had he asked himself that question four months ago, he would have had a straightforward answer. Macario was the patron god of the Majestic Isles, the only one to rule them all. Those who served Him with a pure heart would be blessed. Have a clear path in life and want for nothing.

It was that fierce belief that had seen him through the naval academy and helped him graduate at the top of his class. His parents would've been proud.

"Our men are also faring well, considering we had to cut their rations," Ruiz continued. "Our inventory will last until we make port on the mainland."

Luis nodded, his own stomach rumbling. "If all goes well."

He glanced back at what was left of Tradesman Harbor, the moon casting shadows on a shabby pier and a desolate beach. To this day, he had yet to get a full picture of what had burned their most treasured piers to a crisp and leveled half of Aridia. Witnesses had claimed it was a monster. The Order had declared it the work of pirates and deemed it heresy to believe otherwise.

Guillermo had been tasked with tracking them down, and every day Luis had prayed for his safety. Not that Guillermo needed his little brother's prayers. He'd been leading fleets when Luis was still brushing sand out of his ears from Academy drills.

Yet it had been a relief to read his brother's letters. Luis must have read them a million times, and yet they still made no sense. Walls of water. A girl wielding Macario's legendary scepter. Fire-breathing serpents surrounded by a band of infamous pirates.

Serpents and magic were fodder for fairytales, and his brother was not one to indulge in such things. Had to be some new treachery these Magian pirates invented. They would stoop to any low, including desecrating the Order's faith system to get what they wanted.

It wasn't monsters or magic that had murdered Guillermo or his crew that night. But Luis would find out the truth—and serve justice.

A chorus of temple bells rang in the distance, bringing his thoughts back into focus.

"Advise me when we reach the port," he said, leaving Jaime out on the deck.

His officers stood at their posts, keeping their eyes out for any trouble that might come their way. They had to be on guard for anyone looking to take advantage while their realm rebuilt itself.

And it will never happen on my watch.

Luis finally retreated to his quarters, locking the door behind him. The circular chandelier hanging from the ceiling still burned bright, its light hitting every clean corner of his sanctuary. He unbuttoned his waistcoat, draping it over his desk chair, and glanced over at the parchments stacked on his desk.

The pardon for Elsie, the brothel worker he'd arrested who'd precipitated this trip to Crystal Crest, sat on top—unsigned. And it would stay that way if she didn't uphold her end of the bargain. One always had to wonder whether a sinner's propensity for evil would outweigh the chance for redemption Macario always provided.

Luis unclenched his hands. *This is not the time.*

He strode over to the far corner of the room. Kneeling on the plush red pillows on the floor was a relief, his dark eyes level with the small altar. The unpainted eyes of the small wooden statue of Macario seemed to bore into him. It was as if He saw that Luis's efforts to pray away the anger and hurt brewing in his gut weren't working.

Praise be, you see it all.

Luis bowed his head and allowed a tear to fall. No prayer could erase the hole in his heart created by his brother's death. Every day, week, and month that passed by only caused that hole to grow bigger. That happened when one experienced the death of a loved one.

What he didn't expect were the tendrils of doubt and fear clawing at him because he didn't know his brother's fate or final moments.

He didn't know what had happened at Bluegate. What had his brother seen? A band of bloodthirsty pirates? Or the serpents and magic his brother spoke of in his letters?

"I must know, almighty Macario," Luis whispered.

Who was the pirate that had plunged his sword into his brother's chest? His breath caught at the image flashing in his mind. Blood gurgling out of Guillermo's mouth. The fear in his brother's brown eyes as death took him into the next world. His blood soaking into the wood of his ship.

Luis leaned forward on his hands, sobs escaping his throat.

Macario, I am here to do your will. My life is yours. All I ask is the strength to carry it out. The strength to bring my brother the justice he deserves.

Luis wiped his face with the back of his sleeve, taking deep breaths to suppress the sorrow he'd so carelessly let out.

I'm too close to break down now. He recited the Prayer for Safe Travels over and over until the words were clear, confident, and unwavering.

Straightening his shirt, he rose to his feet and walked to his desk. Sitting down in the soft, blue chair, he took out his ledger from the top drawer. He opened it up to a fresh page before reaching for the ink and quill in front of him to write his daily report.

The voyage from Tara had been an uneventful one. The usual cleaning of the ship, gathering of supplies, and daily fighting drills.

He would have a lot to write about by this time tomorrow.

He would find and arrest the pirates who'd attacked his brother's ship.

They would tell him everything that had happened that night.

He would find out why pirates were attacking their realm. The reason his brother lost his life. He would prove that magic and serpents weren't real. Then he would move on. Be the officer his brother always wanted him to be. Serve Macario with a full and gracious heart.

The sun couldn't rise fast enough.

CHAPTER 4

SERAPHINA

Seraphina's eyes flew open, and she gasped for air. The dream had been much worse than the last time. The smell of soot, smoke, and blood that surrounded her in the beachy dreamscape still lingered.

Her mind knew it was Bluegate, but it looked nothing like it. It was nothing but ash and flatlands. With every wave, more bodies floated to the surface. Lightning ripped through the sky, just like the storm that had almost sunk their ship the night before. A bitter voice had boomed from the heavens.

"Look at what you've done! This is all your fault."

And it was. At least, in the dream, anyway. She never made it to the Secret Library. She didn't get Samara the information she needed to help save the world. Magia was gone, and, as punishment, Macario left her alive to witness the consequences of being too scared and intimidated to do her duty. Play her part.

Find the library.

She turned on her side in her hammock, facing the rest of the hanging beds crammed in the lower deck quarters. Some swung empty, while snores and belches rose out of the others. Slender streaks of sunlight shone through the cracks in the plank ceiling. A rumble of footsteps grew louder as they approached the doorway. Deckhands burst into the room. A short, pudgy man with a large bald spot held up a dented pot and spoon.

"Wake up, you ugly princesses!" he shouted, clanging on that dreaded pot.

The sleepy men cursed as they stirred in their hammocks. Some stretched and yawned before jumping down from the beds. Others grumbled and rolled over. Seraphina stretched out her fingers and rubbed the cramps out of them. It had taken all night to repair the rigging on the mizzenmast.

The pirate banged on the pot again, yelling colorful insults. If he made any more of a racket, her head would ache. There was too much to do.

Much more to worry about before finding the library.

She dropped her feet to the floor and left before the room became too crowded with rude and smelly pirates. The sun stung her eyes as she climbed up the stairs and made it topside.

A handful of men swabbed the deck. The burlier ones tossed the dead fish and seaweed strewn about the deck over the side. The pile of sails by the upper deck screamed for her attention. Her fingers pulsed in pain at the thought. Captain Mari stormed down the steps, grabbing a nearby deckhand by the ear.

"I'm not paying you to stand around and look at the scenery," she sneered.

Seraphina couldn't blame the poor boy. The moss green mountains of Crystal Crest stood at attention in the distance. Despite being so close to the sandy white beach that curved sharply around the cove, she couldn't see beyond the thick line of bright green trees and bushes.

But I do see them. On the shore, crewmen lugged barrels off that beach and into the rowboats swaying in the gentle tide. No need to travel inland. *Are those supplies?* Enough to get them to the Enchanted Cape after they dropped her off on the mainland?

Seraphina walked over to the pile of sails, grabbing a nearby stool. When she sat down and the leather pouch hit her leg, she realized she hadn't untied the sewing kit from around her waist. She was reaching for the flap when a short—yet quite intimidating—shadow fell over her.

"You're coming with me."

Mari's piercing green eyes bored into her, making it impossible to ask the myriad of questions flooding Seraphina's mind. When was she going to the mainland? Would it be today? Tomorrow?

She needed to be prepared, though she didn't quite know what that all entailed. But Seraphina nodded, following the surly captain to the last rowboat. Mari never took Seraphina along on her shore excursions.

Is this it? Were they dropping her off here?

Brody gave her a reassuring nod as Ghad, a dark-haired pirate with a colorful sense of humor, helped her in. Seraphina sat between them, while Mari sat at the head of the boat. When it hit the water, nerves clawed at every inch of Seraphina's empty stomach.

"Captain, may I ask—"

"No." Mari kept her eyes on the shore as they rowed toward it. About twenty of her crewmen were already there, looking at the cluster of barrels on the beach. Their boat hit the sandbar and Brody jumped out to push them ashore.

Mari turned to her. "Don't leave my side and don't say a word."

"Yes, Captain," Seraphina croaked.

Her feet were heavy as she trekked up the dune behind Mari. Their crew parted to let them through. An older gentleman stood in front of the cargo, flanked by two tall and very muscular young men. They all wore the fine rich silks of a typical Godswood trader—brightly colored tunics, flowing vests with rich stitching, and straight-legged trousers embroidered down the sides. Their adorned hats had ridiculous feathers sticking out of the sides.

The old man smiled, deepening the wrinkles in his lightly tanned face as they approached.

"Is this her?" His furry eyebrows rose. "Is this the one who wielded magic to destroy the serpent?"

Of course not. That was Samara. They might have shared the same womb, but she was far from the brave one.

Seraphina opened her mouth to correct him just as a sharp elbow and Mari's lethal stare warned her to shut it.

"The one and only," Mari replied, her tone drowning with sarcasm. She pushed back her black waistcoat and pulled out a velvet pouch from a secret pocket. "We have a deal?"

"Now, now," the old man said. "No need to be so hasty. I would love to see that magic—"

"That wasn't part of the deal," Mari said. "You get to meet Samara, I pay, and you hand over those supplies."

The smile didn't fade from the old man's face. His small brown eyes went from Mari to Seraphina. *Should I smile back? Should I convince him I'm Samara?* That would require lying. Seraphina was terrible at lying.

Mari stepped into his line of sight, holding the pouch in his face. "You have one minute to take this money or we're leaving."

He snatched the pouch from Mari's hand. "Pleasure doing business with you."

He motioned his men to step aside. Mari raised her hand, and ten of her crewmen swooped in and started hauling the barrels away.

"Get back to the ship," Mari said. "Start mending those sails."

Seraphina nodded, facing the rowboats.

"Captain!"

"The trees!"

Seraphina and Mari whipped around. Around fifty soldiers in deep green uniforms poured out from the foliage onto the beach. Their swords gleamed in the sunlight as they descended on the ship like a swarm of angry wasps.

Seraphina gasped, whispering a prayer under her breath. *Way too many to fight.*

"To the ship!" Mari pushed her toward the shore.

Mari wasn't coming with her. Instead, she was running after the old man fleeing up the beach. She pulled a knife out of her sleeve, slowing down to a stop. She flung it through the air, soaring past barrels and men. Its blade landed deep in the back of the old man's skull, his body falling face-first into the sand.

"Get them!"

"Don't let those pirates escape!"

Every muscle in Seraphina's body locked in place, her eyes fixed on her captain. Mari took a breath before spinning on her heels, her sword glinting in the island sun. It looked graceful until she rammed it into the stomach of the Order soldier coming for her. She grunted as she pulled it out, and Seraphina's stomach lurched at the sight of blood spilling onto the sand. The soldier's body fell like a wilting flower as Mari fearlessly ducked the blow of the soldier coming up behind her. She threw sand in his face as she rose, kicking him in the chin as he hunched over. Mari's eyes met hers, her face smeared with blood and sand. She narrowed her eyes, a silent warning to heed her command.

Get to the ship!

Seraphina looked to the beach, but instead of seeing the boats that would take her to the safety of the ship, she saw nothing but the green fabric of an Order soldier's uniform.

"Where do you think you're going, pirate?" he snarled, looking down at her, his tall frame blocking out the sun. She took a step back, and he grabbed her arm. She screamed as he squeezed and reached for the dagger on his belt with his free hand. A large arm wrapped around her captor's neck, and the Order man's eyes went wide. He was dragged backward, his nails piercing Seraphina's skin as he lost his grip on her. She staggered backward, clasping her hands over her mouth as Brody twisted the soldier's neck.

Crack.

He tossed the body aside like a piece of driftwood.

"Time to go, Sister!" Brody's brawny hand took hold of Seraphina's and he dragged her to a rowboat. "Get in!"

The pirates didn't care about the barrels weighing it down. They piled in, leaving a sliver of space for Seraphina to sit.

"What about the captain?" she cried.

"I'll go back for her. You just get in—" His breath caught in his throat as he clutched his right shoulder. Deep red blood poured out, the tip of a blade stuck in it. Seraphina leaped out of the boat, water splashing all about her as she ran to Brody. He sank to his knees, his face twisted in pain. A soldier was right behind him, his sword dripping with Brody's blood. He pointed the bloody tip at her throat.

The soldier opened his mouth to speak, but no words came out. His eyes grew wide, dropping his sword into the shallow water around them. Then his body fell forward, three knives sticking out of his back.

"I told you to get back on the ship!" Mari barked, helping Brody to his feet. The last row boat was halfway out to sea. Soldiers swarmed the last two further down the beach.

"Looks like we may have to swim for it," Mari said, taking off her waistcoat to reveal a white, long-sleeved men's shirt underneath.

"Think you can handle that, Brody?"

The man nodded his head. "If the sharks don't get me first."

"I don't think they like sour meat," Mari said, not cracking a smile.

Brody chuckled, wincing in pain. "Fair point, Captain."

Mari took one arm and Seraphina took the other as they ran out into the water.

Seraphina couldn't remember the last time she swam and, just like lying, she wasn't very good at it. Sitting on the sand reading a book was always a much better idea than getting all wet. The cool water reached her waist before Mari held out her arm to stop them from diving in. Four Order ships came into view, surrounding the *Pursuer*.

Cannons fired, rocking Seraphina to the core of her soul. Shards of wood and smoke billowed into the air around the pirate ship.

Macario, please don't let them sink the ship.

The book and the scroll were aboard. Her sister needed them.

Seraphina gasped as a sharp point pressed into the middle of her back.

"It's over, pirates!" the soldier announced. "You're coming with us."

She didn't say a word, her heart pounding in her ears as a soldier pulled her hands behind her back. Mari grunted, cursing them as they cuffed her, her eyes on her ship.

Those Order galleons were closing in. There was nowhere for the ship to go.

And nowhere for them to run.

CHAPTER 5

MARI

Worm feeders.

Mari scowled as those Order vermin infected every part of her ship. Their stark green uniforms emblazoned with the stupid symbol of the Order swarming over every inch of the *Pursuer*. Snatching patched sails from the mast. Bringing up every barrel her men stored below and throwing them onto the deck.

And she couldn't do a damn thing about it.

She was just like her captured crew—hands bound in front of them, the rope that tied them all together digging into her hips. They were like cattle awaiting the slaughter, herded around the center mast with swords pointed at them from every direction. A barrel crashed, and a month's worth of salted sardines spilled onto the dirty floorboards.

"Watch yourself, sailor," said the one with the tails on his waistcoat. He towered over everyone, his jacket hugging every muscle on his arm. Dark hair slicked back behind his ears, his skin naturally tanned.

The one who dropped the barrel stood at attention, his face quivering as if he wanted to cry.

"Let's not waste any more food than we have to," the fancy man said.

"Yes, Captain Fozo," he said, dropping to his knees to recover the fallen fish.

He turned to Mari and her crew. Those dark black eyes stared at them for a long moment, as if he'd never seen a pirate before.

Sure, they weren't a polished group of mindless brutes, like his people.

They were rough around the edges, lean from the lack of a decent meal, but strong enough to survive a storm at sea or hold their own in a scuffle. Even Seraphina, with all of her lofty ideas and crazy traditions, blended in. A big frizzy braid hung over her shoulder, and there were small bags under those naïve eyes and calluses all over the palms of her hands.

So long as she doesn't open her big mouth, we'll be okay.

The girl's brown eyes darted all over the place, and Mari wished she were close enough to pinch her. She wore the face of a guilty woman, and that wouldn't help their cause in the least.

The captain's gaze fell on Mari, and his hand clutched the hilt of the cutlass sheathed on his side. He pulled it out in one dramatic swoop and pointed its tip at Mari.

"Good day, Captain."

Mari chuckled. "What makes you so sure that I'm the captain?"

He took a step closer, the point of his sword too damn close to her neck.

"You're the one your men have been glancing at the entire time we've been aboard. And the only one not about to piss on themselves at the thought of hanging on an Order noose."

That was never part of my plan. Then again, when was the last time she thought farther than the next score?

"Aren't you the smart one," Mari said, glaring back at him.

One of the captain's men ran up to him with a very familiar book and scroll in his hand. The captain's brow furrowed as he eyed the cover.

Great. That book brought them nothing but trouble. The kind of trouble that had them literally fighting for their lives. The last bloody thing she needed right now.

"We found these hidden away below, Captain Fozo."

Seraphina's bloody gasp was so loud, and the captain's eyes shifted to her.

"Clear the ship and secure the prisoners in our briggs."

Captain Fozo put the sword away with the same stupid velocity he pulled it out with. Mari didn't give him the satisfaction of flinching. She watched him with the same glacial stare she gave everyone who meddled with her affairs.

"This captain will go with me," he said. "We need to have a word."

Mari hadn't realized they'd untied her from the others until a soldier shoved her closer to the other rowboats. Her man-handler dug his fingers into her arm while cramming her into the boat with Fozo and a few other men. The boat sank into the water.

Too close. They were much too close.

She could smell the spice and wood in their cologne and the fresh soapy smell of their uniforms. Hot breath grazed her skin every time they breathed.

"My name is Captain Luis Fozo, head of the Order's naval fleet," Fozo began as his goons began to row away from her ship.

"Don't care." She rolled her eyes for good measure.

"You should if you value your life and your crew."

Mari leaned forward. "I'm not an idiot."

"I never took you for one."

"Good, so you'll know I'll take no deal you're offerin'."

Men like him did deals all the time. They didn't care about random pirate captains plundering their realms. What they wanted was the ultimate prize—destroying Siren's Cove and the Pirate Council, the lifeblood of illegal trade.

Everyone thought it was some mysterious place that no regular person could find. *Any idiot can find it.* But as long as the Pirate Council kept putting thirty percent of all black market profits into Griffin Vale coffers, no naval fleet would get within thirty leagues of its harbor.

"You haven't heard the terms," Captain Fozo said.

"Don't need to."

"I'll explain them anyway."

Mari huffed.

"Charges of bartering illegal goods in an unsanctioned port will have you and your crew rotting inside an Order dungeon for the rest of your lives."

Any pirate worth his salt could work his way out of a jail cell.

"However, an attack on an Order ship and the murder of its crew and captain will have you all rotting in the ground in a few days."

Mari raised a brow. "Now which Order ship would that be?"

Captain Fozo's eyes narrowed. "The *Pontiff's Grace.*"

Bloody hell. Mari normally wouldn't remember the names of every ship they raided. There were just too many to count. But this one she would always remember.

It was the ship they needed to drag that deadly sea serpent back into the underwater hell. A lot of Order men met the wrong end of their swords, though Mari missed out on most of that action. She had to navigate the *Pursuer*, and the ship had been on its last legs before the serpent and all its fury tore it to pieces.

"You must want something if you're willing to let us slide." Mari leaned back.

"I need answers. I need to know what happened on Bluegate the night of the fires."

"Why?"

"None of your concern."

Snappy, aren't we? "So, what do we get for this information?"

He clenched his fists. "You and your crew get to live another day—as long as what you tell us is true and you take your illegal activities elsewhere."

Right. You'll use us like lap dogs and when you're done, hang us by our own leashes.

The rowboat took a sharp left and headed straight to the large galleon docked a few feet away from the *Pursuer*. It looked just as pretentious as its captain. A giant mermaid with her lady parts draped in flowers took up the entire bow. The *Golden Rose* was painted in shiny gold lettering along the side, the many portholes locked up tight with charcoal-black locks.

With her hands tied, it was hard to climb up the rope ladder, but that didn't stop those idiots from shoving her along. When she reached the top, she swallowed down the nasty thought of becoming a turncoat. If she planned to get off this bloody ship, she had to learn every inch of it.

And it started right now.

She counted twenty paces from the port side where the rowboat was to the center mast. Ten men stood along the railings, eyes out onto the sea. The Order rats pushed her over to the center masts, stopping short of the stacked crates tied all around it. Fozo sauntered around them, looking down at her.

"What's your answer?"

Mari spat at his shoes and he raised a brow.

"Fine." He turned to the short, brown-skinned man who hadn't left his side since they left her ship. "Ruiz, fetch me that other young lady pirate. I'm sure she will be much more receptive to my offer."

The short Order vermin nodded. "And what of this one?"

Fozo glared at her. "Throw her in the box. That should calm down her temper."

CHAPTER 6

LUIS

A gust of wind blasted Luis in his face and his eyes fluttered open. The daylight stung his eyes, but the air wasn't stiff and humid. It was arid, ruffling his clothes and sending an unnatural chill throughout his body. He rose to his feet with a heaviness he couldn't explain.

Just as he couldn't explain where he was.

The land stretched out for miles in every direction, void of trees and blades of grass. No ship. Not a rowboat or Order man in sight. Tall mounds of scorched earth covered the ground. Luis took a deep breath and he couldn't even smell the salt of the ocean.

Rubbing the back of his neck, he started walking, his legs heavy as he navigated the narrow passageways around these forsaken mounds.

What in the world are these things? Where was he?

"Ruiz! Bendigo!"

His voice echoed through the gray sky.

Dammit! His foot hit the bottom of those crazy dirt hills, his big toe throbbing through his boots. He looked down expecting to find the rock, but there was none.

A black boot stuck out of the dirt. A boot that looked a lot like his.

He bent down and brushed away the dirt. A boot. A pant leg. A dead hand.

Praise Macario, where am I?

Lightning ripped through the sky, and he cowered.

"Look at what you've done! This is all your fault!"

The voice growled from the heavens, pounding through the air and into the very center of his heart. He clutched his chest, watching as an invisible hand brushed away the dirt from the hill. Thousands of dead Order soldiers were piled on top of each other. Their gray eyes stared off into nothingness. The stench of death made it hard to breathe. He shut his eyes and fell on his knees.

"Stop! Please! Make it stop!"

He opened them again, and he was greeted by the warm light of his room's chandelier. He sat up, rubbing his right temple.

Just a dream. A very disturbing dream.

Luis looked down at the old book he confiscated from the pirate ship. He'd gotten as far as the Chosen One chapter.

"Only the one whom Macario has chosen will wield the scepter and its awesome power," he read, trying to ignore the chills rippling down his spine. "The chosen one will be tested when the sea serpent returns to ravage the Isles once again."

He turned the page, revealing a hand-drawn portrait of a girl with beautiful dark, wavy hair that flowed over her shoulder. Her oval, brown eyes stared back at him with the same aura of daintiness—yet strength—as the young pirate woman he sent for earlier that day. It was hard not to notice the only other woman on the nefarious crew.

Luis got up from his chair, turning to his prayer altar in the corner. He bowed his head and closed his eyes. *I pray for strength, clarity, and empathy.*

He was certain she wasn't like the others. If any good could come from this, aside from getting justice for this brother, perhaps he could save at least one fellow Isle girl from a dark and dangerous path.

Luis took his place at his desk once more, eyeing the scroll next to the book. *I wonder what crazy tale is on this piece of parchment.* The title was the first thing he saw as he unrolled it.

"The Scepter's Prayer," he read aloud. He knew just about every Temple prayer that existed, but this was not one of them.

Praise be to Macario, god, and creator of the land and sea. I pray for light, so

I see the path before me. I pray for the sea to wash away the hurt and pain, so I can let in love and belief. I pray for your mercy, so I can forgive myself. I pray for courage, so I can surrender my pride.

I pray for your blessing so I can have the strength to wield the scepter and all its mighty power. I pray that I am worthy to be Chosen.

Didn't all men pray to be worthy of Macario's blessings? It was a beautiful prayer. Too beautiful to be in the hands of pirates. Yet it'd been hidden underneath a floorboard in the barracks, like a worthy treasure.

He looked up as the door opened and Ruiz entered, the young girl in tow. Her smooth, olive skin was marred with dirt and grime. Her dark hair fell in a frizzy braid over her shoulder. Her brown slacks were tattered, her oversized white tunic streaked with tar-black stains. The baggy sleeves were rolled up to her elbows, her wrists bound in front of her with rope. Yet, despite her appearance, there was an aura about her that he couldn't quite explain.

Jaime gave a quick nod and left the room, shutting the door behind him.

He gestured to the chair, not speaking until she sat down.

"I'm Captain Fozo. And you are?"

She swallowed hard. "Seraphina."

"You don't strike me as a pirate."

"I am a member of Captain Adlam's crew." Her voice cracked as she spoke.

"By choice?"

She took a breath before nodding.

Interesting.

He leaned back, relaxed yet not quite smiling. "I'm having a hard time believing that."

"But it's true."

"And what was your role on the ship?"

Seraphina's beautiful eyes left his and found the book on his desk, the scroll rolled up next to it.

"I'm sorry, Captain Fozo, but what is it you want from me?"

"Information."

"I don't know much."

He leaned forward, folding his hands on the desk. "You know plenty. Just like I know you aren't a pirate, but an Isle girl who lost her way."

"My way is clear, Captain," she said, straightening up in the chair.

"Does your way include taking over an Order ship in Bluegate and murdering its captain?"

She flinched at that. "I don't know what you're talking about."

"Yes, you do." His voice was stern. "As a member of this pirate crew, you're involved in all of their crimes."

"I was never involved in taking over any ship or—killing anyone."

We'll see about that. "I'll be frank with you, Seraphina. I need to know what happened that night on Bluegate between your ship and the Order ship sent there to apprehend you and your crew."

"I wasn't there," she blurted out. "I don't know what happened."

"I find that hard to believe."

"Well, you must, because it's the truth. I'm a horrible liar."

"Yet you take up company with a boat full of them."

She held her head high. "Everyone is worthy of redemption."

"And by Macario's grace and light, they shall find it," Captain Fozo completed.

Was that a smile on her face? "Exactly."

"And is that why you are here? On a religious mission to help these pirates find redemption?"

"No."

He huffed. "I'm trying to understand why someone like you would be in the company of pirates."

"What do you mean, someone like *me*?"

He sat back in his chair. "A woman who seems to know the core tenants of our faith here in the Majestic Isles."

She scoffed. "Of course I do! I didn't spend the last four years in the seminary for nothing."

We're getting somewhere! "What is a sister of the seminary doing on a ship with murderous pirates carrying around an Ancient Order book and scroll?"

She opened her mouth to speak but promptly closed it, looking away.

He softened his voice. "I've always been a man of faith and believer in

Macario's teachings. That much we have in common."

Her soft, brown eyes found his again. "And what do you believe in?"

"What do you mean?"

"Does your belief stop where the Order tells you? Or are you brave enough to follow His will, even if it goes against the government you serve?"

He leaned on his desk, looking down at the book, and then up at her. Seraphina didn't actually believe what was in that book. Did she? And if so, what did it have to do with his brother's fate?

"Trust in Macario above all else," she recited. "Above the opinions of man. Above the limitations of this human world."

"Only He knows our destiny, and so will we if we only listen."

The simple words transported him back to Temple school, sitting at a rickety desk in a crumbling sanctuary schoolroom in Yaton.

"Captain, you asked me why I'm with these pirates." She lifted her chin, her head held high. "I'm with them because I trust in Macario and I'm listening to my destiny."

Is she delusional or just plain naïve? "You mean to tell me that your destiny is in this book?"

"Yes!"

"As the supposed Chosen One?"

She balked. "Of course not."

"And what makes that more ridiculous than everything else in this book?"

Her lips tightened, those brown eyes glassy under the chandelier light. He was losing her. She sat back in the chair, clasping her hands tight as her gaze found the floor.

"You believe everything this book says, don't you?" His tone was soft, attempting to be understanding.

She nodded, refusing to meet his gaze.

He took a breath before continuing. "Are you helping these pirates spread this vicious propaganda, scaring people into thinking there was an actual serpent terrorizing our islands?"

Seraphina's head spun around, and she jumped to her feet. "Propaganda! How dare you call it that? So many people died because of that monster!"

"A monster you pirates created." He pushed back his chair and stood, looking down on her.

"No! A monster that you and the Order refused to acknowledge, burying your heads in the ground. If it weren't for these pirates, you wouldn't be sitting here interrogating me."

"Tell me what happened," he demanded.

"I can't," she said, her voice subdued.

He huffed. "Why?"

"Because you wouldn't believe me."

He stood up from his chair. "Ruiz!"

A short moment later, his first mate stuck his head in the door.

"Bring me the pirate captain," Luis ordered. "Maybe she can give me some answers."

CHAPTER 7

MARI

Mari didn't move a muscle when the lock to her prison chest clanked open. She squeezed her eyes shut, almost expecting a burst of air heavy with incense. Madame Mirielle lit dozens of incense sticks in the Harmony Room to mask the smell of piss from the girls locked in the box.

A box just like this one.

The first few times the madam locked her in the box, she'd been terrified. She'd vowed to never make the mistakes that landed her in there—telling the wrong joke, not smiling enough when the men came in to choose, dirtying her dress.

But when she moved up from a scullery maid to a woman of the Pleasure House, the box was her escape. No man could see her, let alone touch her without permission. It was better than getting whipped or forced to watch the other girls eat while she starved.

There, she got to think about what her life could be outside of the Enchanted Cape. Running her own tavern, filled to the brim every night.

Seeing the world on my own damn ship.

That was the image she'd held onto while she lay in that cramped box.

Now, the lid swung open, and she blinked her eyes. The two Order sailors standing over her didn't say a word. They just reached in, grabbed her arm, and pulled her out. Her knees cracked and her back muscles screamed as she stood up straight. Her white, button-down shirt stuck to her chest, her dreads a sweaty, matted mess.

Doesn't matter. I'm getting the hell off this boat and getting my ship back.

They dragged her out of the empty cell, right up the stairs and onto the deck. The still night air was heavy with humidity, the moon struggling to shine through the clouds. The lanterns burned bright through the haze, shining down on the unfortunate sailors tasked with swabbing the deck.

Her captors maneuvered around them, dragging her up the stairs to the captain's quarters. Her breath caught. For a moment she was a young girl back at the Cape, being brought to a man's room in the middle of the night.

What level of danger waited for her behind that door? Would he be gentle, but go all night? Or was he a fast one, but wielded a heavy hand?

Curses, Mari! Pull yourself together!

The door opened, and the men shoved her into the room, giving her a glimpse of Seraphina, standing there all wide-eyed.

"Leave us," the Order captain said, and his men scurried out, closing the door behind them.

"Two women in one night," Mari said. "A little ambitious, don't you think?"

He walked around his desk. "I'm done playing coy. Are you going to take my offer, or not?"

"I'm not."

"Then you'll both hang."

Seraphina stepped in front of them. "Now, just wait a minute!"

Luis glared at her. "You had your chance to tell me what happened at Bluegate."

Wow. She kept her mouth shut.

"You're wasting your time, Captain."

"We can agree on one thing." Fozo crossed his arms as if that was supposed to scare her.

I should cut your throat and take your ship.

A bright light burst in the room and they all whirled to face the desk. Seraphina's book, the one that'd caused them a whole heap of trouble back in Lucia, flipped open, light bursting from its pages.

Seraphina ran right over to it as Luis drew his sword. Mari eyed the brown hilt of a dagger sticking out of his boot.

"What is happening?" Luis glared at them. "Whatever you're doing, stop it at once!"

"It's not me," Seraphina said, staring down at the book like a child inspecting a fruit tart. "It's magic."

Luis shook his head. "Magic is not real."

"Then how do you explain *that*?" Mari said, sliding closer to him. His eyes darted from Seraphina to the glowing book. *He's good and distracted. That dagger is mine.*

She slowly knelt on the shiny wood floor.

"Out of all the times to show me the way, you pick now," Seraphina said to the book, wrinkling her nose.

"Stop that!" Luis asserted. "I command you."

"You can't command the magic of the gods," Seraphina said.

Mari inched her hand closer to the dagger. Just a few more inches and she'd free it.

"I knew there had to be a reason for all of this." Seraphina's hands touched the open page. "Oh, no."

Mari's fingers touched the hilt of the dagger and Luis's hand clamped down on her wrist. Mari tried to wriggle free, but he was a lot stronger than he looked. He yanked her to her feet and pushed her up against the wall.

"Did you really think you could take my dagger?" he said, the sharp blade of his sword just inches from her face.

"Captain!" Seraphina took a step away from the book. "I wouldn't do that if I were you."

"You best listen to her," Mari said.

"Look at this!" Seraphina waved them over.

Luis, who still had way too hard of a hold on her wrist, tugged Mari over to the desk and looked over Seraphina's shoulder at the book. On the blank page formed a drawing of the Pontiff's Palace, complete with wrought-iron gates and fancy gardens on the page. A cavern below it. The words *The Oracle's Athenaeum* beat with the light right under it. Then, as if written by an invisible hand, a set of coordinates appeared in black ink at the bottom of the page.

"That wasn't there before!" Seraphina pointed out.

What other crazy magic could happen in a night?

I spoke too soon.

The book's magic continued its drawing, adding the shapes of three people. A portrait of Seraphina included her now-signature side braid, as well as the circular birthmark on her shoulder that made her sister, Samara, the Chosen One.

The second person was the Order captain. There was no mistaking the slick black hair and sharp facial features. The third drawing made Mari step away, her heart pounding in her chest.

The girl had the same long dreads, cold stare, and the tricorn hat she'd lost in the storm off Bluegate. *It's me.*

"Whatever joke you're trying to pull, Seraphina, this is not funny," Mari shouted, her breath quickening by the second.

Seraphina looked up at her.

"This is no joke. Macario has made his will very clear."

"And what is that?" Luis growled underneath his breath.

"That we're all meant to find the Secret Library."

Bloody hell.

The light evaporated, and the book looked ordinary again. Captain Fozo grabbed Mari's wrist, yanked her over to the chair, and slammed her down into it.

"You're bloody lucky my hands are tied!" Mari's voice bounced off the quarter walls.

He strode over to Seraphina, cornering her between him and the desk. "What just happened?"

She shook her head and shrugged her shoulders. "I don't know."

"What is the Oracle's Athenaeum?"

"You wouldn't understand if I told you."

He swung around the table, and before Mari could open her mouth to protest, he stood behind her with his blasted blade at her throat.

"Talk," Luis said through his teeth. "Now."

Seraphina took a deep, resigned breath. *She's gonna need it for all that rambling she's about to do.*

"The Secret Library is where the Ancient Order kept records on the prophecy about the end of the world."

"Prophecy?" Fozo pronounced every single syllable of that word.

"The Ancient Order foretold that Bedros would return and destroy the world if the Chosen One didn't stop him. The sea serpent was just the beginning."

Fozo lowered the sword and Mari pushed it away, jumping up from the chair.

"You can have this conversation without that blade to my neck."

"You expect me to believe there is a serpent out there?" Luis said, shaking his head.

"Actually," Seraphina said, "there *was* a fire-breathing serpent."

"Don't think the captain here cares about that," Mari said.

He ran his free hand through his hair. *Please, drop that sword.*

"That cannot be true," he said.

"You want something bigger than a book lighting up and writing its own pictures to convince you?" Mari snorted.

He took a breath, sheathing his sword and straightening his waistcoat. "It's clear neither of you will take up my offer."

"This is so much bigger than what happened at Bluegate," Seraphina said. "The fate of the world is at stake."

He banged on the door and a few moments later, the short Order man walked in. "Take these prisoners back to their cells," Fozo said, not having the decency to look them in the eye. "Make sure everything is prepared for when we dock on the mainland in the morning."

CHAPTER 8

SERAPHINA

The sounds of hammers and wood reached Seraphina's ears long before Tradesman Harbor came into view. The wooden frames and poles jutting out of the water were a shadow of the crown jewel of the Isles.

There weren't scores of trading ships dotting the harbor, their flags and sails flapping in the summer wind. Instead they were only ferries carrying workers lined the two miles of shoreline. The wall that divided the harbor from Aridia was gone, with no signs of being rebuilt. The shops that the tidal wave destroyed were now piles of stones being carted around.

Seraphina craned her neck to see, the ropes scraping against the skin of her wrists. The clouds floated away, and the sun beat down on her and Mari again. The sailors continued to scrub the deck in unison, paying no mind to the two women tied to the mainmast.

"Anchor down!" a sailor called.

"Prepare to disembark."

The sailors on the deck put the sponges into the buckets of dirty water with impressive precision. They shuffled across the deck in a single line, putting them down in front of the mizzenmast. As if on cue, they dispersed to their respective posts, grabbing the rigging to pull in the rest of the sails. Mari ceased tugging at the rope with her teeth, spitting out the bits of material in her mouth.

"You don't plan on escaping right now, do you?" Seraphina whispered.

Mari didn't answer, wriggling her hands until they danced around Mari's wrists.

"Rally the prisoners!"

Ten sailors in short naval jackets wove through the busy deckhands. *They must have seen Mari trying to get out of her ropes.* Mari must have thought the same, for she went still and assumed her usual glare. The men strode past, the heavy clanging of chains behind them. Seraphina almost broke her neck to see what was going on, but the mast blocked her view.

Clanking.

Stomping.

Moaning.

The eerie pattern of sounds grew closer until she saw the lanky frame of the *Pursuer's* cabin boy. He struggled to lift his head under the weight of a heavy chain around his neck. Another rusty chain was hooked to Ghad, who shot her a glassy look as they marched him on. All of Mari's crewmen marched by, chains around their necks, hitched up to each other like a herd of animals.

Seraphina bit her lip, her heart plummeting to her boots. *What is Captain Fozo doing?*

Did he not see what the book revealed last night? Macario's magic revealed the location of the Secret Library. Until then, only she had seen such a miracle, sitting on the beach when her sister left for the Griffin Vales.

Letting Luis see it had to mean something. And that look in his eyes. Half scared and half amazed, darting around as if his brain were combing for answers.

Probably how I looked when I saw my sister wield that godly scepter for the first time.

That had made her a believer in what the Order deemed impossible— magic and prophecies.

An evil taking over our world.

"We have to help them," Seraphina whispered. "We have to do what the captain wants—"

"Quiet!" Mari snapped, biting her bottom lip as they watched their crew march across the deck and down the gangplank. Where were they going?

Two men swooped down on Seraphina, untying her from the mast and yanking her toward the gangplank. She looked back at Mari, who followed behind her. The captain watched as the soldiers led them onto the pier, the wood creaking under their feet. The crew was already on the beach, surrounded by more guards as workers toiled away in the background.

Would she be slaving away at Tradesman Harbor? It would certainly be better than being sentenced to death. When she saw a caged carriage waiting for them where the beach ended and the road began, she itched for a hammer. Her steps slowed and her captor dug his fingers into her arm as he dragged her along.

Just like the last time.

Priest Sanchez had her arrested right after the tidal wave took out half of Aridia. She had pleaded with them to believe her, but it'd fallen on deaf ears. She told Priest Christian the truth about her sister and the scepter. He responded by sending her to the gallows. If it weren't for Samara and the pirate captain Baz Blackwater, she wouldn't be standing there.

I wouldn't be getting into another cage to face another death sentence.

Mari cursed as they threw her inside. The heavy door slammed shut, the lock creaking as the soldier turned the key. The sky rumbled in the distance, the clouds strolling past the sun. Captain Luis Fozo took his time coming down the pier, reading a piece of parchment while another sailor trailed behind him with a leather bag.

Are the book and scroll in there? Please, let them be in there.

Stealing them from him would be much easier than stealing them from aboard a ship. *By Macario's grace, Seraphina, you're talking about stealing from the Order.* It wasn't like she hadn't done it before with her sister's help. And, as she looked at Mari, who was already studying the ropes around her wrists, she would have to do it again.

Fozo disappeared around the front of their carriage, and she took a seat on the far side of the cage.

"Where do you think they're taking us?" She rubbed her sore legs.

"Don't know," Mari muttered before gnawing at the ropes again.

Their carriage jolted forward, settling into a rocking motion as they traveled away from the harbor. The road twisted away from Lucia and the breezy shore. The Golden Rose faded from view, nothing but desolate dunes on either side of them.

Seraphina braced herself as the carriage took a sharp turn, the road sloping downward to enter a forest of thick palms and brush. The canopy of rich green leaves kept out the sea breeze, the air heavy and humid as the sky darkened. A trio of calm and melodic bells rang in the distance as they cleared the dense jungle. Fire pits formed a winding line down the middle of the rather large clearing. They cast shadows on the slick brown rock face behind her, which extended well beyond the lights of the camp.

And it indeed was a camp. Three neat rows of perfectly pitched tents lined either side of the fire line. The last of the dusk clouds faded away, the full moon already glowing.

"Where are we?" Seraphina grabbed the bars as she stood.

"Don't know and don't care," Mari said, the ropes now loose around her wrists.

"Do you have a plan to get us out of here?" Seraphina whispered.

Mari looked up, her face unbothered by their present predicament.

"What do you think I've been doing the whole time you were daydreaming over there?"

The pirate captain stood up and went to the side of the carriage that faced the camp. Two soldiers stood with their backs to them a few feet away. They whispered to each other, a short and very scrawny one glancing back at them.

"What does a girl need to do to relieve herself around here?" Mari called out, her tone uncharacteristically sweet.

Both guards turned around, the fire behind them casting shadows on their scarred faces.

"Depends on what she's willing to do," the short one said, stopping beside the caged wagon.

Mari pressed her face to the bars, her words just above a whisper. "Open up this cage and I'll show you."

The soldier smiled, and Seraphina's stomach lurched. No. The grumpy pirate captain wouldn't stoop so low as to— She shook her head at the thought as the guard opened up the carriage door.

"If she plays nice, you may get out too," his companion sang, his eyes searching Seraphina's face. She backed up into a corner as the cage door opened. The men ogled her as Mari sauntered out.

Was that a smile? Is Mari flirting with them? The door clanged shut behind Mari, and Seraphina ran toward the bars. They closed in on Mari like wolves stalking their prey. Instead of heading for the tents and bonfires, they went around the far side of the carriage, disappearing into the shadows cast by the rock wall behind them.

What is she doing? This is not the Mari I know. Or had she ever known her?

Seraphina jumped at the loud thump and muffled cry that followed. The carriage rocked, and a body slumped against the bars before sliding to the floor. Mari stepped into view, leaning over the soldier's limp body, tugging the keys from his hip.

"Are they dead?" Seraphina whispered, running to the bars.

Mari didn't say a word, running over to the cage door and unlocking it. "Hurry!" she said through her teeth, and Seraphina rushed out.

Mari shoved a soldier's coat and hat into her arms.

"Just like the Justice House, I see," Seraphina said with a smirk, remembering the disguises they donned trying to get back the book from Priest Christian.

The book.

She gazed out into the darkness beyond the camp, putting her thin arms through the wide and sweaty sleeves. Escaping sounded like an excellent idea. A safer idea. An idea that wouldn't get her killed.

Mari pulled the Order hat down over her eyes, holding up a dead tree branch.

"Head for the horses while I start a fire."

"No." The word escaped her mouth before Seraphina could overthink it. There was no turning back now. "I can't leave without the book."

"I'm not stealing a damn thing."

Seraphina straightened her jacket, hoping it would instill the confidence she needed.

"Fine. I'll do it."

CHAPTER 9

LUIS

Touch my spirit so I may overcome my fears and bless me with the clarity to understand you will.

There was more to the Prayer for Guidance, but Luis couldn't bring himself to finish it. From the moment he closed his eyes to perform his evening prayer in his tent, all he could see was the light emanating from that book.

The coordinates. His portrait drawn right next to those pirate girls.

The Ancient Order foretold that Bedros would return and destroy the world. The sea serpent was just the beginning.

The Ancient Order were crazy heretics. A group of women who broke away from the Temple Order, creating confusion and chaos in their faith system. The Order eradicated them, so they couldn't corrupt anyone else.

Does your belief stop where the Order tells you? Or are you brave enough to follow His will even if it goes against the government you serve?

By Macario's light, he didn't know what to believe. Was his brother this tormented? Did he see the serpent this girl spoke of? Capturing those pirates was supposed to give him answers. Put his grief to rest. But as the tears welled in his eyes, it just made everything worse.

"Macario, I pray for answers," he said, squeezing his eyes shut. All he needed was to know what happened to his brother. Not prophecies, monsters, or secret libraries.

Just the pirate who ran his brother through.

We're all meant to find the Secret Library.

Luis got up from his knees, looking back at the Ancient Order book on his desk. A map of the main island poked out from underneath it. With careful steps, he walked over to it, opening the book like it was made of glass. He took his time flipping through the pages, his heart skipping a beat when he came to that page.

Fifteen degrees north. Twenty-three degrees south.

He reached into his pocket, taking his brother's compass into his palm. He savored the warm metal for a moment, then released it and withdrew his hand.

Wish you were here to make sense out of all this.

He pulled out the map, a red pin marking their current location. He ran his finger along the line of the mountains, past Santa Dolas to the far west to a patch of painted trees to a waterfall.

Only a day's journey from here.

The faces of the three people Macario supposedly called upon to find this place stared back at him. The seminary girl's eyes looked just as pure on paper as they did in person.

"Captain, I need that book back—right now!" Seraphina stood at the front flap of his tent, a sword trembling in her hand.

"How did you escape?"

"That doesn't matter." She strode over to him, pointing her cutlass at him.

"Where is your captain?"

Her eyes darted from the tent flap back to him. "Not here."

Her brown eyes followed him as he walked out from behind the desk.

"You're not going to hurt me."

She rushed him, the tip of the sword probing his neck. "I really don't want to."

"You won't get out of here." His eyes darted toward the flap of his tent, expecting his men to come charging through any moment to let him know about the prisoners' escape. *The book will be the least of your worries.*

"I will because you and the book are coming with me."

Luis scoffed. "I'm not going anywhere with you."

MJ MCGRIFF

Shouts permeated the tan fabric of his tent. He moved to see what was going on, wincing as the tip of the sword nicked his neck.

More shouts and screams. "Fire!"

"Get the water buckets."

Luis's eyes narrowed. "What did you do?"

"What we had to do."

Flickers of light grew outside his tent. *That blasted pirate.* The tent flap flew open and the devil herself rushed in.

"Seraphina," the pirate captain growled, "put the sword down before you hurt yourself. We gotta go."

The young girl drifted away from him. He snatched the sword out of her hand, slicing his own. Shaking off the pain, he grabbed her arm and pulled her against him, the crook of his arm around her neck. With his free hand, he grabbed the dagger hidden in his belt and held it to her neck. The pirate captain snarled, revealing the blades of the daggers in her hand.

"I'll kill you where you stand," she sneered.

"No!" Seraphina said. "No one is killing anyone. We have to find the library—together."

"I'm not finding any library," the pirate captain said.

"I hate to say this, but I have to agree." Luis smirked.

Smoke filled his nostrils, a glint of light on the edge of his vision. He swiveled to the right side of his tent. The fabric blackened and curled under the flame rising up the middle of the paneling. He couldn't keep Seraphina from running *and* her captain from trying to kill him.

But if we stand here and argue, we'll burn to death. He launched the dagger in Mari's direction, aiming just above her head. She hit the floor and Seraphina slipped out of his grasp, diving for the book. She barely had it in her hands when he grabbed her wrist and dragged Seraphina out the back of the tent. Smoke filled the night air like a mist. Dante, his all-black mare, tugged on his reins, just as eager to get out of the burning camp.

"What are you doing?" Seraphina cried.

"Get on the horse!"

His tent was engulfed in flames, the pirate captain nowhere to be seen.

He'd hunt her down later. Seraphina turned to the tent and then to him, her eyes wide and untrusting.

"If you want to live, you'll get on that horse," he said, his tone calmer despite his entire camp burning down around him.

She struggled onto the horse, Dante still skittish. He untied his horse and mounted behind her. With a hard tug of the reins, they raced out into the camp, thick black smoke all around them. Dante trotted to a stop, Seraphina clutching the book to her chest, her body shaking with every cough.

You know the way out, Luis.

He closed his eyes and saw the entrance to the mountain pass in his mind's eye. He and his men had scouted it out during his last visit. General Souza swore it was safe and well-patrolled, but he needed to be sure.

Didn't trust him then, and shouldn't have trusted him to secure these pirate girls.

He opened his stinging eyes and pulled Dante back to the mountainside, the horse taking careful steps. A ball of smoke rushed by, revealing just enough of the path to the rock face.

"Where are you going?" Seraphina cried.

"Somewhere safe," he said, flicking the reins and sending Dante into a full gallop.

The ground sloped upward, and the smoke thinned as they started up the narrow passage winding along the side of the mountain. Dante snorted and charged on. The ground leveled, a thicket of fern trees shielding them from the rest of the world. The chaos of the camp faded behind them until there was nothing but crickets and rustling trees.

Then, just as he remembered, the mouth of a small cavern came into view. He rode toward it, bringing Dante to a slow stop at the entrance.

"Are you all right?" He could feel Seraphina's eyes on him as he tied up the horse to the nearby tree. He could only imagine the flush of red on his neck. He looked up at her and offered his hand.

She held the book to her chest. "I'm not going anywhere with you."

Of course, you're not.

"You plan to spend the whole evening up there on the horse?"

She narrowed her eyes. "If it means not being tied up again or going into a creepy cave, then yes."

The rumble in the distance brought his attention to the sky. Gray clouds rolled across the full moon.

"Even if it means getting caught in the rain?" He smirked.

She narrowed her eyes and grabbed his hand, almost stumbling on the way down. He pulled out his spare knife from his side belt.

"You can't be serious!" She eyed the blade before glaring at him.

"Can never be too careful with pirates." *Not even a pretty one like you.*

The sound of pounding hooves drew closer.

Good. My men are already on their way.

CHAPTER 10

MARI

Dammit! Mari dove out of the bloody tent and rolled, the heat of the flames searing her arm and burning through her jacket.

And damn that stubborn nun.

She pulled off the jacket and threw it right into the arms of a soldier heading her way. Mari took off for the southern end of the camp. Black smoke billowed into her face as she wove through the tents that weren't on fire. The soldiers were too busy scrambling to save their own asses to notice her.

Mari cracked a smile. Her little diversion had worked.

The sound of pounding hooves in the smoke in front of her made her skid to a stop, pressing herself against a rock wall. A gray and black mare burst through the smog, its empty saddle flapping against its sides.

Perfect. She jumped out in front of it, holding out her arms, and it skidded to a stop.

"Easy there, now!" It stood on its hind legs, whinnying and kicking before coming back down.

"I'm not crazy about this idea, either,"—Mari lowered her voice to a soothing murmur—"but we either get out of here together or burn to death."

The horse cocked its head to one side, and she took that as an accord. She held her breath and walked over to it carefully, not letting out her breath until it let her grab the saddle. It took a few tries to hoist herself up, the animal stamping its hooves as the shouts grew louder.

"The stable's on fire!"

"Get those damn buckets!"

"Looks like we go north." She patted the horse on its mane. "Just don't knock me off, or I'll have you for dinner."

Mari grabbed the reins and snapped them hard. The horse took off like a bolt of lightning. She ducked as tent tarps whizzed past her head. Men jumped out of their path, making pathetic attempts to chase after them on foot. The tent in front of them burst into flames and the horse reared. Mari held on for dear life.

It landed hard, and it bolted for the rock wall. She tugged the reins to the right and the dumb animal stopped and trotted in circles. Black smoke surrounded them and the damn air stung her eyes. Blinking away tears, she straightened out the horse and yanked the reins, pots and pans bouncing off the ground as they rode past.

Then, by some miracle, the smoke parted. A black horse with two riders clattered up a rocky path away from the camp.

Damn, Seraphina.

The nun should've listened to her. Followed the plan.

Instead, she marched right into the stupid captain's tent, waving the sword at him like a child. All for a stupid book.

Mari had no time for anyone on her crew to disobey her—on or off her ship. She should just kick the damn horse and head north, through the narrow path that wasn't on fire. Double back around and head to Tradesman Harbor and save her crew from crushing rock and laying stone. Poor Amrit wouldn't last a day out there.

And he shouldn't have to.

But Seraphina was also part of her crew. And despite her dumb decisions, she wouldn't make it out there with Fozo either. All that man needed to do was flash that pretty boy smile and she would tell him everything about her crew.

Dammit!

Mari steered the horse onto the mountain path, kicking the animal in the sides. It took a leisurely trot up the narrow path. The beast must've felt her nerves, for it took careful steps until it reached the protection of the trees. The sky rumbled, lightning striking through the air.

As soon as the sky opened up, those clowns down there would have the fire under control and be combing the forests. She flicked the reins and her horse quickened its steps, the grassy path twisted before coming to a small clearing—and a cavern with a horse tied outside.

Mari drew the sword at her side, the rain pelting her face.

"Let's go," she whispered, digging her heels into the mount and charging toward the cave. She was halfway across the clearing when the captain stepped out, sword in hand.

"Where is she?" Mari demanded, bringing her horse to a short stop.

Seraphina stepped out of the cave, clutching the book. The captain blocked her path with a restraining arm.

"She's not going anywhere, pirate," Fozo spat. "And neither are you."

He raised his sword, its tip pointing between her eyes.

"Really, now?" Mari raised a brow.

Seraphina looked between them, scowling in obvious dismay. "You two must stop this!"

"Unless you want to join her at the gallows for escape and sabotage," Luis said to Seraphina, "you'll do well to go back into that cavern."

Mari dismounted, twirling the sword in her hand. "Somehow I doubt your pompous pontiff will get a noose around this neck."

Luis eyed her coldly, standing his ground. "You don't want this."

"Take your own advice, lawman." She lunged at his gut. He sidestepped, blocking her sword.

You're not the only one with quick feet, soldier boy. Mari slid away as he came at her quick and fast, swinging high, then low, and—just for show—whirling around to catch her on her left side. She blocked every one of his swings without even breaking a sweat. Not that she could tell the difference, since the rain fell in sheets and ran into her eyes.

Now it's my turn.

Mari swung at him—high right, low left—and stabbed at his chest, where their swords crossed before he pushed her back.

Just as she expected.

She tossed her sword to her left hand, flashing him a wicked smile.

"You Order men are so predictable."

He lunged at her, and she swerved out of the way, gliding with the mud under her feet. The Order captain swung low, and she blocked him with her sword.

"Do they not teach you how to fight with your other hand?" She grinned as his tanned face grew red.

With her left hand, she came at him hard, every block of his becoming more labored, though he tried not to show it. With the tree only a foot behind him, Mari kept swinging, pushing him closer to it.

Just a bit closer.

Their swords locked and her arm shook under the weight as he inched closer to the tree. She flicked her right wrist and the knife hidden in the sleeve slipped into her hand. She swung it around and cut his arm.

"Damn you!" He pushed her to the muddy ground and shook his right arm.

Mari jumped to her feet, just in time to block his sword over her head. He bore down all of his weight, but—like holding a helm in a bloody hurricane— she pushed him away just as his sword caught her in the thigh.

"Not so fun, is it, pirate?" He backed away, dark eyes glinting at his little victory.

Mari bit her lip as hot pain shot up her left leg. The cut wasn't deep enough to kill her. *So, shake it off, Mari.*

She assumed her fighting stance—sword in her right hand this time and the knife in her left.

"Haven't had enough, pirate?" Luis rolled his shoulders back.

"I'm just getting started."

Thunder boomed, and they both flinched, the horses leaving them to rot. Then lightning. Streaks flashed one after the other, like angry fireflies trapped in a bottle.

"Get inside!" Seraphina screamed, the rest of her sentence drowned out by the thunder. A blinding bolt hit the tree just a foot behind her.

"Look out!" Luis rushed Mari, grabbing her with both arms until they hit the ground. Another lightning bolt hit the ground where she stood.

"Bloody hell!" Mari pushed Luis off of her. Deadly strikes fell from the sky without mercy, creating a gauntlet of lightning between them and Seraphina. The nun-turned-pirate fell on her knees in the mouth of the cave, clasping her hands. *She'd better be praying for a miracle.*

Luis scrambled to his feet, slipping on the mud, and Mari matched him, clutching the sword.

"Don't you ever put your hands on me," she growled.

"Fine." He sniffed, flinging his head to shake back his wet hair. "I'll let you burn next time."

Firebolts kept falling from the sky, hitting the same patches of grass in front of them.

"We have to get in the cave." Luis scowled.

Mari glowered back at him, unmoving. "You will not tell me what to do."

Another strike hit the ground, vibrating through the mud and into her feet.

"I told you," the captain said, his eyes on the sky. Seraphina's head was still bowed in prayer clutching the book to her chest like she sat in a temple instead of in a cavern in the middle of a bloody lightning storm.

A gust of wind blew the rain in Mari's face and the sky went dark. Mist rose from the scorched earth. Seraphina leaped to her feet, her eyes wide as she ran over to them.

"What in the blazes was that?" Mari barked.

Seraphina shook her head. "I don't know."

Luis shoved past them both, and Mari pointed her sword at his chest. "Get back, Order rat."

"You would kill an Order officer and sentence yourself to death?" Luis crooked an eyebrow.

I'd rather not.

But facing down a fire-breathing serpent could change someone's perspective. Things hadn't been this eerie since the day they sailed to the Misty Isle to steal the scepter. Prophecies and monsters weren't so far-fetched now.

But my crew comes first.

And all the other stuff had to wait.

"Don't think you'll get away with this," he said, the rain slowing.

Trust me, I am.

Her fist struck him dead in the nose. She led with her shoulder, knocking him backward. He grabbed both her arms, and she head-butted him.

"Mari! Stop!" Seraphina waved her arms as if that would do anything.

Another punch to the face, and his head hit the wet ground. Hard. His eyes closed and his body stilled.

"What in the world are you doing?" Seraphina wrung her hands, staring at Mari like she'd lost her mind. "We need him!"

I don't have time for this. Mari grabbed her by the arm and dragged her away into the drizzling rain.

Screw prophecies and libraries.

My crew comes first.

CHAPTER 11

SERAPHINA

Seraphina's wrist pulsed with pain under Mari's grip. The captain dragged her through the trees, around rocky walls, and down slopes of wild grasses. When they reached a small clearing, Mari let her go. Seraphina shifted the book to the crook of her arm, rubbing her wrist and glancing at the line of identical palm trees surrounding them.

The slick green palms were wide and thick, shielding from view any easy way to get through them. The sky still loomed gray and foreboding, threatening another unnatural lightning storm any minute.

Mari didn't seem to care, sucking her teeth as she dug into her pocket. She pulled out a shiny, gold compass. Much too shiny to be hers.

"Did you—" Seraphina began.

"Yup," Mari said, flipping it open and focusing on the spinning arrow. "That's the least Fozo could do after putting me in that stupid box."

"You didn't have to knock him out." Seraphina sighed. "We need him if we're ever going to find the library."

Mari held out the compass, taking careful steps left, then right, her eyes on its spinning dial. She took a careful turn and her face soured.

"Crap. We gotta double back." She snapped the compass shut. "It'll take us at least three days to get back to the harbor."

Seraphina shook her head, taking quick steps toward Mari.

"No!"

Seraphina scared herself with how forceful that response came out.

Mari whirled around, her eyes narrow and cold as Winter Tide ice.

"What did you say to me?"

Seraphina swallowed. "We can't go back to the ship."

"Since when do you give me orders?"

"I'm not. I just—we can't..."

Mari put her hands in her pockets. Seraphina flinched. "All I'm saying is we shouldn't go back. Not yet, anyway."

Mari's features relaxed just a bit, scoffing as she looked away. "You know what? I think I'm quite done saving your ass for one day."

"It's not that I'm ungrateful for all that you've done for me..."

"Could've fooled me." Mari spun on her heels and headed to the tree line.

It would be so easy to shrink down and follow her through the known dangers of the Order to go after the crew in Tradesman Harbor.

But then what?

"You can't save the crew by yourself!"

Mari was good, but not that good. The Pontiff's men were already combing the forests looking for them. And after the bruising she gave Luis, they would take extra care to make her life miserable for as long as she still had one.

"Watch me, nun." She waved her hand in dismissal.

Say something, anything. Make her stay! To find the library they all needed to be together. *Even if hell has to freeze over to do so.*

"You won't make it out of the harbor."

Mari's footsteps didn't even falter.

"Another summer storm will ground the ship, at best. If it's a lightning storm like earlier, the ship will sink to the bottom of the sea."

The captain stopped short.

Praise Macario, this is working.

"Whether you believe it, all of this horrible weather is just a sign of what's to come."

She couldn't know for sure. But with a slighted and powerful god on the cusp of coming back, the world wouldn't be right. Weather included.

"If any of us are going to make it out of this realm alive, we need to know what we're dealing with."

Mari took long, casual strides back to Seraphina, not stopping until she was a breath away.

"What are you not telling me?" She poked Seraphina's shoulder hard. "And don't lie."

"I don't know how the end of the world is supposed to happen. But what I do know is that the library has the information we need to stop it."

Mari crossed her arms.

"And maybe treasure," Seraphina added.

"I don't risk my neck for 'maybes.'"

"What better way to duck Order guards than to go to a place they don't know exists?"

Mari raised a brow. "Except for your little boyfriend back there."

Seraphina's face warmed. He knew because the book wanted him to know.

"Only the coordinates. Besides, once we get in, you can lock him up, tie him to a tree, or whatever seems fair to you. We just need him to get inside."

At least, she hoped so.

Mari rolled her eyes and Seraphina's shoulders relaxed. "You and your sister are just alike—a pain in my ass."

Seraphina held up the book. "This book helped save us the last time. It will do it again. I promise."

Mari snatched it out of her hands, flipping to the page with the coordinates. She dug out the compass, flipping it open as her eyes darted from the page to the spinning arrow in her palm.

"Do you know the way? Is it far?" Seraphina's stomach knotted.

Mari closed the book and shoved it back into her hands.

"Does it look like I have a map? I only know the general direction." She pointed to the trees behind her. "And it's nowhere near where we need to go."

"The only thing waiting for us back there are Order soldiers. And what good will we be to our crew, then?"

Our crew. Who knew she would ever say those words?

But she couldn't ignore how her heart tore as she watched them march onto the beach in chains. They were good men behind their sweat and foul language. They accepted her for who she was, and without realizing it, she'd returned the favor.

But what about Mari?

Will she trust me the way she put her trust in Samara and Baz that night back in Bluegate? Believe in the unbelievable? Do what is right for the world and not just for herself?

"Mari, you are a brilliant captain. Baz wouldn't have chosen you otherwise."

Her lips tightened. "Don't you dare play that card with me."

Seraphina hugged the book to her chest. "I'm a terrible liar and you know it."

"What did you tell Fozo?"

"The truth. The three of us are destined to find the library. I don't know why, but after everything we've been through, I find it better not to question Macario."

The sky lightened, the gray clouds thinning. Just yesterday she was on the Pursuer. *Now, I am so close!*

"Mari, please."

"Son of a sea monkey," the pirate captain murmured, storming off into the trees.

A green palm snapped behind her. Seraphina trembled. *She left me.*

Just like that. After everything they went through. The serpent. The storms. How could she believe Samara, but not her?

She'd proven herself. Made herself a valuable member of the ship. Held up her end of the bargain she made back when the Pursuer was just a wrecked ship careened on a beach.

"Now what?" Seraphina mumbled to herself.

The sky was clear now, the orange rays fading. She turned in the direction Mari pointed earlier, breathing through the fear of what might be hiding in the shadows of those palms.

"Nothing can be as bad as a sea serpent," she reminded herself.

Or a tidal wave. Or the fire in the Quarter.

I can brave whatever is in that forest, right?

The cracking of tree limbs sent Seraphina staggering backward, her breath caught in her throat. The palms parted and Mari charged through.

Seraphina's heart jumped, a smile forming across her face.

Mari scowled. "You comin' or what?"

CHAPTER 12

MARI

Whatcha going to do, Captain Adlam?

She tightened her grip on the stolen sword, wishing it was the polished wood of the Pursuer's helm. She just needed to get back on her damned ship. Save her crew. Prove that she deserved the title of captain.

Instead, she was out in the middle of nowhere thinking about going after that stupid library. If it even existed.

That's what you said about the scepter, remember?

She was there the day Baz came back onto the ship from Siren's Cove, waving around the last piece of the map to the Misty Isle. He totally abandoned their normal pirate life to chase it down, promising it would be the score that set them up for life. He would be on the pirate council and any crew member of a Siren Cove leader would be treated like royalty. That meant free food, booze, and a cut of every haul in and out of the pirate haven. They would only raid if they wanted to, not because they needed to.

Instead, that treasure turned out to be one piece of powerful magic and Seraphina's impulsive and hard-headed sister Samara was the only one who could use it. Yet Baz took a chance, and in the end, he got everything he wanted—to live life on his terms and no one else's. That was what this captain's role was supposed to do for her. The chance for her to live her own life. *Not lose my ship and my crew to Order rats.*

She could only imagine the pirates of Siren's Cove laughing at her once news reached the Cove. Awful news always did. She could never show her face there until she redeemed herself.

Could stealing something from this supposed library do the trick?

It worked for Baz. He'd probably had songs written about him going to a cursed island, finding magic, and then slaying a monster.

She grimaced at the thought. *How can I live up to that?*

Mari pulled out the sword from the sheath on her hip and headed into the trees. *This is the damn Misty Isle all over again.*

Except this time, she was the one cutting through the untamed jungle, instead of keeping her distance in case any wildlife decided to show up. Luckily, Seraphina couldn't see her flinch with every swipe, hoping there weren't snakes or giant palm lizards lurking behind those cut palms. Fortunately for both of them, the only thing under their boots was rich, dark soil.

She stopped short, and Seraphina almost bumped into her as she spun around.

"You have five minutes to tell me everything you know about that library."

Seraphina cracked open her precious book, turning to the fated page. She handed it to Mari, who scanned every inch of the page. "The Oracle's Athenaeum is the proper name, and according to this picture, it's beneath the Pontiff's Palace."

The mountains. The fancy palace sitting on top of it. A cavern with a building inside, bookshelves lined with manuscripts.

"All the information Samara needs to save the world is in that library."

"Save the world from what?"

I need to know how all this mumbo jumbo affects me. And my ship and crew.

"This book says the serpent was just the first of many monsters that will be unleashed. Just like the War of the Gods."

An amusing tale Mari had heard in her travels around the Magian seas. Five gods roaming the Magian realms, showing off and whatnot. When one couldn't keep it in his pants, the other four went to war with him. Needless to say, it wasn't a fair fight.

"This book also says that Bedros will return and there will be another war."

Mari looked up. "Sounds like you got all the information you need."

"No." Seraphina shook her head. "We don't. The stones in Lucia showed how the serpent would attack us. But we don't know what other monsters may come and how. More importantly, we don't know how to defeat Bedros."

She took a breath. "The Order did a phenomenal job burying this prophecy. If they are going to such great lengths to kill us for even speaking about it, you know this is serious."

More monsters meant more ways for her plans to go wrong. She hated when Seraphina was right. Sailing into the open sea without knowing what other crazy shit she might come across was sailing into a squall. Mari closed the book, handing it to Seraphina.

"Do I smell palm fruit?"

Seraphina gasped, and Mari's stomach clenched with hunger. The sticky, sweet smell overpowered her nose. She cut away a large cluster of palms to reveal a gravel path. The narrow trail snaked around the forest of tall trees, heading in the general direction of the mountains.

Seraphina pushed past her, snatching up the big balls of orange fruit lying on the ground. Her fingers pierced the skin with precision, and she dug in face first, slurping happily. Mari sighed.

They needed to keep moving. There was no telling when Fozo and his landlubbing friends would catch up to them.

But I'll be damned if I do it on an empty stomach.

Taking out the knife tucked away in her boot, she sliced into the ball-shaped fruit lying by her foot. The squishy and syrupy-sweet fruit hit her, and her stomach ached for more of it. It was just her and that island fruit, Mari chewing so fast she almost bit her tongue.

"Palm fruit is especially sweet at this time of year."

Mari startled and looked up, dropping the fruit and grabbing her sword.

Captain Fozo stepped out from behind a tree a few yards in front of them, twirling the sword in his hand. Four more soldiers came out of the forest, flanking him on each side. *Clever Order rat.*

"Was wondering when you'd catch up," Mari said as Seraphina scurried behind her. "Enjoy your nap, captain?"

His jaw clenched.

"Fozo, please!" Seraphina pleaded. "You know the task Macario has given us!"

Her little boyfriend's eyes locked on hers.

"Surrender now and you won't get hurt," Fozo declared.

Mari took a subtle step backward.

"Come now," she said. "I hate to beat you in front of your little friends."

Seraphina took a step closer to her.

"What are we going to do?" she whispered.

Create another distraction.

Mari slowly lowered her sword, gripping the handle of the small dagger in her other hand.

"There is no need to make this any more difficult than it needs to be," Fozo said, stalking forward. "You're outnumbered."

"Clearly," Mari said, half-smiling as she tossed the sword to the ground. Fozo lowered his sword a touch, his shoulders relaxing. One of his men drew closer to him, closing rank.

Perfect.

Mari glanced at the man on Fozo's left. She took a breath and threw the dagger, not waiting to watch it slice through the air and land square in the Order man's neck. Mari turned on her heel and shoved Seraphina.

"Run!" she yelled, and the former nun turned on her heels and took off down the path. Mari wasn't far behind, running with no weapon and no plan.

Great job, Mari.

The road twisted and turned, bringing them deeper into that godforsaken forest. The heavy boots and swords of the soldiers chasing them were a little too loud for her taste. She couldn't keep running like this forever.

They came around another bend, and she pushed Seraphina into the dense forest on their right. The poor girl almost toppled over, but recovered quickly and skipped around those trees. Mari did the same, the slower pace giving her a chance to catch her damn breath. This would slow them all down for sure.

Long enough for her to think of what to do next.

"Stop!" Luis called out. "You can't keep running forever!"

Just to spite you, that's exactly what I'll do.

"Keep going!" she yelled after Seraphina.

If Mari didn't know any better, she would've thought Seraphina grew up in this forest, dodging trees while maintaining a good amount of distance between them. The Order captain continued to yell, but his voice was drowned out by rushing water ahead of them.

First these blasted trees. Now waterfalls. *Can this day get any bloody worse!*

Seraphina cleared the trees and skidded to a stop—mere inches away from the edge of a cliff. Mari slowed her steps, her heart dropping to her boots. Holding onto Seraphina's arm, she peered over the side. The ground plummeted straight down at least one hundred feet before disappearing under a roaring river at the bottom.

Seraphina looked at her, wide-eyed, her bottom lip quivering.

"What do we do? Where will we go?"

Curses. I wish I knew.

"Why don't you ask that benevolent god of yours?"

CHAPTER 13

SERAPHINA

Mari glanced back at the forest and Seraphina's heart sank. By Macario's grace, why was Luis still chasing them? They were headed in the right direction. After everything, why didn't Luis believe?

The captain and his Order men emerged from the forest, forming one straight line. Their swords gleamed in the sunlight.

"Please, Captain," she pleaded. "Everything I told you was the truth."

"So true, you knocked me unconscious?"

Seraphina shook her head. "Let's go to the coordinates in the book. If nothing is there, we'll go with you willingly. Punish us as you will."

"Speak for yourself," Mari snapped, reaching for a sword that wasn't there.

"I won't be falling for that again," Luis said. "Those coordinates place you down there in that roaring river, and that is the last place I want to be."

Seraphina clutched the book tighter to her chest. *That can't be true.*

She looked over the edge, the water fast and violent.

And something else.

The water twinkled, but it wasn't with sunlight. It pulsed and glimmered until it was so bright she couldn't even see the water.

And she couldn't hear it either.

"Don't move!"

"You're going to kill yourself."

Their voices were muffled as if she were underwater. She closed her eyes, and the world went quiet.

Until she heard the whispers. She couldn't understand a word, she reached out her hand, trying to see them in her mind's eye. Her body felt light as if she were floating, and when her eyes opened, she saw the water rushing at her. Nothing but air under her.

She was falling.

She opened her mouth to scream, but it choked in her throat.

This is it. I'm going to die.

Tears streamed down her face, and she closed her eyes, not wanting to see her demise when it came.

Instead, she thought of her parents. Her father lost at sea. Her mother, who died of summer fever. She would open her eyes and see them again. Just like Samara did in her dream before she took off for the Griffin Vales.

Her body no longer felt light. She slammed into a hard surface, her arms outstretched. She moved her hands, something dry and light crunching between her fingers. *Leaves?*

Her eyes flew open, and she rose to her feet. The book hadn't mentioned Macario's kingdom looking like an untamed jungle. The tops of the mile-high trees created a canopy so thick the sun struggled to shine through. The dead palm leaves formed a circle around her, the only clear space in a sea of brush and floor vines.

Crickets sang. Frogs croaked. The heat in the air sent beads of sweat down her back.

Samara.

She'd failed her. She'd got herself killed falling off a dangerous cliff nowhere near the secret library. Sobs caught in her throat as she fell to her knees.

"I'm sorry!"

It was all she could say.

A gust of wind blew through her sweaty hair. A blinding light surrounded her until she couldn't see anything.

"Dammit!"

The light flashed away, and Mari lay on the ground in front of Seraphina. The captain locked eyes with her and scrambled to her feet.

"What the hell just happened?!"

Seraphina tried to find the words. Sure, everyone was redeemable and deserved a chance to be in their god's kingdom for all of eternity.

But Mari made it here? The afterlife was full of surprises.

"One minute you're falling off a cliff, and the next you disappeared in mid-air," Mari ranted. "And then that bastard—"

Another white light flashed around them, and Mari cursed under her breath. Seraphina used her arm to shield her eyes, not taking it away until the light faded.

Captain Fozo lay at Mari's feet. Before she could say a word, his hand shot out and grabbed the pirate captain's ankle. He yanked her off her feet, and she landed hard on her back. In a flash, he was on his feet, standing over Mari with the tip of his sword at her neck.

"Give it to me!" he growled.

"We just fell off a bloody cliff, almost died, and you're still crying about this?" She held up the shiny gold compass in her hand.

"It doesn't belong to you," he said through his teeth.

"Captain!"

His eyes moved to Seraphina, his face flushed with sweat. She almost wanted to scold him for shedding blood in Macario's kingdom. *But something tells me this isn't the place people go when they die.*

No, this was something else entirely. But what?

Luis's eyes darted to her and then to the trees, his face twisting in confusion. Mari kicked him between the legs, rolling out of the way as his sword nicked her neck.

He doubled over in pain. "You damned pirate!"

Mari rolled to her feet, tucking the compass away as she walked over to Seraphina's side. Luis took a breath and shoved himself upright again.

"What just happened? Where in the world are we?"

"I was trying to figure that out before you came crashing in," Mari said. She didn't take her eyes off him as she wiped the blood off her neck.

"I didn't ask to be here!" He snarled and lifted his sword again. "What manner of evil magic is this?"

Mari snorted. "You shouldn't have lunged at me. It's your damn fault we ended up here."

Seraphina laid a trembling hand on Luis's arm, swallowing her nerves. *Macario, please help me keep these two from killing each other. We just got here.*

"Captain, we were meant to be here. You said so yourself. The coordinates were in the middle of the river."

And, by some stroke of magic or divine intervention, they were there together in this strange-looking jungle. Luis bit his lower lip, jerking his arm out from under her touch.

"Start explaining, Seraphina," Mari ordered, not taking her eyes off the captain. "This idiot isn't convinced and I'm tired of having a sword at my neck."

Seraphina shook her head. "I can't. I can't explain any of this. Before you two arrived, I thought I was dead."

"Well, you're not." Luis snorted, indicating Mari with the tip of his sword. "Otherwise, this heathen wouldn't be here."

"This heathen will gladly kick your ass—again."

Mari took a step toward him and Seraphina grabbed her arm.

"This is not the time to fight amongst ourselves," she said. "It's clear we are on the path to finding the library—together."

They both scoffed at the same time.

"I'm not finding anything," Luis declared. "Except a way out of here, so I can bring you two to justice."

"We're not going anywhere with you." Mari spat.

With one quick swipe, he sliced the blade across Mari's chest. His free hand grabbed Seraphina and pulled her to him. They stood but a breath apart, the tip of his sword at her neck, and his black eyes looking straight through her.

She should've felt afraid of being this close to a sword. Maybe she was naïve, but she knew he wouldn't hurt her.

He could've left her to burn in that camp. Or hurt her in the cavern. He wasn't just a blind lawman. The small altar he had to Macario in his quarters was proof.

And the god that they both fiercely believed in put them together for a reason. A part of him had to know that. Otherwise, he wouldn't have made it this far.

"Tell me how we get out of here," he said, his breath warm against her skin.

"I don't know."

"What does your book say?"

"I can find out if you put the sword down." Her voice was calm and even.

He lowered the sword, taking a few steps back.

"If I ever get my hand on a sword, I'm going to gut you," Mari swore, staring down at the fresh tear in her shirt. Blood stained the ripped edges, a nasty cut peeking through.

"It's just a scratch," Luis said. "You'll live."

And I thought my sister was exasperating!

Seraphina cracked open the book, praying for a ray of light to shine through its pages and show them what to do next. *If we stay here any longer, those two will kill each other and I will never find the library.*

The frogs and crickets went silent. Maybe they were tired of those two arguing. She flipped to the last page and sighed. Nothing new. Only shadows danced along the parchment. She looked up, the sun still shining through the palms. Also nothing out of the ordinary.

"What does it say?" Luis pressed.

Seraphina opened her mouth to answer, but a loud, unnerving sound made her shut it again.

Hiss.

They all froze, Seraphina afraid to breathe.

Hiss.

It was too loud to be coming from a garden snake, though the slithering black creatures scared Seraphina to death. *By Macario's grace, please don't let this sound come from anything bigger.*

She slowly turned to Mari, whose eyes drifted upward. The pirate captain cursed fluently under her breath.

"This is why I hate bloody jungles!"

CHAPTER 14

LUIS

This wasn't a divine or holy place. This was a pit of hell.

Three giant snakes coiled overhead, their boulder-sized heads slipping down from the canopy of palms stories above them. Their blood-red tongues flicked back and forth, their yellow eyes fixed on the three humans. Their green and black scales gleamed in the sunlight, their writhing bodies wide enough to swallow a small boat, sails and all.

Not even pirates deserved to die at the hands of these monsters.

Luis took careful steps toward the pirates. Seraphina took her time closing the book, inching closer to Mari, who'd gone pale. Behind them, a narrow path covered in vines disappeared into the foliage. Any one of them might trip and sprain an ankle.

But it's better than staying here to be swallowed by these monsters.

He tightened his grip on his sword, the blasted leaves cracking under his feet. Mari's wide eyes went from the snakes to him. She opened her mouth to speak, but he signaled for her to be quiet.

Snakes usually had horrible eyesight. No need to help them by making noise. He gestured to the path and they both turned around. Mari started first, taking careful steps down the path.

He motioned to Seraphina to follow, but she stood frozen in place, her eyes wide in horror. Luis gently tapped her shoulder. She jumped and unleashed a scream he swore Macario himself could hear.

She just invited those monsters to eat us!

Luis glanced up at the snakes, which were a hundred yards above, their eyes staring right at them. On cue, they opened their mouths, flashing their fangs. Swallowing down the fear clawing up his throat, he turned to Seraphina. But she was halfway down the path, jumping over vines with surprising grace. He took off after them, his pace slowed down by those treacherous roots. His foot caught on one of them, sending him flailing until he regained his balance.

Hiss!

He made the mistake of glancing back.

Liquid dripped from the snakes' fangs a mere five yards behind him, their bodies slithering across the dead palms. Fear caught his breath, his body moving with a renewed sense of energy. He wasn't running anymore, but gliding over the roots. The girls were far ahead of him, rounding the corner into a thicket of trees.

Maybe that was a good thing.

With his sword still tight in his hand, he charged forward, rounding the corner like a crazed man. More dead palms, more twisted vines. But no pirates.

Of course, they left you behind to be snake food. They're pirates.

Luis jumped over a vine, only to have his foot catch on another. He landed on his chest hard, knocking the wind out of him. He shook it off, rolling quickly onto his back and coming face to face with a snake towering over him, jaws open wide.

Not today. He had no intention of becoming its meal.

The monster met the wrong end of his sword, its point slicing through the roof of its enormous mouth. It wriggled and writhed, bearing down on his shaking sword hand. He turned his head to create more distance between him and those wet fangs. The sword was only aggravating it, not killing it.

Praise Macario, I do not want to die like this.

It screeched, its head ripping off his sword, and Luis scrambled to his feet. The serpent's body went limp, its head hanging from the ax lodged in its neck.

"I'm going to need that back." Mari stepped out from behind the trees. "Unless you want to get eaten by them." She gestured to the other two snakes hissing with fury as they slipped closer, their scales rasping on the vines.

I don't know what just happened, but we'll sort this all out later.

He rushed over to the dead snake, his hands wrapping around the handle of the double-headed ax. He had seen nothing like it before—where had Mari gotten it, anyway?—but thank the Magian gods it was there.

Before he could even attempt to dislodge it, the second snake's large black tail wrapped around his waist. Luis coughed for air. *Don't let go.* The ax came free from the monster carcass as the snake lifted him in the air. The jungle swirled around him and the beast twisted him to meet its beady-eyed gaze. It opened its mouth, displaying gigantic fangs.

It would share its comrade's fate.

As its mouth came down, he pulled back the ax, slicing its bottom jaw in two. Hot coppery blood splattered all over him, and the serpent's tail loosened its grip. He sailed to the ground, the carcass of the dead snake breaking his fall.

A scream ripped through the air and he scrambled to his feet. The third snake slithered over its brethren, straight for Mari. He ran to her, and she looked back at him, hand outstretched. Without thinking, he tossed the ax, and she caught it. She whirled around, the ax high above her head, and brought it down on the last snake's skull.

The pirate captain stepped back, watching with indifference as the monster convulsed to its death. Seraphina emerged out of the trees, her hands shaking as she held the book to her chest.

"I thought we were going to die," Seraphina said, peering at the dead monsters.

"Nope. Not today." Mari sauntered over to the beast she'd killed. She grabbed the handle of the ax sticking out of its skull.

Luis blew out his breath, questions swirling in his mind. Where did those snakes come from? What was this cursed place? Where did those two disappear to? Where in Macario's name did they get that ax?

"Why did you help me?" The question tumbled out of his mouth.

After a few tugs, Mari pried the ax free. She wiped the tar-like blood on the skin of the dead snake before resting the ax over her shoulder.

"If anyone is going to enjoy killing you, it will be me." The pirate captain smirked, looking dead in his eyes.

She didn't make any sense. The pirate who took part in the carnage on Bluegate went out of her way to save him. They could've left him to die. It would have certainly made their escape that much easier.

But escape to where?

"The ax is mine." Mari gestured to the serpent that almost ate him. "I'm sure that animal didn't swallow your sword."

She's insufferable. That was for sure. As much as the thought of fishing for his sword in the mouth of a dead snake made his empty stomach churn, he wouldn't dare travel this forest without a weapon. He couldn't be at the mercy of whatever else lay in the forest. Or these pirates, for that matter.

Seraphina gasped, and he and Mari looked at her.

Her magic book. It was glowing again.

She knelt on the ground and opened it, furiously turning its pages. He stepped quickly to her side, dropping to a knee beside her. Mari peered over Seraphina's shoulder, shaking her head.

Seraphina stopped at a blank page, light encircling the edges. Then the magical ink appeared. In the top left corner, an invisible hand drew a jungle of tall palm trees, snakes dangling from the canopy.

"That would've been helpful a few minutes ago," Mari mumbled under her breath.

A snaking path led to a tall gate with the letters SS written on the front. As quickly as it came, the light disappeared, leaving them with a rudimentary map.

"What does this mean?" Luis ruffled his sweaty hair.

"It means this is the next place that will lead us to the library," Seraphina said, her voice cracking.

He was not here to find a library. He needed to get those two into custody and back to the mainland. If there even was a mainland.

Don't get ahead of yourself, little brother. It was as if his brother were right next to him, keeping him on task. Making sure the pirates met the hand of justice was the ultimate goal.

But first, he had to survive this evil place.

Then, he'd find out the truth of what happened to his brother.

He rose to his feet, not saying a word as he went to retrieve his sword out of the dead snake's mouth. After a few pulls, it slid free.

"So, we are all in agreement then?" Seraphina looked at Mari and then Luis.

"What am I agreeing to, exactly?" Mari narrowed an eye.

"That we won't kill each other before we make it to the next destination on that map."

Luis grimaced as he tore off a section of his shirt to clean the serpent's blood off his sword. The shirt was a loss anyway.

He glanced up at them, sheathing his sword. He couldn't achieve either of his objectives without gaining their trust.

"Fine," Luis said. "As long as she returns my compass to me."

Mari glared at him, casting a sideways glance at Seraphina.

The nun gave the pirate a pleading look. Mari rolled her eyes, digging into her pocket and pulling out the only thing he had left of his brother. She tossed it like it was a piece of trash, and Luis strained to catch it.

"I won't kill you today Order rat," she said. "Can't make any promises about tomorrow, though."

Neither can I, pirate. Neither can I.

CHAPTER 15

MARI

Mari's new ax grew heavy in her hands as she trailed Seraphina and that Order rat, Fozo. The giant snake-infested jungle they'd magically landed in was behind them.

Good riddance.

Though she should feel relieved, she wasn't crazy about their new surroundings, either. A sea of burnt brown grasses spread out for miles on either side of them. The blades extended well over their heads and into the dusky orange sky, providing plenty of cover for any other oversized creature to hide.

But the Order captain forged ahead like a stupid hero, using his sword to cut their path. Mari took one look at the change of scenery and hung back, her ax ready for any crazy thing to come at them.

Finding that weapon among the bones of some unfortunate fool was a stroke of luck. If only the cursed forest hadn't been so thick. The tree trunks had twisted into a thorny wall so high it was impossible to climb.

So, instead of running off and letting those snakes make a snack out of the Order rat, she had to kill them—and, unfortunately, save him.

"Sounds like there's a river up ahead!" Fozo called out. "We'll make camp there."

Mari opened her mouth to protest, but her growling stomach forced it shut. *Let's hope this godforsaken place has some nice-sized fish to eat.*

Fozo gave one good swipe, and the river came into full view. Though it was at least a few yards wide, the waters ran clear and calm. It should be passable.

Man-sized rocks lined either side of the bank, patches of rich, black dirt separating them from the grassy lands they'd spent all day crossing. A few paces away, a lone tree with a thick trunk clung to the bank, its naked branches curling over the river.

"I thought we would never get a chance to rest!" Seraphina plopped herself down on one of those gray rocks. Mari rolled her eyes. *Spoiled nun.*

"You'll also get a chance to starve if you don't get off your ass and help me get some wood for a fire." Mari stomped off toward the tree. She didn't turn around to see if the nun was following.

Ship or no ship, she was still Seraphina's captain.

"No bother, I'll get it," Luis called out.

"We've got it," Seraphina called back, shuffling to Mari's side. Seraphina stood there and watched as Mari searched the trunk for a foothold.

"I think he's starting to trust us," Seraphina said in a low voice.

"Don't get your hopes up." Mari sucked her teeth, settling for using a low branch to pull herself up. Putting the ax in her left hand, she squatted down and jumped, barely catching the branch.

"We're making progress," Seraphina continued. Mari's arms shook under the weight of pulling her body up and onto the branch. "Once we get to the library, he'll believe us. Then, there's no way he will arrest us when we get back."

Ah. There was that insufferable optimism again.

Mari shook her head. *If we get back.*

From her vantage point in the tree, Mari could see the acres of dull brown grass beyond the river. There wasn't a mountain, a cluster of trees, or even another body of water. The orange rays of the setting sun shone on a sea of absolute nothingness.

The perfect way to die of starvation, thirst, or heat exhaustion.

A splash in the water diverted her attention back to the river. Fozo stood waist-deep in the water, his tattered shirt lying on the bank. Using his sword, he trapped a fish against the river bottom. When he got a good grip, he pulled out a large, wriggling fish.

Perhaps you're not worthless after all.

Yet fishing without a shirt was unnecessary. Unlike other girls—she shot Seraphina a pointed look—Mari wasn't swayed by a nice set of stomach muscles. She'd seen enough naked men in the Enchanted Cape to last her a lifetime.

A man she could trust, rely on, who was strong enough to deal with her brusque personality? Now *that* was attractive. Like a pirate on her crew. A pit formed in her growling stomach.

What were they doing to her men back in Tradesman Harbor?

No, Mari. Survive today. Worry about tomorrow when it comes.

She put the ax in her right hand and took to chopping the branches above her. After missing the first two she dropped, Seraphina caught the others. She created a neat pile beside her. When they had enough wood for a decent fire, Mari took a breath and jumped down.

"Captain, I just want to say thank you." Seraphina flashed Luis her most charming smile.

Mari snorted, twisting a handful of dried grass into a bird's nest.

The Order captain looked up from skewering his catch. "For what?"

"Believing me," Seraphina replied. "Together, I just know we'll find the library and help Samara."

Mari grunted, giving the nun a sharp look. "Just because I haven't killed your little friend over there doesn't mean I believe anything. When I figure out how to get out of here, we are getting our crew back. Library or no library."

She walked back to their makeshift camp, putting an end to any more of that stupid conversation. The sun was setting, and she worked quickly to arrange the wood into a loose cone shape, standing twigs in the center and placing the bird's nest in its heart.

Mari reached for the flint and steel in her pouch, striking a few sparks and blowing gently until it caught. Flame curled up, the smoke stinging her nostrils.

She didn't have to think about it, her hands knew what to do. Building a fire was one of the few talents she held onto from her life before the Enchanted

Cape. Everyone back in her tiny Godswood village knew how to build a fire before they could walk.

When Fozo finally splashed out of the river, the flames had caught on the kindling, sending smoke into the starry sky. He had two fish in each hand, their grayscales shimmering in the firelight.

"Are those safe to eat?" Seraphina leaned forward, clinging to her perch on a rock.

"If they're ugly, you can eat them," Mari answered, taking a seat on the soft soil between Seraphina and the captain.

"Your friend is right," Luis said, laying the fish down on a flat rock beside him.

"Of course I am," Mari snapped, eying those fat fish as her stomach growled again.

He didn't come back with a retort, focusing on not burning himself as he pulled out three sticks from her perfect fire pit. Mari opened her mouth to curse him, but then, how else would they get that fish into her belly? She would let it slide for now.

"How did you learn how to fish?" Seraphina watched intently as he skewered the first fish on the sharpened end of one of the sticks.

"My father was from a fishing village outside of Mazas."

"My papa was a fisherman, too," Seraphina said, sounding a little *too* happy.

Mari rolled her eyes. How disgustingly cute.

Fozo picked up the fish skewer and offered it to Mari. "Consider this a truce while we figure our way out of here."

Mari glared at him and snatched it out of his hand. "I consider it my dinner."

She looked to her piece of fish and the fire, trying to concentrate on how good it would taste when it was cooked.

"What did you see while you were up there, Captain?"

It took a moment to register that Seraphina was talking to Mari, and not her little Order boyfriend.

"A whole lot of nothin'," Mari replied.

They wouldn't make it far without water or food. Tomorrow, she had to get that Order boy to catch more fish. She also had to find something to use as a canteen before she even thought about going back into the wild.

"Did you see any trees, water, anything we can use for provisions?" The Order captain raised an eyebrow.

"What part of 'a whole lot of nothin'' did you not understand?" Mari said, turning her fish over to roast the other side.

"We've made a mistake charging into this mission blindly," Luis said, getting comfortable in his seat on the ground. "In the morning, we'll gather enough fish and water before we continue on this quest."

Gee, wish I'd thought of that.

"But with what?" Seraphina frowned. "We don't have any satchels or canteens."

"Judging from the look of that ax, there were people here before." Luis shrugged. "I'm sure we can find something."

Mari looked up at him, his eyes boring into her.

"So, your idea is to get even more lost trying to find the comforts of home?" Mari clicked her teeth. "You've lived in your gilded Order cage far too long."

Unlike the Order rat, she'd spent her entire life making do with very little. From the dirt floors of her childhood home to the decks of her pirate ship—it was another skill she'd been forced to learn.

Mari pulled her fish out of the fire, inspecting its darkened skin.

"What do you suggest?" The kindness act was starting to fade.

She held up her skewered fish. "Plenty of wood for carrying fish."

Mari gestured over to the dark path that brought them to the river. "From what I remember, snakeskin makes for great canteens."

"We would lose an entire day going back for those," Fozo declared.

Seraphina gagged, almost spitting out the fish in her mouth. "Please tell me you're joking."

"Since when have I ever joked around with you?" Mari said, though she had to admit, the idea made her stomach lurch a bit too.

Being thirsty was even worse. The ache in her throat. The delirium. Her brothel madame loved to withhold the basics of survival when her girls didn't have a good night.

Mari bit into her fish, the bland skin crackling in between her teeth. Luis began eating his. Seraphina picked at her meal. The crackling of the fire was the only thing breaking the silence between the three of them.

Seraphina wasn't going to volunteer to go back to that forest and skin a snake. From the way Luis sat there with nothing to say, he wasn't going to do it either.

Mari sighed, resigned. "Since the last thing I want to do is die of thirst out here, I'll go back and skin the snake."

Cowards.

CHAPTER 16

SERAPHINA

Sunlight warmed Seraphina's face, bringing her softly out of a deep sleep. And she'd slept quite well. The adrenaline of being chased first by men and then by monsters had subsided as soon as she ate the last morsel of her roasted fish. Add to that an extremely long day of walking through unknown grasslands.

She hadn't cared if she had to sleep in the dirt. All she'd wanted to do was sleep.

And keep sleeping.

Seraphina rubbed her eyes before opening them, expecting to see those tall brown grasses. Heaven knew she grew tired of staring at them, afraid something would jump out at them.

Except they weren't there.

Lush, green, gently rolling hills went on for miles. Seraphina scrambled to sit up, reaching for the rock behind her to help her to her feet.

But that wasn't there either.

She whipped around. No rocks. No river. No sea of nothingness.

More green. More hills. Tall, thick trees with blinding green leaves and branches that intertwined with each other to form a barrier. From what, she couldn't see. Sweet song jerked her eyes upward. Flocks of bright blue birds flew overhead, creating intricate patterns in the sky.

"Where in the bloody hell are we?!" Mari leaped to her feet, the ax at the ready.

Luis struggled to stand, drawing his sword. His eyes squinted in the sunlight, his clothes disheveled.

"What is this place?"

They both looked at Seraphina as if she had all the answers.

"I don't know!" She shrugged. "I'm just as surprised as you are."

At least the Ancient Order book was right where she'd left it, its cover dirty from being next to her all night. She shuffled the pages until she reached the one with the map.

It looked just as it had a day ago. The path curved out of the jungle and around the blank parchment until it came to a gate with SS in the middle of it. She glanced up from the page to the line of trees and tilted her head to the side. With enough imagination, those trees could resemble a gate.

"What is it?"

Luis's voice made her jump. The Order captain peered over her shoulder.

"I think those trees over there form the gate in this picture," Seraphina said, trying to ignore the sparks of nervousness going down her spine because he was standing so close.

"And this library is beyond those trees?

Why are you standing so close to me? "I don't know. I'm just following this map."

Mari walked over to them, wiggling the ax at her side.

"That blasted book has been nothing but trouble. First, we fall off a bloody cliff and land in a jungle. Now the damn terrain is changing while we sleep?" She huffed. "I didn't sign up for this crap."

"Neither did I." Luis took a step away from Seraphina and she could finally draw in a shaky breath.

"But," he said, his voice even and calm, "our only option is to move forward and hopefully find a way out of here."

"Macario wants us to find this library," Seraphina added. "We need to know what we're up against."

The pirate captain put her free hand on her hip, slapping the ax against her thigh.

"Mari, we can't do this without you," Seraphina said, edging toward her. "You're one of the bravest people I know."

"Stop kissing my ass." Mari shot a mean glance at Luis before turning back to Seraphina. "Let's get this over with."

Luis took a step toward the tree-gate, then Mari did the same, each of them eyeing the other, ready to pounce like mountain cats. *When will they realize that it takes less energy to trust one another than hate each other this much?*

Their great god, Macario, had chosen the three of them to find one of his most sacred sanctuaries. He was leading the way, the magic book in her hands.

This was an honor.

Terrifying, but an honor all the same. With every step she took, the knot in her stomach grew heavier. Was the library behind those trees? Did it look like the Old Seminary outside of Mateo, with cracked stone walls and slimy moss?

And she couldn't forget about the trap door in the floor where she first found the Ancient Order book. The Order went to inordinate lengths to get the book and bury the prophecy, along with her too.

Had it not been for Samara and the others, Seraphina wouldn't be walking across those rolling hills toward an unknown line of trees. Was Samara just as close to finding the Spell Keeper as Seraphina was? Was Macario leading them both to the answers they needed to save the world at the exact same time?

How amazing would that be?

When they reached the top of the last hill, the trees came into full view. A builder could have carved an entire ship out of one tree trunk. Seraphina craned her neck to see its crown as it rose at least thirty feet into the sky. The thick branches of each of the twelve trees twisted up into the canopy of man-sized green leaves.

Luis stepped close to Seraphina, Mari joining on her other side. The small gaps in between the trees only gave glimpses of more greenery behind them.

"Look at that." Luis pointed his sword to the middle trunk. Two large Ss' were carved into the dark wood.

Just like in the book.

"What's that stand for?" Mari walked over to get a closer look.

Seraphina sighed, looking up at the sky hoping for an answer in one of those powdery clouds above them. If finding the library depended on the lessons about Macario and his might that she received back in the seminary, they would find it before nightfall.

But all she knew about the Ancient Order, the religious predecessors of their present government, was in the book. Which, for being a magical manuscript, wasn't exactly being helpful and forthcoming. Other than the details of the serpent attack that had already happened, she didn't know much.

And I should. She'd been so foolish to think she could find this place with only a rudimentary map.

Faith, Seraphina. Rely on your faith.

"I'm sure we'll find out," she said, ignoring Mari's rolled eyes.

Throwing the ax onto her shoulder, Mari ducked through the narrow opening between the massive tree trunks. Seraphina took a breath and followed her through, bumping into Mari's back. The pirate captain stood frozen in awe. Seraphina didn't know whether to be amazed or afraid.

Either reaction would be warranted given this unbelievable situation.

Stems rose out of the white-speckled soil, reaching almost as high as the trees shielding them. Flowers at their tops swayed overhead in the gentle breeze. The red and yellow petals reminded Seraphina of the island tulips she and Samara used to pick in the inland forests on their home island of Bluegate.

"This place just gets stranger and stranger." Luis paused at her side, eyeing the oversized patch of flowers.

"These are beautiful." Seraphina smiled.

Mari snorted, quickly glancing at Luis, then turning back to the flowers.

"The prettier they are, the more dangerous they can be. The Misty Isle taught me that much."

"You've never been to the Misty Isle," Luis scoffed.

"Of course she has," Seraphina said. "Where do you think my sister got Macario's Scepter?"

Luis raised a brow. "Am I supposed to believe that?"

"Believe whatever you want, Order rat," Mari said. "If this crazy place hasn't made you a believer by now, there's no hope for you."

As if on cue, the book began to glow.

Finally. Seraphina welcomed the light emanating from the pages. Eyes wide, she opened it to the last page. Tall flowers appeared behind the gate, a winding path going straight through them. It led straight out into the blank page, ending at the mouth of a cavern.

Could this be the library?

"A trip through the flowers," Seraphina said. "What can go wrong?"

Luis drew his sword. Mari twirled her ax. *Sure. What could go wrong?*

Luis charged into the field of flowers first, Seraphina following him. The path was narrow, and she had to step carefully to avoid knocking into the oversized stems. If they were delicate like the ones back home, they would topple right on top of them.

And who would want to die at the hands of a big flower?

Their petals remained closed, pointing to the sky, where the birds still sang.

Seraphina, don't tell me you're afraid of flowers?

It was something Samara would say if she were here. What was she doing now? Was she experiencing something just as fantastical? Or was she safe and out of trouble?

Seraphina huffed a breath of laughter.

Out of trouble? We know better than that!

She glanced over at Luis, her breath catching. His dark, enchanting eyes were on her, and he gave her a confident nod before continuing on. Seemed like she'd acquired her sister's tendency for trouble.

A loud cracking noise ripped through the air, and all three of them came to a halt. Fat green stems surrounded them on either side. Too far to turn back now.

"What was that?" Seraphina whispered.

Mari and Luis didn't say a word, their eyes scanning every inch of the surrounding stalks.

Crack.

Pop.

Seraphina's eyes locked on the rich soil under her feet, her heart drumming in her chest. *There's nothing up there. No snake trying to eat us. Or anything crazy like that.*

"You gotta be kidding me," Mari mumbled under her breath.

"We have to move!" Luis whispered.

Mari slid up beside her, her dreads tickling Seraphina's arm. She jumped, and her pirate captain clasped a hand over her mouth.

"If you scream, we're dead," she whispered, tilting her chin upward.

Mari removed her hand, and Seraphina looked up. Fear crawled up her throat. The petals were open, the flower heads dancing around as if looking for something.

Something like us, perhaps.

One tilted slightly, revealing the insides of its petals.

Teeth.

Rows and rows of jagged, skin-piercing teeth.

Praise Macario, what kind of place is this?

Mari shoved her along after Luis glancing back every so often to make sure they were following. It was the longest path she had ever taken, clutching the book to her chest in a feeble attempt to slow down her beating heart.

But her feet kept moving, weaving through the writhing stems.

Writhing stems. Macario, see us through.

He must've heard her silent prayer, for the path widened to reveal a small clearing. They all picked up the pace, Seraphina keeping her eyes on the exit, the place of safety from these bizarre, people-eating flowers.

They would survive. Maybe even find the library by nightfall. *You can do this. It'll all be worth it.*

A sharp pain shot up Seraphina's foot, and before she could blink, she fell forward—right into the sea of twisting flower stems. She grabbed one to break her fall, the stem pulsating under her grip. She let go and fell hard to the ground, rolling herself back into the path.

Luis was halfway out of the lethal flower patch before he heard her cry and spun around. Mari huffed, helping Seraphina to her feet. They stared upward, hoping for a moment that the flowers hadn't noticed.

Then one shrieked. A sound like a dying seagull ripped through her ears.

The other flowers joined in, shooting downward into the path.

Straight at Seraphina and Mari.

"Run, dammit!" Mari pushed Seraphina away, sending her staggering. But she kept her balance and darted at Luis, who ran right at them, sword in hand. She clutched his outstretched hand, and they ran, not stopping until they were halfway across the clearing.

"You monstrous bastards!" Mari shouted.

Seraphina spun around and her eyes widened in horror. A man-eating flower had Mari in its grasp, one of its leaves twisted around her waist. Her ax lay on the ground, her hands pounding at the creature as its petals snapped open and shut, excited to make a meal out of her.

By Macario's light!

How were they supposed to survive this?

CHAPTER 17

LUIS

Giant carnivorous plants.

In all his years of training in the Order naval army, nothing could have prepared Luis for this insane adventure. First, oversized serpents. And now, flowers ruined by height and teeth ready to pierce the flesh of their grumpy pirate captain.

Seraphina shoved the book into his hands and took off for the patch of carnivorous foliage.

That poor girl is going to get herself killed.

"Stop!"

She ignored his calls. Sighing, Luis set the book down and ran after her. One of the flowers shot out in front of her, flashing its teeth. He grabbed her arm, pulling the nun-turned-pirate behind him. The petals leaped at him and he brought down his sword, slicing one of the lethal petals right off. The flower yelped and pulled away, clearing the path.

Seraphina tried to dodge around him so he tightened the grip on her arm. "You can't go back in there!"

"We have to help the captain!" She yanked her arm away. Her lip quivered, yet she spun and headed into the madness.

And heaven knows I can't let her go in there alone. Luis took off after her, swinging his sword at anything that wasn't human.

Teeth-filled petals.

Wriggling stems.

More pesky petals.

Unlike the monstrous snakes, these things were no match for his sword. But they did test his energy. He was a sailor, not a soldier.

"Mari!"

Seraphina screamed and Luis whirled in time to see the pirate captain falling from the sky. Before she hit the ground, a petal from those man-eating flowers grabbed her leg.

"Hold on, Mari!" Seraphina scrambled toward the flower stem, Mari's ax in hand. Luis only made it two steps in her direction before another flower blocked his path. It took two swipes with his sword to get it out of his way.

Seraphina was already hacking away at the flower petal. She screamed, giving one more good swing before she split the petal in half. It let go and Mari spiraled straight to the ground. Luis jumped over the fallen foliage, arms stretched out to catch her.

Mari crashed down on top of him, knocking the wind out of his chest as they both hit the ground. He waited for a shot of pain that came with a broken bone. It wouldn't be his first.

"You bloody idiot!" Mari cursed, rolling off him. Luis sucked in a breath, his ribs burning as he struggled to his feet.

"Are you all right?" Seraphina knelt over her. The flowers squawked and screeched.

"No!" Mari winced, holding her right arm. "I fell from the sky onto an Order rat."

This Order rat should leave your pirate butt right here.

He grabbed her good arm and yanked her to her feet.

"We have to go! Now!"

Seraphina wrapped Mari's good arm around her shoulder, and once again, Luis began clearing their path. He ignored the ache in his sword arm, focusing his irritation on cutting down the monstrous plants until they reached the tree line at the edge of the clearing.

"Let me go, dammit!" Mari cursed as Seraphina helped her sit down against the tree. The pirate captain cradled her arm, a tear escaping her green eyes. Seraphina collapsed beside her, closing her eyes as she set her head back against the tree.

"Praise Macario, what did I just do?" she said, shuddering.

Something foolish. Brave but foolish.

He stood over Mari, hands on his hips. "Is it broken?"

Mari glared up at him, her face twisting in pain. She turned away, taking a sharp breath.

"It's dislocated," she said.

Easy fix. It'd happened a few times to some of his crewmen who weren't as cautious as they needed to be climbing the rigging.

"I'll help you pop it back in," Luis said, bending down.

Seraphina's eyes flew open. "Pop it back in? Won't that hurt?"

"Only for a moment," Luis said. "I'm sure the captain here can handle it."

"You touch me, I'll gut you," Mari said through her teeth.

Seraphina laid a hand on her good shoulder. "Mari, please! Let us help you."

"I'm captain to you!" she shot back.

Seraphina swallowed hard. "Captain—he's only trying to help."

"He just wants to keep me alive so he can kill me himself."

Luis scoffed. "I'm keeping you alive because it's the right thing to do." *And the only way I'll get answers about what happened to my brother on Bluegate.*

"Keep telling yourself that," Mari strained. "Shit! Help me up!"

She grabbed Seraphina's hand, not waiting for the seminary girl to answer. But Seraphina helped the rude pirate captain to her feet. Mari pushed her hand away, struggling to turn and face the tree. Mari leaned her head on the tree trunk, taking in a long breath.

Don't tell me she's going to—

Mari leaned back and slammed her shoulder into the trunk, screaming as loud as the flowers that tried to eat them. She hugged the tree, a few sobs escaping her lips as Seraphina rubbed her back comfortingly.

He'd heard pirates were impulsive. Crazy even. But snapping her own shoulder back into its socket was just as brave and as foolish as Seraphina running back to save her.

Would any of his men be able to do that? He couldn't be sure.

Fool pirate. Should have just let me help.

Mari straightened and Seraphina took a step back as her captain lifted her head and turned to face him. Sweat poured down her face, her breathing labored.

"See? I didn't need your help."

"You'll need a sling. Unless you can create one with one hand, you still need my help."

He looked down at the dirty long sleeves on his shirt. Too hot for sleeves anyway. He tore each one, leaving just enough cloth to cover his upper arms. He fashioned them together into a suitable sling, the way his brother taught him. Guillermo had a nasty habit of breaking bones when they were children.

He handed it to Seraphina, and she gave him a courteous smile. Mari rolled her eyes but didn't protest when Seraphina put her injured arm into it. With her good hand, Mari grabbed the ax that'd been dropped on the ground.

Seraphina's hands flew to her cheeks. "The book!"

Luis pointed to the patch of ground a half a foot away from them, where he'd set it. She ran over to it and picked it up, wiping the dirt off its cover.

"Let's go," Mari said, turning on her heel and venturing into the forest of oversized trees.

"You're welcome!" He called after her, picking up his sword.

"I'm sure she's grateful," Seraphina said.

"I doubt it."

"She left instead of cursing you." Seraphina flashed another of her innocent smiles before turning to follow her captain into the forest.

***

Praise Macario, the rest of the journey into the forest was an uneventful one. Aside from the occasional curse from Mari, it was a quiet trek. It gave him time to breathe. To think.

To get some answers.

Seraphina's attempt at small talk made the time fly, the conversations polite and superficial. And easy. Unless she was super cunning or manipulative, it was hard to believe she was lying about not being there when his brother died.

That didn't mean she didn't know what happened, though. And as the sunlight faded behind a darkening sky, it was the perfect opportunity to find out.

"Berries!"

Seraphina's voice jolted him out of his thoughts as the girl ran toward a small bush growing at the base of a tree. The palm-sized purple fruit looked delicious, yet foreign. Seraphina took a large bite out of one, her eyes closing as she chewed on it.

"Let's hope those things aren't poisonous," Mari said, her gaze slow and tired. She dropped her ax, taking a significant effort to sit down on the ground. Making camp wasn't a bad idea. He, too, was weary from the day.

And those berries look delicious.

"Sun's going down," Luis said. "We should just camp here tonight."

"What a brilliant observation." Mari winced in pain as she adjusted her arm.

Luis shook his head, taking up the task of gathering wood for a fire, which wasn't hard. Unlike the river, this forest had plenty of wood, as well as berries. By the time he had the fire going, Seraphina had picked enough of them to last a few days.

But the refreshingly sweet fruit was addicting, and after eating his fifth one, he still hadn't had his fill.

"Captain, you've barely eaten anything." Seraphina looked over at Mari. The pirate lay flat on her back, her face pale in the firelight. She'd pushed herself too hard. She'd taken quite a fall, not counting how those plants had jostled her around.

"I just need to sleep," Mari said, turning her head away from the fire.

"Will she be all right?" Seraphina spoke softly, her beautiful brown eyes staring into his.

He cleared his throat. "Some rest will do her some good."

She looked down at what was left of her berry. "Thank you for helping me save her."

"You didn't leave me with a choice," Luis said.

Seraphina gave him a shy grin. *There's that smile again.* He would miss her company, when...

She cleared her throat. "I'm usually not that impulsive."

"Really? I couldn't tell."

Her nose wrinkled. "My sister is the impulsive one. She'd run into a burning bungalow without thinking twice."

"Where is she?"

Her smile faded. "The Griffin Vales."

Mari let out a soft snore. Good.

"Were you two close?"

She nodded. "As close as twin sisters can be."

Twin sister? Interesting. "So, why isn't she here with you?"

She sighed, turning her gaze to him. "Because Macario has a different path for her."

"What path is that?"

"You wouldn't believe me if I told you."

"Try me."

Luis leaned forward, resting his arms on his knees. She shook her head, looking back at the fire.

"You still don't believe any of this."

"It's pretty hard to deny the impossible after what's happened here the last two days."

"Yes. This place is hard to make sense of."

"So, help me make sense of it." *Help me make sense of what happened to my brother.*

"It's not my place." She shook her head, pointing up at the darkened sky. "Macario will give you the answers you need."

"Will that be your answer to every question I ask you?"

She flashed him a nervous smile and he swore his heart skipped a little. "Not when you start believing."

"But I do." At least in giant snakes and man-eating flowers.

"Only because you've witnessed it all yourself. But true faith comes in believing what you don't see."

He surely wouldn't have believed he would be sitting in a cursed jungle getting a lesson in faith from a pirate. The only pirate he didn't mind being around. *This jungle is clouding my senses.*

Seraphina ate the last of her berries and knelt on the ground. She bowed her head, clasping her hands together in prayer.

Prayer.

It had been days since he prayed. *No wonder I feel so conflicted.*

Wiping his hands on his pants, he knelt down, closed his eyes, and bowed his head. His brother's face appeared in his mind's eye. He was a foot taller than Luis, with their father's wide jaw and stark nose. They shared their mother's ebony hair.

Macario, I will endure whatever you put in my path. Even keep these pirates safe. So long as I find out what happened to my brother. Please.

He sniffed back a tear, refusing to show any weakness. If he was going to survive out there, he had to keep a clear head. And, just maybe, an open mind.

CHAPTER 18

MARI

The flapping of sails and swooshing of the sea filled Mari's ears. Her eyes shot open, and she sat up. The quarterdeck rocked up and down.

"That bastard Ghad has left my helm unattended." She cursed, rising to her feet.

Wait. Why the hell am I out here sleeping on the upper deck?

She ran her hand through her dreads. Her right hand. The one she shouldn't even be using because she hurt her shoulder. *I mean, I hurt it, right?*

Mari ran to the side of the ship, hoping the crisp blue ocean lapping against her ship would give her the calm she so desperately needed. But the sea wasn't blue, or clear, or even crisp. Blood-red water left stains on the wooden siding of the ship.

What kind of fresh hell is this?

"Amrit!"

She called out, waiting to hear his boots shuffling behind her. But her heart knew better. She was alone. As alone as she'd felt since Jules died, and Baz left for his adventure.

Mari breathed back tears, spinning around. The ship still cut through the stained sea though the helm was fixed in place. She ran over to it, placing her trembling hands on the polished wood spokes. Heat pierced the skin of her palms as she tried to turn the ship around.

Back to where?

The red ocean spread out for miles in every direction, not a piece of blasted land in sight. And how in the bloody hell did she get back on her ship? Where was Seraphina and her little Order boyfriend? Where were the Majestic Isles?

"And what in the blazes is that smell!"

A mix of smoke, rotting fish, and dead animal carcass hit her in the face. Mari leaned over the helm, coughing for air. The ocean boiled like the seafloor was one big fire pit. Mari spun the helm around, not caring if the ship tipped over.

But the Pursuer didn't budge, still approaching a horizon she couldn't even see.

There has to be something wrong with the blasted rudder!

Mari stormed down the deck steps, the sails still flapping in the foul-smelling wind. As she passed the banister, she saw something out of the corner of her eye. She stopped in mid-step, whirling around to peer over the side.

The body of a man lay face down in the sea, the reddened water lapping over the leather of his pants and stained white shirt. Dark hair swirled all around him.

Mari didn't need to see his face to know who it was.

Baz.

When the body of a woman floated up to the surface, she clasped her hand over her mouth. Brown curly hair stuck to the woman's deathly pale face, those stubborn brown eyes staring blankly up at the sky.

Samara.

Mari backed away from the banister as more dead bodies rose to the surface. The smell of death overtook her, sobs escaping her lips as she gasped for clean air.

She backed into the mainmast, sliding down to the floor, trying to shake away what she saw. She couldn't afford to think that way. A shudder went through her body.

Lightning crashed through the sky, and a voice boomed from the devious clouds overhead.

"Look what you've done! This is all your fault."

Mari covered her ears, the voice ripping through her soul. She didn't ask for this! She didn't ask to go after a cursed treasure, or face down a bloody serpent, or even be captain of this damn ship. She didn't ask to end up in some godforsaken forest killing serpents and monster flowers.

How were the deaths of her pirate family and all those other nameless faces out there in the ocean *her* fault?

"It's not my bloody fault!" she screamed back. "I didn't ask for this shit!"

The sky roared in anger, and Mari squeezed her eyes shut. A hand grabbed her shoulder. Her eyes flew open, grabbing a wrist.

"Captain!" Seraphina's girly brown eyes stared down at her. "It's me! It was just a dream."

Mari shot up, pain blasting through her hurt shoulder. Sunlight shone through the giant trees all around them. A pile of ash was all that remained of the fire last night.

The spot where we made camp, and I passed out.

Luis sharpened his blade with a rock on the other side of that ash pit, looking at both of them with disinterest. *Great. I've made a fool of myself in my sleep.*

Yet she could still see Baz's dead body floating in the ocean. That awful smell of smoke and death still hung in her nostrils. And just thinking about that booming voice sent goosebumps all up and down her skin.

"You had the dream, didn't you?" Seraphina said, kneeling next to her.

Mari shook her head, letting go of the nun's wrist to rub out the pain in her sore shoulder.

"Don't know what you're talking about."

"Sounded like a vivid dream to me," Luis said, not looking up from his sword sharpening. "You kept screaming that it wasn't your fault."

"Were you on a beach all alone with a horrible smell of smoke and death?" Seraphina pressed. "Were there dead people in the water? A loud voice telling you that it was all your fault?"

Mari's heart pounded in her chest. Sure, she wasn't on a beach, but everything else Seraphina had described was accurate. *I'm not crazy.* But then why were she and the Chosen One's sister having the same horrifying dreams? Who was that voice condemning her?

Why was everyone she cared about dead in the ocean?

She glanced over at Luis, who met her gaze steadily, looking quite interested in her answer.

"No," Mari lied. "I don't have crazy dreams like that."

She took a deep breath and struggled to her feet. Every muscle was taut and sore from her battle in that cursed garden the day before. She needed at least a few days to rest, in case this forest had other unworldly surprises in store.

Look at what you've done. It's all your fault.

She knew for sure that her crew's lives hung in the balance. If she didn't get out of this horrible place and free them, they could very well be dead bodies floating in the ocean. The quicker they got out of this place, the better.

I just don't know how I'm supposed to do that.

"Doesn't that blasted book of yours tell us what strange monstrosity we're going to face next?" Mari bent over to pick up her ax.

Seraphina shook her head. "No. Just a line that ends at a mountain cavern."

Mountains. How lovely. Maybe they would have to beat down a herd of mountain cats. Or rocks that moved like people. Maybe an oversized bat or two.

One thing was certain—she wouldn't be caught unawares.

She took a bite into a berry, surprised at the right amount of sweetness for being so oversized.

"At least where there's a mountain, there should be freshwater." Luis stood and sheathed his sword. He gestured to the stack of firewood. "For now, we use these sticks to take these berries with us."

Who died and made you the king of this expedition?

Yet she would've come up with the same idea.

The Order rat and Seraphina got to work skewering as many berries as possible on the sticks, Mari painfully using her ax to knock them off the vines. Using a nearby vine, Luis tied them all together, carefully hoisting them onto his shoulders.

Good.

Then off into the cursed forest they went, Mari leading the way with Luis in the rear. She kept a brisk pace, though her body was already punishing her for it. She couldn't risk Seraphina asking her any more questions about that dream.

Even if Mari told her the truth, it would only fuel her crazy notion that the three of them were destined to find this library and save the world. Serpents or not, she wasn't here for some prophecy.

Do you really think Macario is writing in that book of hers?

That wasn't easy to explain away, but she didn't have to. It was showing them the way. And it better show her the way out of this blasted place, so she could rescue her crew. Get back to pillaging the coffers of the Enchanted Cape.

Yes. I like that plan much better than any ancient prophecy.

CHAPTER 19

SERAPHINA

Mari had the same dream. I just know it!

In all her time aboard the Pursuer, Seraphina had never seen Mari so scared. Her screams had startled Seraphina out of a deep sleep.

"It's not my bloody fault!"

"I didn't ask for this shit!"

Mari had held her hands to her ears, a tear strolling down her cheek and eyes squeezed shut. Only Macario knew what she saw in her sleep when having that horrid dream. It had been a while since Seraphina had a similar dream. Not since she was on the *Pursuer* headed in the wrong direction.

But then, she didn't need reminding of the task that lay before her. She'd heard Macario loud and clear. Now she was traipsing through a magical forest, following the magical map in the book clutched to her chest.

Was Macario speaking to Mari, too?

Was that the reason she charged through that forest with so much purpose and determination, not even caring that Seraphina and Luis trailed behind her? If only she could find out what changed Mari's mind. How Macario made a believer out of her...

"You shouldn't worry about your captain." Luis came up beside her, smirking in Mari's direction. "She's a tough one."

"Even the toughest people need someone to care about them." Her sister Samara was a prime example.

"True. But I doubt an unpleasant dream will rattle her."

"That wasn't an ordinary dream." As soon as the words came out, she bit her lip. Yet another reason for the Order captain to think she'd lost her mind.

"And how would you know?"

"Call it a feeling."

"Is this the same feeling that made you leave your seminary and join Mari's pirate crew?"

Oh, how he made that decision sound so simple. It was fear for her sister's safety that made her leave the security of her home in Santa Dolas. Then it was a quest for the truth behind Macario's Scepter that led her into the dank ruins of an Ancient Order temple. Once she learned of the prophecy, it was the sheer belief that saw her through the rest of that arduous journey.

"That was faith," she said.

He nodded, though he didn't seem satisfied with that answer.

"Don't you find it hard to be a faithful servant of Macario when you keep company with the likes of pirates?"

"If I have learned anything in the time since I left the seminary, it is that everyone's path to Macario's light is different. For some, it is a straight line. For others, it may be a winding path."

Or, in Samara's case, a path that had to send her off a cliff before it righted itself again!

"My sister is the perfect example. It took a lot of poor decisions before she could find her way, and it was those mistakes that made her strong in the end."

Luis thought for a moment. "In other words, your sister is a pirate."

Once upon a time. Seraphina shook her head.

"She is much more than that." Before he had the chance to ask anything he could use to incriminate them later, she changed the subject. "And what about you? Why did you become an Order naval officer?"

"The standard answer would be, out of a sense of duty and unshakeable faith in our patron god."

"I don't recall asking you for the standard answer."

He chuckled, his face relaxing. "The honest answer is, I joined because my older brother did."

"So, serving in the Order is a family business, then?"

"Something like that."

"Well judging from the size of your fleet you've done quite well."

He rubbed the back of his neck. "It's not the fleet that I really wanted. It was the ship. I would watch it sail by every day with my brother, wondering what it would be like to command her."

A man who not only had big dreams but achieved them. How admirable. *And incredibly conflicting that I'm admiring the man sent to arrest me.*

"I'm sure your brother is so proud that you finally have that ship." *A shame I spent more time in the brig than admiring it like he did.*

"I would like to think so."

"Where is your brother?"

The brightness in his face dulled, his eyes lowering to the grassy ground. "He passed on."

From the way his face stiffened and his body tensed, it must have been recent.

"I'm sorry," she said. "I know what it's like to lose someone."

"Do you?" His voice was sharp.

"Yes. My father went to work one day and never came home. His ship was lost in a storm. My mother passed away a year later from a summer fever."

A warm breeze graced the awkward silence between them.

"Did they ever find your father's ship?" He let out a shaky breath.

"No."

"Were you able to give him a proper funeral?"

"No." Just a wreath of sea lilies sent out to sea.

"So, I imagine you would give anything to find out what happened to him?"

"In the beginning, I did, but—"

"That's how I feel about my brother. He's dead and I don't know why."

His voice trembled on those last words. Before Seraphina could offer a comforting word, or a prayer even, he brushed past her and stomped on ahead. She wanted to go after him. Needed to go after him, but held back, hugging her arms instead.

"About damn time!" Mari was yards ahead of them, disappearing through a cluster of trees.

Seraphina picked up the pace, though her feet ached with each step. She would wear through the soles of her boots any moment now. By the time she reached the trees, she could hear rushing water.

Praise Macario.

She pushed past the branches to find a winding river of crisp blue water flowing in front of them. Luis set down the skewers of food on a nearby tree stump. Mari was already kneeling along the bank, scooping water into her mouth. Luis didn't even look in their direction as he went a little further down the shore to get his fill of water.

So, she found a spot between the captains, setting down the book behind her. She dipped her hands in, the water cool and soft against her skin.

Thank you, Macario, for this wonderful creation.

She splashed the water in her face, the days of grime washing away. But it wasn't fast enough. She dipped her entire head in, the currents taking away all the hardships her body had endured.

Sweat, dirt, and thirst.

Seraphina lifted her head, smiling as the water dripped down her scalp and the tips of her hair. After drinking so much water her stomach almost burst, she sat back on her hands to let the air dry her face. Mari took a seat beside her.

"I'm going to ask you a question," she said gruffly, "and you're not allowed to ask me anything about it."

Seraphina turned to her and nodded.

"Let's just say, I had a dream like you said. What does that mean?"

Macario did speak to her! She was meant to be on this journey. She opened her mouth, ready to blurt out a ton of questions, but Mari held up her hand.

"Simple answer. No questions."

"I don't know for sure, except that it's confirmation that you're on the path Macario wants you on."

"Why?"

"Because I had the same dream, too."

She raised a brow before her eyes shifted behind Seraphina. She turned around to see Luis approaching.

"Say nothing about this," Mari said. "I'd hate to cut out your tongue."

"I'm rather fond of my tongue, so I won't be saying a word."

Luis wiped his hands on his pants, pausing beside them. "We should follow the river."

"Why?" Mari didn't take her icy eyes off him.

"Because the cavern we're supposed to go to is right up ahead." He pointed upriver. Lo and behold, the river led into the mouth of a large mountain. The mounds of jet-black rock rose until they disappeared into the ring of clouds above.

This was it. The library was just a half day's journey away.

Butterflies of excitement mingled with the knots of fear in her stomach. She would finally learn everything about the prophecy, the monsters Bedros would unleash, and, just maybe, how her sister and the mysterious Spell Keeper could defeat him.

But then what?

How would they get back to the ship and rescue the crew? From the scowl on Luis's face, there was no guarantee he wouldn't resume his mission to see her and Mari hanged.

You have to change his mind, Seraphina. You have to make him believe.

That meant earning his trust, telling him everything that happened leading up to this moment. That meant getting Mari to divulge what happened that night in Bluegate, a night Luis was inexplicably obsessed with…

This is not going to be easy.

But she owed it to her sister and the world to try.

CHAPTER 20

LUIS

Don't forget why you are here.

Luis kept his distance as they trudged up the river bank toward the foreboding mountain. He'd enjoyed his conversation with Seraphina, letting his genuine interest in her show. He felt comfortable, as if they'd known each other forever, a list of questions a mile long swimming around in his head.

He'd almost not minded that they were going after something that didn't exist. Shaken off the guilt he felt for saving a pirate—not once, but twice.

But when she asked him about his brother, the reason he was even talking to her in the first place, reality rose up and bit him in the heart. Suddenly, he didn't see an attractive girl with a faithful heart in front of him. She was a pirate, no matter what led her down this dark path. And, like a pirate, she'd used her charm to put him at ease, so it would be easier to take advantage of him later.

And now they were walking into another dark and dangerous place. That danger could take the form of an oversized plant or insect. He could see that coming. But that danger could also be the two pirate women walking in front of him.

If he let his guard down, they would have the advantage.

And I will never let the enemy catch me unawares.

The grassy lands sloped upward, his boots crushing the clusters of weed flowers growing among the sea of green. The line of giant trees far off to the west thinned, giving a clearer view of the orange-streaked sky. No one could tell by the gentle breeze or the subtle bubbling of the river that this place was cursed with gigantic serpents or man-eating flowers. Even the mountain, the lone stone structure in an otherwise flat landscape, reminded him of the range at the western edge of the mainland.

Don't forget why you are here.

He was here to learn the truth about his brother's death. To find out which one of Mari's crew killed him that night on Bluegate.

And it was no serpent.

He refused to believe that.

"We camp here tonight," Mari said, stopping just short of an enormous boulder placed in the middle of the grassy clearing. Seraphina shook her head.

"Captain, we are so close." She pointed to the mouth of the mountain a good fifty yards away.

"Too close to get my head chopped off or eaten by whatever the hell is in that cave," Mari said. "And I'll be damned if that happens in the dark."

She took a seat on that rock, taking care not to move her arm too much in the sling.

The sling he'd given her.

This wasn't good. He was caring too much. Maybe that was part of their plan all along. He set down the sticks of food, his shoulder aching from their weight.

This will be the last time I'm stuck traveling with the food. He sucked his teeth as he gathered wood for the fire—again. Mari gazed out at the river, refusing to look in his direction. Seraphina knelt down a few feet away from her, head bowed and eyes closed.

Is that an act, too?

The thought of it made his stomach turn, his hands rubbing the twigs faster to spark the fire. He needed to pray, his muscles tense with an anger that would make him reckless.

Anger clouds judgment.

His brother always sounded like a wise old man. Maybe if he were still alive, Luis wouldn't be so angry.

"What did you do to my crew?"

Luis looked up to see Mari glaring at him across the fire, ax in her good hand.

"What happened that night at Bluegate?" Luis countered, returning her death stare.

Seraphina almost burned herself trying to step between them. "We are about to step into a piece of history. We are on the holiest of missions—"

"I don't give a damn about this mission," Mari said.

My sentiments exactly.

"I'm only here to get my crew back." The pirate captain stared at him.

"Your crew isn't going anywhere," Luis snapped. "They are right where they belong."

Mari shot up from her seat, but Seraphina put up a hand to stop her from going any further.

"They will pay for their crimes."

Seraphina's head snapped around. "That was NOT their doing!"

"So, who did it? Some ancient monster?" He scoffed.

"Exactly!" Seraphina said, so infuriatingly matter-of-fact.

He stood to face them. "Do you take me for a fool?"

"It's about time you caught on," Mari said, rolling her eyes.

Luis raised his sword, and Seraphina laid a hand on his arm. Despite the anger swelling in his gut, it was hard to ignore the shot of welcoming warmth that radiated from her touch.

"The last thing we need to do is kill each other before we even get inside the library," she said. "Despite how uncomfortable this is for all of us, Macario brought us here for a reason."

Mari twirled her ax, but Luis refused to flinch.

"He brought me here to get answers," he said.

"Why are you getting your petticoats in a bunch over what happened at Bluegate?"

An image of taking his sword to her throat flashed through his mind. Maybe under the threat of death, she would finally give him the answers he so desperately needed.

But she would never cower. She'd rather die first.

"Please, tell him what happened," Seraphina pleaded, her eyes soft in the firelight's glow. Mari leaned over and spat.

"I'm not telling him shit until he tells me what's going to happen to my crew."

Seraphina turned that beseeching look onto him, and he could feel his resolve wavering. But he wouldn't let himself falter.

"I am a captain of the Order's navy. I owe nothing to the likes of her."

"In case you haven't noticed, we are a long way away from the Majestic Isles." Seraphina narrowed her eyes, her gaze accusing. "Out here, we are nothing more than Macario's servants, going wherever he leads us."

He is leading me to the truth.

"It was her, wasn't it?"

Seraphina squinted as if she didn't understand the question.

"Your captain there was responsible for the deaths of those brave men on that ship dispatched to Bluegate a month ago."

She opened her mouth, but shut it again, lowering her eyes.

Mari might not cower, but Seraphina would. He directed his sword at her, its tip a mere inch from her neck. Mari took a step, but Seraphina held up a hand.

"I will gut you where you stand, if you so much as nick her."

"Not before I get answers," Luis said, his heart twisting in his chest. This was the last thing he wanted to do to Seraphina. "Now, talk."

"All I know is, the serpent that destroyed Tradesman Harbor attacked my home island. Mari's crew and my sister were there to stop it from hurting anyone else."

"You lie," he said through his teeth.

She looked him in his eyes, a nervous strength he hadn't seen from her before. "I told you I was a terrible liar."

"Say nothing, Seraphina!" Mari commanded. "He's not going to do a damn thing to you."

Seraphina shook her head. "The only way we can move forward and get answers is to tell the truth." She took a breath. "After helping some of my people get away from the monster, I retreated inland." Her eyes turned to Mari and so did his.

"Put the damn sword down," Mari said. "She told you everything she knows."

"Not until you tell me what happened. I bet my life you were right there."

"Captain Fozo." Seraphina's voice was low and surprisingly calm. "I told you my truth. Tell us where our crew is, and I'm sure Captain Adlam will tell you what you need to know."

Mari huffed. "What makes you so sure of that?"

"Because I'm betting my life on it." Seraphina straightened her back, standing firm at the wrong end of his sword.

So, this is what it means to take a leap of faith.

"Your crew will do hard labor until they restore the harbor. What happens after that is up to the Pontiff unless I help sway him otherwise."

Mari slapped the ax against her thigh, biting her lip as her eyes searched the sky. She'd better make the right choice. Hurting Seraphina was the last thing he wanted to do.

"Dammit it, Seraphina," Mari hissed, tightening her grip on the ax and looking at Luis. "She was right about the serpent. Damn monster had the entire coast on fire. Between the cannon fire and her sister's wicked magic, that beast was pushed to the bottom of the sea."

"The ship!" Luis voiced cracked.

"It was just getting in the way. I wasn't the captain. Just the damn navigator. While we were trying to kill the monster, it was stubborn people like you who just wanted to arrest some damn pirates."

Luis's jaw clenched.

"Some died in the fight on deck. Some jumped overboard and became fish bait. Satisfied?"

"And what of the captain?"

Mari raised a brow. "That's why you've got your britches in a knot? The captain was a friend of yours?"

Seraphina yelped as the tip of his sword nicked her neck. *Dammit!*

"I warned you," Mari began, but Seraphina waved her off.

"Just answer his question," she said.

"The captain died when we took over his ship to kill the monster. I sure as hell wasn't the one who ran him through."

"Then who did?" The angry whisper squeezed through his tense jaw.

"I don't know. There was a lot of fighting. You know how these pirate raids go."

His brother died protecting his ship. The pirates did kill him. If she couldn't tell him who dealt the final blow, they would all hang for his death.

Even though she saved his life.

His eyes met Seraphina's, and he swallowed back the bile in his throat. This was not the way. He lowered his sword, and Seraphina let out a breath of relief.

"So, is this the part where you try to kill me?" Mari tensed, her ax at the ready.

He shook his head. Killing her would make him no better than a pirate. He was an Order captain. She'd face justice the right way. He'd lost his cool once already.

"I'm a man of my word. As Seraphina said, we are here on a holy mission and we've all told our truth. Now we will see this thing through."

Mari didn't look convinced, but Seraphina smiled.

"I'm sorry, Seraphina," he said, unable to meet her eyes. "I let my anger get the best of me. I will never raise my sword to you again."

"I accept your apology," she said, taking back her seat at the fire.

He slowly sat down too, laying his sword down at his side. As they all dug into the fruit, the sound of the crackling fire spilling into the space between them, the anger in his gut still churned. *There will be time for that later.*

First, he had to indulge them in this secret library quest until he found a way to get them out of this cursed place.

After that, he owed Mari Adlam nothing.

CHAPTER 21

MARI

"Hurry it up! I ain't got all day!"

Mari's injured shoulder was sore as hell. But she hadn't let that stop her last night from scavenging for vines to make a holder for the heavy ax. Going out into the night with just an ax in a cursed grassland wasn't the smartest thing. But she'd be damned if she fell asleep before that Order rat.

Look at him, chatting it up with Seraphina, like he was her friend. Never mind the fact that last night he'd put a sword to her throat.

They were taking their sweet time following her to the mountain. She could smell the moss growing on the side of the eerie cavern. Mari made it over the last grassy hill and paused at the gaping mouth of the cave.

If this weren't such a wretched place, it would be perfect for hiding an entire ship. The opening offered plenty of room to tow a ship into the cave, and the river flowed into it, disappearing into a darkness that made her skin crawl.

"By Macario's grace, there's a boat!" Seraphina joined Mari at the top of the hill, panting.

The "boat" she mentioned proved to be a raggedy dinghy lying on its side on the bank right at the cavern entrance. The Order captain also caught up with them, keeping a safe distance away from Mari. He shot her a sharp look, and she was more than happy to return the favor.

"Let's get this over with," Mari said, leaving them to gawk as she headed for the boat. Her face twisted in annoyance. The wood was on the verge of cracking, the boat's sides covered in moss. Weeds grew through the gaps in the boards.

"Is it still good?" Seraphina took a moment to catch her breath.

"It's a piece of shit." Mari sniffed.

"You said the same thing about the *Pursuer* once upon a time. Yet you made her seaworthy."

Yeah, but I don't have a month and I don't have a blasted crew.

"There's only one way to find out if she can float," Luis said.

He stepped right past them, grabbing the side and flipping it over. Dirt covered the wooden benches, grass poking out of the tiny holes along the sides. Surprisingly, the oars were still inside, their wood a grayish-green.

"I'm not getting in that," Mari said.

"We can't swim," Seraphina said. "And your shoulder— "

"My shoulder is fine!"

When would the irritating nun stop giving her little Order boyfriend the idea that Mari was weak and injured? *They're both insufferable.*

"We get in that," she said, "and we'll be swimming anyway."

Fozo didn't care. He pushed the boat into the water. It landed with a hard splash, swinging around to face the Order captain, who held the tie line in his hand. It bobbed a bit in the water but didn't sink.

At least, not yet.

"It seems to be holding up just fine," Luis said. "I'll hold her steady, while you both get in."

So we can both drown? I don't think so.

Seraphina looked at Fozo and he gave her a reassuring nod.

"It'll be fine," he said.

With shaky legs, Seraphina lowered herself down into the boat. It wobbled under her weight but still stayed afloat. *More blasted magic, no doubt.*

"That wasn't so bad," Seraphina said with a nervous smile.

"After you," Luis said, his face almost unreadable.

Mari looked at the boat and then into the cavern. Not a sliver of dirt in that entrance, the black water too deep to tread for long. And her shoulder hurt like the dickens, the ax weighing heavy on her other shoulder.

She gritted her teeth and stepped into the boat, grabbing the crumbling side to steady herself. Luis went in after her, taking the bench at the head of the dinghy. Mari sank down next to Seraphina. Those two didn't need to get any cozier than they already were.

Luis grabbed an oar and Mari went for the second, but Seraphina stopped her.

"I'll do that, Captain," she said. "Can you just hold this for me?"

Seraphina handed her that blasted book, and the thought of tossing that troublesome thing into the water almost brought a smile to Mari's face. Then Seraphina and Fozo started rowing into the dark mouth of the cave, and her joy faded away. The darkness swallowed them whole in a dingy that could sink at any moment.

Great.

A loud whoosh filled the air around them, and the cavern lit up. Fire burst from dozens of wall lanterns lining the cavern walls.

"Praise Macario," Seraphina whispered, her expression matching the Order captain's wide eyes. Mari's heart clamored in her chest.

Just how many cursed places can one island realm have?

"Look!" Seraphina pointed straight ahead, where the river water pooled. A short stone pier lay a few yards ahead, a set of stone stairs carved into the wall behind it. The Order rat saw it too and started rowing harder.

"Those must lead up to the library!" Seraphina sang under her breath, struggling to keep up with his strokes. Hopefully, the optimistic nun was right this time. Mari wasn't sure how much more of these random, unexplainable occurrences she could take.

Mari was the first one out of the boat when they made it to the dock, wincing in pain as she tied it down. Seraphina stepped out—with the help of the Order rat, of course, who stowed away the oars before stepping out himself.

Mari stared at the stairs leading straight up into a lot more nothingness.

You would think a library would be a bright, sunny place. This light is horrible for reading.

Not that she did much of it in the Enchanted Isles. The madame didn't like educated girls in her brothel. Neither did the Godswood, where peasants were painfully discouraged from taking up the same hobbies as its royal idiots.

But her uncle Azmi didn't think so. Like her, he didn't accept their station in life. A station dictated by a royal family. He said just as much every night after dinner when she snuck away to go to his room in the stables. He would be there, waiting with a patchwork blanket and her favorite book.

The High Seas Adventures of Suhaib of the Sun. Those stories of magic and monsters never got old. She'd only wished Suhaib was a woman.

"A woman is just as capable of sailing a ship," she used to squeak. Azmi would smile, deepening the wrinkles in his creamy skin.

"You can do whatever you set your mind to, my little Suhaib," he would say before asking her to continue reading to him.

Well, uncle, does that apply to surviving whatever is at the end of these very creepy stairs?

The Order captain took a torch, and Mari snatched it out of his hand.

"After you," she mocked, raising a brow. He didn't say a word, stomping past her and up the stairs. Seraphina took the book from her hand, casting her a disapproving look.

"Don't expect me to bat an eye at him," Mari whispered. "And if you like living, I would suggest you cut that out."

Ignoring Seraphina's rolling eyes, Mari started climbing the stairs after him, Seraphina's shuffling steps right behind her. Each step seemed much steeper than the next, the walls slick under her sweaty palms. A good twenty minutes later, the Order captain came to a stop, taking careful steps before disappearing behind the rock wall.

Mari picked up the pace, her ax slapping against her back. She was out of breath when she reached the top, halting beside him, too winded to care that she stood close to him.

I hate heights! A long, rickety bridge stretched out in front of them, crossing over the dark depths below. Her legs growing weak, Mari leaned against the rock wall for support.

"I don't do bridges," she said.

"Doesn't look like we have much choice."

Seraphina peered over their shoulders. "Please tell me we don't have to cross that bridge."

"Unless you've got some wings in that magic book of yours, that's the only way across." Mari crossed her arms. "How badly do you want to read a bunch of dusty books?"

"Macario," Seraphina whispered, "I pray for the courage to journey forward on your path, and your continued protection."

Mari snorted. She should've prayed for a set of wings.

The Order rat turned, sweat pooling on his brow. "Seraphina, are you sure this library is on the other side of this bridge?"

Seraphina's eyes shifted between them. "We need answers. If that means crossing an incredibly dangerous bridge, then so be it."

Despite the shakiness in her voice, she stepped out from behind Mari.

"Macario will protect us."

The only thing Macario has been trying to do is kill us ever since we set foot in this forsaken place.

"Very well," he said, stepping aside and letting her through.

Mari shook her head. *Samara's sister is going to get us all killed.*

CHAPTER 22

SERAPHINA

Stating her confidence in Macario's help crossing the bridge was one thing. Actually crossing it was something else altogether.

Seraphina set her foot on the rope bridge, and the wooden plank swayed under her feet. Her free hand shot out for the rope railing, the strands as frayed as the damaged rigging back on the *Pursuer*. The other end of the bridge seemed miles away. Her stomach dropped to her feet.

This is something Samara would do.

If her twin were here, she would be halfway across this bridge already. She'd hardly blink an eye. She wouldn't be gripping the ropes for dear life, her heart sinking every time the planks groaned under her feet.

"The bridge will hold," Luis said over her shoulder, and she managed a breath.

"How can you be so sure?"

A gust of wind made the bridge wobble. She lost her balance, and his sturdy arm grabbed her waist. He pulled her up, her back pressed against his stable chest.

"If it doesn't, I'll be right here to catch you," he said in her ear, sending an electrifying tingle down her back. He held her a moment longer than he needed to before letting her go.

"If you're both done cuddling now, I would like to get the hell off the bridge," Mari called out.

Seraphina flushed, turning carefully to see Mari picking her way closer, her eyes trained on the Order captain. She'd been eyeing him as if waiting for him to do something malicious to them on that bridge.

But he wouldn't, would he?

Her hand went to her throat, touching the small scab where his sword pricked her neck the night before. His angry outburst had frightened her. And yet, she was sure he wouldn't hurt her. Not intentionally, anyway.

Now who's being naïve, Seraphina?

Her time away from the seminary had taught her so much. Just because a man wore holy robes didn't automatically make him trustworthy. In the same vein, just because someone was a pirate didn't mean they were all terrible people. Jules, the worn-faced pirate boatswain, had made her feel welcome from the moment she stepped on board the *Pursuer*. Then there was Priest Christian, who wanted to see her hanged just for speaking the truth.

So, what about Luis? Was he like her, a person who would follow his heart and his faith? Or an Order man who followed orders, no matter what?

I want to believe the former.

Seraphina took another shaky step, making the mistake of looking down. A small sliver of black wood separated her from the dark pit of death below her. Just how far did this trench go? How did something so vast exist on an island?

The same way giant snakes and man-eating flowers existed on an island.

"Just keep your eyes on the ledge in front of you." Luis's voice, calm and reassuring, stayed close to her as they moved across the bridge. The ledge drew closer,and Seraphina was able to see torch lights twinkling on either side of the entrance. Praise Macario, they were almost there.

A loud crack broke the silence, and they all froze in place.

"Seraphina, was that you?" Mari hissed.

"No." She ventured a look at her feet.

Crack.

Groan.

"This was a bloody bad idea!" Mari cursed.

The bridge jolted. Luis and Seraphina locked eyes.

"Run!" he cried. "Now!"

Seraphina sprinted for the ledge, the snapping of ropes filling her ears.

A final crack. Her feet met the air. The bridge sailed sideways. Luis grabbed her waist, bringing her into him as his other arm stretched out and grabbed the wooden planks. She clutched the book to her chest. Mari's screams bounced off the cavern walls.

No! She's fallen to her death! It's all my fault.

Seraphina and Luis slammed into the rock face, many of the wood planks crumbling under her weight. The one right above her was still intact, and she grabbed it.

"You all right?" Luis's eyes were soft and caring.

Seraphina nodded, warm tears streaming down her face.

"I'm just fine! Thanks for asking!" Mari's grumpy voice echoed off the mountain walls.

Seraphina sighed. "Thank heavens, Mari! I thought you fell!"

"I wouldn't give you two the satisfaction," she snapped back.

Luis dragged his arm out from around her, peering over his shoulder as he extended a hand to the pirate captain.

"Keep your damn hand," Mari said. "Just move your tail before the rest of this bridge decides to fall."

Luis grunted and Seraphina looked up. The top seemed so far away. She looked down at the book. How would she climb with one hand?

The bridge wobbled. The book, the very thing that brought them all together, slipped from her hand and tumbled into the darkness. She bit her lip, tears flowing.

It's all my fault.

How was her sister supposed to save the world now? Was this punishment for foolishly thinking she was even up to this task?

Look at what you've done. It's all your fault.

"It's gone, Seraphina," Luis said gently. "And if we don't climb up, we will be too."

Seraphina looked up at the wood bridge-turned-ladder.

Just climb. You've done this before.

The last time, she'd been climbing out of the Quarter—the illegal sector of brothels and bars that had burned to a crisp, thanks to the serpent terrorizing the Isles. She would've died in those flames, if not for her sister's magic. Samara had created a makeshift ladder out of the rock. Seraphina had once doubted they could ever survive any of the other perilous situations she'd found herself in thereafter.

But, somehow, she did.

And she would survive being suspended over a dark pit hanging onto an ancient bridge. Even if it meant ignoring the wood groaning under her weight as she kept climbing. Not thinking about just how painful falling to her death would be. When her palm reached the cool rock at the top, she let out a nervous laugh.

Praise Macario. I'm not going to die today.

She pulled herself up and backed away from the edge, staring down into the dark. The loss hit her again, like a blow to the stomach. She'd lost the book. How could she be so clumsy? Tears welled once again in her eyes.

Luis launched himself over the edge, and Mari struggled up over the side, rolling onto her back.

"Are you hurt, Captain?"

"I'm fine," Mari and Luis said in unison. Mari glared at him, taking a few breaths before struggling to her feet.

"I told you that bridge was a terrible idea," she said, brushing past Luis to grab the wall torch over Seraphina. "For your sake, there better be enough gold to buy an entire Order fleet in this place."

Since she'd risked her life more than once, Seraphina hoped there was too. Mari walked through the doorway, the light from her torch trailing behind her. Luis offered a hand and helped Seraphina to her feet.

"Are you all right?" He squeezed her hand. All she could do was nod, feeling herself getting lost in his dark eyes. Her breath came in short, excited bursts. Heart beating fast, but not out of fear.

It was something else. Something she wasn't supposed to be feeling around him.

She slipped her hand out of his. "We should go in."

He took the remaining wall torch and handed it to her.

"Lead the way."

The narrow tunnel was just like the underground one her and Baz Blackwater took to escape the Order guard in Lucia. Narrow walls. A winding passage. Nothing but darkness around them. Only the faint glow of Mari's torch up ahead to indicate they weren't alone.

She couldn't wait to see her sister again. Tell her everything. She would be so proud of her. Shocked, but proud.

She'd learned how to be part of a pirate crew. Got captured by the Order. Escaped the Order—twice. Survived monsters and even a rickety bridge. Samara would find all of it hard to believe at first. She was the impulsive one, the twin that got into the most trouble.

Now she's not the only adventurer in this family.

For the first time, she could understand why her sister ran toward danger. The adrenaline rush was addicting, she had to admit. And afterward, one had a story worth telling to just about anyone.

What would Mother Rosa think of all this? The old woman would most likely order her to pray every minute for the rest of her life just for mentioning it aloud.

The passageway widened, a large swath of flickering light appearing at the end. Mari stood in the center of it, holding her torch high. Moments later, Seraphina reached the pirate captain, and her mouth fell open in surprise. The chamber could fit a small village.

A maze of stairs and bridges connected stone archways. The entire room was lit by the firelight of man-sized wall torches. A giant altar stood at the center of the atrium, a faded map of the Majestic Isles etched on the floor.

Just like the Ancient Order Seminary back in Mateo.

If they were looking for anything else, she would be in awe of this piece of lost history.

But that was not Macario's mission for them. They had to find answers for Samara and discover how to save the world.

"This is a strange-looking library." Luis's eyes scanned the room.

"Especially since I don't see a bloody book in sight," Mari added.

Nor shelves, tables, or even a chair. But this had to be it. The book showed this place in a mountain on the mainland.

Remember, things are not always as they seem.

She wouldn't leave this place without some answers. She hadn't survived that horrible, rickety bridge for nothing.

CHAPTER 23

LUIS

Luis combed his mind, trying to find the words to explain this place. It looked nothing like a library, more like the setting of a story he listened to as a child. Guillermo was the best at telling stories.

The way the stairs crisscrossed one another, creating a maze of mysterious rooms around an ominous altar, reminded him of the story of the evil sorcerer. He hid maidens away in a lair like this, using his altar to make his human sacrifices to Bedros, the god of life and death.

As his brother would tell the story under the ratty covers of their beds, Luis would imagine that evil man in a dank place like this one. Dim torchlight creating shadowy corners. Deathtraps like snakes, lethal plant life, and a dangerous crossing just a few magical measures to keep this place hidden.

And what part do you play in this story, Luis? Was he the shining warrior sent by Macario to banish the sorcerer and save the maidens? Or just another sacrifice to an evil cause?

"Try not to get yourself killed, Seraphina," Mari said, making her way around the altar.

"Where are you going, Captain?"

Mari shot him a scornful glance before answering. "To look for what all pirates look for—treasure."

She jogged up the first set of steps, disappearing into the first room. Seraphina walked up to the altar, passing her hand over the dusty surface.

"What are you searching for?" He surprised himself that he wanted to know.

She paused a moment before replying. "Answers."

"To what?"

Seraphina looked over at him, giving Luis a smile that could calm angry giants. "To how my sister will save the world."

She left him, disappearing into another chamber on the far side of the vast room. Luis sighed as he watched her go, running a hand through his damp hair.

Why was *he* here?

The captain died when we took over his ship to kill the monster.

There was a lot of fighting on that ship. You know how pirate raids go.

Mari had confirmed what he already knew. Someone on her crew killed his brother. She would face the consequences when they returned.

But what of the serpent? Was that true? Did it exist?

Seraphina said so. Her cynical captain agreed. And his brother wrote of a fire-breathing serpent in his letters.

Why couldn't he just get a straight answer?

When the world seems askew and clarity eludes you, leave it in the hands of our almighty God, Macario.

Luis dropped to his knees, his body aching from all the danger and adventure it had endured the last few days. He lowered his head, closed his eyes, and fought to catch his breath. This wasn't the time to be overcome with emotion. He needed to clear his head.

This was supposed to be an ancient, holy place. Perhaps in prayer he would find his answers.

Macario, I pray for strength, clarity, and courage. I confess I don't know what you are asking of me.

How could he explain what was happening to him? This was supposed to be a straightforward mission. Even when things took a turn, the pirate captain told him about his brother's fate.

But he couldn't believe her. It wasn't safe. Out here, he had no leverage. No crew to lock up. No Justice House to bring them to justice. Out here, he was an Order man in name only.

He was no one.

How did he get himself into this situation?

You fight too much, Luis. Sometimes you just have to let go and believe.

Guillermo would say that every time he didn't ace an academy test. Luis would pray so hard the night before and be angry when it didn't come to pass.

Just like now.

He rose to his feet, sheathing his sword as he strode to the staircase. For now, he would entertain the notion that this library held answers to unworldly questions—like a serpent and a girl wielding magic. As he walked up those dusty steps, he would imagine that in one of those very rooms, he would find all the answers to the questions causing him grief.

Or discover something new about the world he thought he knew so well.

He would believe, just for now, that this was the magical place Seraphina believed it to be.

The staircase curved upward with no banisters to protect him from a fall onto the altar below. He kept going, climbing to the top of the cavern. It led him to a room with a rounded doorway, just tall enough for him to walk through without crouching. When Luis crossed the threshold, he jumped back. The multi-candle chandelier overhead flared to life, lit with unseen hands.

Or unseen magic.

He took a careful step inside, his eyes landing on the enormous table in the middle of the room. Maps drawn on yellow parchment paper sprawled out on top of it. He moved in to get a closer look, comforted by the familiarity of such paperwork. A map of the Majestic Isles lay on top. It charted every city in its rightful place on the mainland.

Except for Tradesman Harbor.

The large bay was there, complete with drawings of waves and ships. But the long, expansive pier and the circle denoting the town of Aridia were missing.

Just like they are now.

Aridia had never fully recovered after the attack, many of its townspeople fleeing the crumbling city to settle elsewhere. With trade ships getting diverted to the north side of the mainland, the only people who stayed behind were those working to rebuild it.

He checked the rest of the islands before going to Bluegate. Crab Cove was on the far western end of the island. A naval ship was along the coast, the Order insignia drawn on its sails. Right beside it was another ship with black sails and no other defining features. There, right in front of the ship's pointed bow, was the head of a large black serpent. Its yellow eyes were trained on the ship. He squinted to see a figure with a blue light over its head.

He should've looked away—left that room, those pirates, and this cursed place behind. But he'd crossed an imaginary line of dutiful ignorance into knowing what couldn't be possible.

I have to know.

He touched the Order ship, the one that looked so much like his brother's craft. At least he wanted it to be. He wanted to believe that everything Mari told him was true. It would make it that much easier. Blowing out the torch and setting it down, he rolled up the map and tucked it in his back pocket.

If Mari's story matched the map, perhaps he could believe. There was nothing remarkable about the other maps on the table. The Griffin Vales. The Godswood. Even the Winter Tide, which wasn't any more detailed than his maps back home. Very few people traveled that far north, the realm just as mysterious as this mountain structure.

He looked up from the table, the drawings and letters on the wall in front of him catching his attention. As he approached it, he realized the whole thing was written in the language of the gods, the symbols drawn in perfect columns. Except for the last line at the bottom of the wall. The letters were written in fancy red script.

His breath quickened, his heart beating out of his chest like when he was dangling off that blasted bridge.

Never betray your values and always do what's right.

Trying to believe this was a secret library was one thing.

But how in the world did his brother's intimate words end up on the wall of some ancient cavern?

I need answers. Now!

CHAPTER 24

MARI

To hell with this place!

Mari turned over the table in the middle of the room, the dusty scrolls on top of it tumbling to the floor. Three rooms. Three bloody rooms she'd gone through so far and not a speck of gold. Not a sliver of a jewel. Not even a fancy compass to replace the one she'd stolen from Fozo. She'd found nothing that would justify everything she'd put up with since she fell into this miserable place.

Baz Blackwater was an idiot. He should've never made her captain.

All she did was royally screw up. No ship. No crew. No bloody treasure.

And I'm stuck in a cursed place that I have no business being in to begin with. She leaned against the dusty wall. Crossing her arms, she stared up at the chandelier that had lit itself when she first walked into the room.

What now, Mari?

Staying in that dusty place to starve to death seemed like the only option. The bridge back to the river sat at the bottom of that pit. The light flickered, the painting on the ceiling twinkling. She squinted to get a better look. It wasn't a painting exactly. More like a large circle with four black ink points.

Cardinal points.

She uncrossed her arms, stepping away from the wall. She damn near sprained her neck trying to get a full picture of the compass. And figure out why in the world someone painted one up there. She twirled until she saw the longest line of them all—the one that always pointed North. It pointed to the far left side of the room, toward the only wall made of stone brick.

Why didn't I notice that before?

She strode over to it, starting at the top brick. She pushed and pulled at each one, waiting to hear some sort of click or clank. Curses, she needed something! Pressing her lips together, she pushed another random brick. It sank into the wall, the sound of wheels clicking and turning bouncing off the room walls. Mari took a few steps back, reaching for the handle of the ax strapped to her back.

The damn wall is moving.

Like a twirling wheel, it flipped around, exchanging the wall of unassuming bricks for one with a compass on it. Inside the bright golden circle were the classic eight points that every sailor lived by. Each one labeled on the large arrow mounted in its center, the point facing southeast.

Fancy compass or not, it was a crime to have that arrow pointed in the wrong direction. She marched right up to it, using her good hand to turn the dial. Despite the cobwebs, it moved freely, clicking into place at the northern point.

Another clank.

Another brick that wasn't supposed to move. This time it was one right next to the fancy N, but instead of sinking into the wall, it slid upward. A dusty red box stared back at her, and she smiled.

Now we're getting somewhere.

She reached up and pulled it down, her shoulder giving her a painful reminder that it was still healing. Did it contain gold that these Ancient Order folks were too foolish to spend? Jewels they stupidly offered to some magical god who had no use for them, anyway?

She looked over at the now-toppled table, wishing she hadn't been so rash as to destroy the place. Sitting on the floor would have to do.

Mari sat down cross-legged, setting the box in her lap. She wiped off the layer of dust, revealing a gold double S engraved in the reddish-brown wood. Whoever this S person was, Mari had found the precious treasure that he or she took so many precautions to hide. She opened the lid, and the glint of silver twinkled.

Three daggers in black velvet holders. Mari could see her ragged reflection in the silver blades, as if someone had just polished them. The handles were just as pristine, the redwood smooth under her fingers. She should shut the box, tuck it under her arm, and get to work finding a way out of this blasted place.

Instead, she swallowed back the sudden lump in her throat, her skin prickling with feelings she'd thought buried a long time ago.

It was bad enough she'd been thinking about her time back in the Enchanted Cape way more than she liked. But seeing those blades brought the memory of the night she'd escaped that deplorable place.

Jules, the late and great boatswain of the *Pursuer*, met her where he always did, in the dank wine cellar under the brothel. With hair just as long, streaked with gray, and a smile as warm as the summer sun, he came through on his promise to help her. The first man to keep his word since her papa and uncle back in the Godswood.

Now that she bloody thought about it, Jules had given her a box just like the one in her lap. Inside were the three blades that would secure her freedom.

"You have a good eye," he had said. "I know you won't miss."

At the time, she wasn't so confident wielding a weapon, but she'd only nodded in response.

"I promise you a better life than this one," he said. "Just make sure you get to the dock before sunrise."

It hadn't mattered to her if she scraped barnacles off the hull of his pirate ship for the rest of her life. If she spent one more night in that hell hole, she would send herself to the afterlife. With a reassuring nod, he'd handed her the box before slipping back into the shadows of the cellar.

Jules was right then, and every day since, until the day he died.

She did not miss.

The first dagger slit the throat of the last man she would ever service.

The second landed in the back of the patrolling guard's skull, securing her exit.

But she couldn't leave until she'd served the last dagger. She made sure it struck true and fast. That madame didn't even see it coming until blood was gushing out of her chest.

It was then that she'd realized daggers were always meant for her. It was the moment she'd known she would never let anyone take advantage of her ever again. On the fateful day when Baz announced he'd found the last piece of the map to Macario's Scepter, she already knew what she would buy with her cut.

A set of three, very expensive daggers, with her last name engraved on each handle.

She never saw a dime from that scepter.

Yet here she sat, on the floor of some dusty room, holding a secret box with three daggers, each engraved with her name on the handle.

Her bloody name.

What sort of magical crap was this?

She slammed the box shut, her lip quivering like a stupid little girl about to cry.

And I'm not a stupid little girl.

Whatever was going on, she shouldn't have any part of it. But to see her name glaring back at her—not once, but three bloody times—in fancy silver lettering made her heart stop mid-beat.

"I bloody forgot who I was," she whispered to herself.

Ever since she'd taken on the mantle of captain, she second-guessed every damn decision. She'd fought her way out of the brothel. Worked her way to being the best damn navigator on this side of the Magian seas. Survived a cursed jungle, broke in and out of an Order jail, faced down an Order ship while fighting a sea serpent.

She picked up the middle dagger, the handle perfect in her hand. She'd done so much. Things a poor village girl from the Godswood couldn't even dream of doing. Couldn't even imagine surviving.

And dammit, she wasn't quite done with this life just yet.

So, what are you going to do, Mari? Get your crew back and do more of the impossible?

She twirled her new dagger in her hand.

Sure. Why the hell not?

CHAPTER 25

SERAPHINA

Macario, god of the Land and Sea, and whom I adore very much. Please tell me why I have yet to find a single book in your ancient library?

The chandelier lighting itself when she stepped into the room didn't even surprise her anymore. This was the fifth chamber she'd walked into, and it looked like all the rest.

Bare stone walls. A dusty table in the middle. Not a single, solitary book in sight. She hadn't heard from Mari or Luis, so either they didn't find anything or they'd gotten themselves lost.

Maybe I'm the one who's lost.

Coming to this library was supposed to be like all the other times she stepped into Ancient Order locations. A book she could pick up that would cause another to appear out of the floor. The Prayer Circle in Lucia, where the order of the serpent's attack was painted on the stones. Or she'd touch a picture and a scroll that would unlock magic would appear.

She made her way to the table, resting her head in her hands. *This was not how it was supposed to go at all.*

What she had to find was much too important. Macario chose her sister to defeat an evil god. The battle with the serpent only scratched the surface of what she could do with the scepter.

And the prophecy. All they knew was Bedros was coming and unleashing his monsters as he did in the War of the Gods. But what monsters? And where? And how was her sister supposed to defeat them all?

Seraphina leaned on the dusty table, holding her head in her hands. *What made me think I could do this?*

She wasn't Samara. Her twin was fearless and brave. It was why Macario chose her to save the world. Maybe Seraphina should've taken her up on her offer to stay and help her find the information she needed.

She shifted her weight from her left foot to the right to stretch out her sore legs. The brick under that foot sank into the floor. Seraphina grabbed the table, hoisting herself up, the floor trembling around her.

This is it. Her stomach fluttered and her legs went weak. The floor sank into steps that led into darkness. The room stilled, the swift and musty breeze from the secret passageway ruffling her clothes. She opened her mouth to call for Mari, but closed it again.

No. I can't always count on other people to save me.

She'd promised her sister she would take care of herself. No better time than now. Even if it meant going down dark and creepy stairs. Grabbing a large candle from the chandelier above, she lowered herself down to the first stair.

Macario, give me strength.

She wiped her sweaty palms on the side of her pants and started down the stairs. Another swift wind made the flame of her candle dance, and Seraphina cupped her hand around the flame. It was hard enough that she was going down there alone.

She didn't need to do it in the dark.

Just like the stairs that brought them to that scary bridge, they seemed to go down forever. Or maybe it just seemed that way because she went down very slowly.

She could trip and tumble into a pit. Or some giant animal or insect could jump out. The candle shook in her hand, the light only allowing her to see the slick walls closing in on either side of her.

Seraphina shook her head. *This is an awful idea.*

She took another step and heard a click. She froze in place. Flickering light streamed down a few steps below her, revealing a landing and an arched doorway. Two golden S's adorned the top.

What does that mean?

Her steps quickened, clearing the last step, and she rushed through the doorway. She was met by a long stone hallway, reminding her of the library back at the seminary. Instead of ceiling to floor bookshelves on either side of the polished walkway, there were columns the same brown speckled stone as the chambers upstairs.

The sounds of bubbling water filled the enormous cavern, and Seraphina's feet whispered against the stone.

Did the Ancient Order women walk this very hallway? Did Macario's godly presence grace this place?

The thought sent nervous shivers down her spine. She reached the end of the hall and found herself on the top of a set of steps. They were long and wide, creating a perfect square around a pool of turquoise water. The torchlight from the simple wall sconces twinkled on the pool, its waves lapping against the stone as if an imaginary wind pushed them along. An unexplainable light gleamed from the bottom, making the water appear even more magical.

She could continue to stand there and marvel at the prettiest thing she'd seen since arriving in this strange place. However, the stark white pedestal in the middle of the pool caught her attention.

The stone structure looked freshly carved, without a speck of dust or a cobweb on it, and perched on top of it—an open book, just waiting to be discovered.

Seraphina blew out the candle, setting it aside before going down the steps. She stopped short of the water, peering down into it. It was shallow enough to see clear to the bottom, not a deadly fish or flesh-eating insect in sight.

I hope.

She took off her boots and sweaty socks, taking a moment to stretch out her toes. She rolled up her trousers to her knees and stepped in. Despite looking warm and inviting, the water was ice cold, stinging her skin as she waded her way to the pedestal. Her teeth began to chatter, and she was waist-deep in the water before her foot hit a hidden step at the base of the pedestal.

Seraphina staggered up the step, her cold, wet pants weighing her down.

But when her eyes read the first line of that book, her face became as bright as the water below her.

> *We now call upon the Sacred Sisters.*
> *The women Macario, in all his infinite wisdom, anointed to carry on his legacy and safeguard his magic. The Sisters in faith, pure of heart, married to their faith and bestowed with the sacred duty of passing on the knowledge of the Second Coming of Bedros. The Sisters who will dedicate their lives to training the One in the ways of their almighty god, cleansing her in the sacred waters of this Sacred Mountain before accompanying her to the Oracle's Athenaeum to train her.*

Seraphina looked up, trying to find her breath as she digested this revelation.

This place was not the Secret Library.

The SS stood for the Sacred Sisters.

The Library would help her sister learn how to fight the monsters, just as she'd hoped.

I just waded through a pool of sacred water.

She turned the page and hope filled her heart. A full, detailed map sprawled across the two pale yellow pages. In the top left corner was the mountain, the sacred water pool drawn in the middle of it. A black path wound through green grass and palm trees, stopping at an open-air temple in the middle of a forest.

The path continued—through rough terrain, more jungle, and even down a river ending at another mountain. Bright yellow lines shone behind the words The Oracle's Athenaeum.

All praises to Macario!

She had a map and a plan. She might pull this off after all.

Stifling her excitement, she removed the book from the pedestal, the cold water no longer a bother as she waded back to the steps. Fumbling to put her boots back on, she raced to the steps, almost slipping in the massive corridor.

Perhaps this day wasn't a disaster.

I can really do this.

Mari would be grumpy once she realized this wasn't their final destination. And Luis seemed to still barely tolerate them since learning the truth about what happened at Bluegate.

But they would continue, the proof right there in her arms.

She reached the stairs and stumbled as the ground shook beneath her. She grabbed the wall for balance, pebbles, and dust raining down on her.

Crash!

Boom!

Seraphina whirled as a third column crashed to the ground, the ceiling coming down with it. Using the wall for support, she made her way up the steps, the world rocking all around her. Dust filled her lungs, her throat burning as she coughed.

But she made it to the top, tripping on the last step and falling onto the table. The chandelier rattled above her, and Seraphina got to her feet, holding the book to her chest.

"Seraphina!" Luis's voice was nearly drowned out by the rumbling and crashing that filled the air. She staggered to the doorway, holding onto the archway with a free hand. The book was heavier than the Ancient Order one.

The one she dropped into the pit of the nothingness.

She spun around in time to watch the rope holding the chandelier snap. The large lamp crashed down. Luis grabbed her arm and pulled her out of the room. Rock and dust fell all around them, Mari barely visible by the altar below.

They started down the stairs to meet her, Luis pulling and pushing her out of the way of the stones falling all around them.

They'd almost reached the bottom when one big jolt sent Seraphina flying down the last bit of steps. The book sprang out of her hands, her knees scraping the steps as she slid the rest of the way down. Her palms stung as she hit the floor, and Luis once again helped her to her feet.

"Just when I thought we were going to have a quiet day in a mountain tomb." Mari picked up the book that slid to her feet.

"I don't know what happened." Seraphina stumbled, catching herself with her scraped hands.

"I'll ask you about this later," Mari said, holding up the book. "Right now, we've got to get the hell out of here. I'm not partial to getting buried alive." She shoved the book into Seraphina's arms.

Luis nodded.

"But there's no way out." Seraphina's voice quivered. "The bridge was destroyed."

Luis and Mari scanned the room, using their arms to shield themselves from the falling debris.

The map!

Seraphina opened the book, furiously turning the pages until she came to the beautiful map. She found the mountain, the bright blue of the sacred water fountain almost glowing off the page. Even the altar was there.

And that was where the dark line started. The line that took them out of the mountain and onto that jungle path to the library.

"The altar!" She pointed to the stone table. "There's a secret passageway under the altar!"

At least, I hope so!

Mari and Luis looked at her, at the book, and then back to the altar. As if they had some sort of secret captain communication, they both ran over to it and each took a side, using all their strength to topple it over.

It hit the ground, breaking into two uneven pieces. Careful not to get crushed by a piece of falling rock, Seraphina rushed over to them, stopping short of the dark hole at their feet.

Mari looked at Luis, giving him a sly smile. "You first, Order rat."

CHAPTER 26

LUIS

Had this been any other circumstance, Luis would've gladly pushed that smug-faced pirate into the pit below. But this mountain cavern was falling apart, and he had no intention of dying that day. He took a nearby stone and tossed it down. It hit the ground a second later.

Falling to his death wasn't happening that day either.

With a swift motion, he jumped down, squatting as he landed on his feet. The air was as musty as it was humid, the walls slick and wet.

"Hurry!" he called up.

He stepped aside as Seraphina jumped down, almost losing her footing— again. Mari wasn't too far behind, stones crashing behind her. She pushed them both out of the way, the cavern bathed in total darkness as the rocks blocked the entrance.

No turning back now.

A hand grabbed his arm. From the way the slender fingers clutched his skin, he knew it was Seraphina.

"In case we get lost," she said, and a small part of him wished that wasn't the only reason. The ceiling rocked above them, dusting them all with dirt.

"We've gotta move," he said, moving forward, using his free hand as a guide.

The wall stayed straight, Seraphina and the pirate following close behind.

His eyes adjusted to the darkness. The passage seemed to go on forever, until finally a sliver of sunlight came into view. As if they'd planned it, they quickened their steps. They rounded the gentle curve, and sunlight poured into the passageway, revealing the uneven rock walls that had guided them. Seraphina let go of his arm, and Mari charged past both of them.

"We're finally out of this bloody mount—" She skittered to stop just short of the threshold. She stepped back, her spine straight. Seraphina came up beside her and peered over her shoulder.

"What is it?"

Luis didn't wait for an answer. They stepped aside, revealing the small ledge that separated them from a hundred-foot drop into the tangle of shiny green palm trees below.

For Macario's sake!

"This cannot be happening! This was supposed to be our way out of here. The map to the library said so."

Luis scowled. "You mean, this wasn't the library?"

Was he wrong about her? Was the sweet seminary girl thing all an act?

From the way Mari was glaring at Seraphina, the pirate captain didn't know anything about this either.

"I was going to explain it all when we got out of here," Seraphina said, holding the book to her chest.

Mari raised a brow. "Well, we're stuck up here, so feel free to run your mouth."

Those two can have their little spat. He would figure out a way down. It was useless to have a secret passage out of the mountain that ended up in a fall to one's death.

"I didn't even know there was a secret passageway," Seraphina rambled. "I mean, not until my foot hit a brick on the floor and then whoosh! A set of stairs."

"Just get to the part where this place isn't the bloody library," Mari snapped.

Luis grabbed a firm hold of the rock wall, kneeling so he could safely peer over the side. Clusters of thick, brown vines grew out of the same-colored rock. It reminded him of the ones that grew along the rocky cliffs of Yaton.

After temple classes, he and his brother would sneak off to the cliffs to watch the ships sail up and down the Isle straits. Then, Luis's brother would challenge him to grab one of those vines and slide down to the beach below.

The thought of Sister Marta finding even a speck of sand in his shoes was enough to deter Luis. She made discipline a sport. Every time he would watch his brother tempt fate, grabbing those vines and praying the entire time it wouldn't snap under his brother's weight.

"I was getting ready to find you, but then the whole place started falling apart!" Seraphina's voice jolted him out of his thoughts.

"So, because you grabbed another damn book, we're going to die out here on a ledge." Mari crossed her arms over her chest.

"This book has a map! It has everything we need—"

"You said the same thing about the last one. And where is that one, by the way?"

At the bottom of the pit.

He squinted down at the vines, so deceptively sturdy, just like the one he'd grabbed a hold of in Yaton. He'd grown tired of his brother taunting him every day. He took his time trying to find the fattest one, thinking it was the sturdiest.

Back then, he had a choice. Now, this plant life was their only option.

Luis rose to his feet, whipping his head around at the sound of Mari growling.

"You and books are nothing but trouble," Mari declared, her voice bouncing off the cavern walls.

"It's an important piece of history!"

"It's just another book of mumbo jumbo that has us stuck up on here between a crap ton of rocks and a fall to our death!"

"Did you just call this book—" Seraphina's eyes widened and her nose flared.

Mari didn't flinch. "We are going to die because of a stupid, dusty old book!"

Seraphina dared to point her finger at her. "You may not have respect for this realm or our culture, but I do. This faith system is my entire life. It's what kept me alive and so far, our lives too."

Mari scoffed and Seraphina's face turned red.

"All I ask is for a little common courtesy!" Seraphina jumped at her echo. "Trying to help my sister save the world from utter destruction is hard enough without having to tolerate your pigheadedness!"

She looked at Luis, but he wasn't sure what to say. What to think. What to believe. Everything he swore was true was being proven wrong at every turn.

But he couldn't ponder that while stuck on a mountain.

"We have to climb our way down. The vines I found along the side should hold."

"For some strange reason, I don't feel any better." Mari's voice oozed with that annoying sarcasm. She could rot in that mountain for all he cared.

Seraphina grabbed the book off the ground, wiping away the dirt from the gorgeous cover. He had to admit, he was quite proud of Seraphina for standing up to Mari. But, as much as he would like to thumb through those pages, there was no time for that.

Because you also have to admit you want to know if the library is real. He reached into his back pocket to make sure the map he'd taken was still folded inside.

Mari slowly looked over the edge. "You're going down first, Fozo."

He remembered watching his brother go down those vines on those seaside cliffs a thousand times. So much so, he'd felt confident being the first one to go down that fateful day. That confidence was quickly lost when the vine snapped when he was halfway down. It took weeks for his arm to heal and many more to survive Sister Marta's wrath for disobeying her.

"Climbing down is the only way to get out of here?" Seraphina squeezed the book to her chest.

"It is," he replied. "But they're sturdy. We will get down safely." He pointed to the book. "But you'll need both hands."

Her shoulders dropped in disappointment. "We need the map, Luis."

"I know." He held out his hand. "I'll gently rip it out and take it with us."

Her lip quivered and she searched his eyes for a bit before handing the book to him.

"I'll be careful." He gave her a soft smile before setting the thick tome on the ground in between them. He cracked it open and it landed right on the map. She looked away as he tore away the map with a steady hand and a gradual pace. Once it was out, he slowly folded it up and handed it to her.

She took a breath, forcing a smile as she tucked it away in her back pocket. "All right. Let's go."

CHAPTER 27

MARI

Bloody. Hell.

The sun burned into her back, making Mari's hands all the sweatier. And sweaty hands around a stupid vine on the side of a mountain were not the best companions.

She worked up the nerve to glance down, where Seraphina and her annoying Order boyfriend were scaling down side by side. He looked so comfortable, like a stupid little monkey. And the nun?

Wading in a stupid pool and escaping a collapsing cavern put some fire in her gut, standing up to Mari like she could best her in a fight. Mari didn't know whether she should be pissed or proud.

But right now, she was damn near petrified.

Frozen in place like an idiot, instead of sliding down the rock face like a pirate captain. She would face a thousand sea serpents or oversized plants rather than fall to her death.

Just the thought turned her legs to jelly, every ounce of confidence retreating into a shell, leaving behind the memory of the Scarlet Mountains in the Godswood. The elders in her childhood village would say they got their name because of all the blood that spilled during the War of the Gods.

Even as a little one, Mari didn't believe in any of those silly stories, and, being a pig-headed person, she wanted to prove them all wrong. Her older brothers, Sahl and Záměl, chased after her, begging her to turn around the whole half-day trip up there.

That stone wasn't stained red with blood. It was red clay.

Slippery red clay.

But that didn't stop her. She made it halfway up to its summit before stopping to take in the view. She could see clear to the southernmost port. But the rolling hills of green, purple, and red, mixed with clusters of wooden rooftops and snakes of crystal blue water, stole her breath away.

Too dazzled to watch her step. Too enamored to realize the clay was extra slippery. By the time she realized what was happening she was already in the air, the clear blue sky flying away from her until the world went dark.

She should've died.

Uncle Azmi told her she had the favor of Redal, the god of men and beasts. That celestial being had nothing to do with it. It was sheer luck, and she vowed never to tempt it again.

Yet here she was, inching down a mountain on a vine that could snap at any bloody minute.

And, just as she thought of it, the vine slid under her slippery hands, sending her down further and faster. She got control of her feet, pressing them against the rock to bring herself to a jolting stop. She let out a shaky breath. If the fall didn't kill her, a heart attack from the fear would do her in first.

She looked down. The Order captain picked up his pace, his feet able to touch the tree tops below. Seraphina hadn't moved much. For once, Mari couldn't blame her for being scared. Sweat poured down her face, her dreads wet against her skin.

If I don't move, I'll bake to death too.

Mari started down again, nice and slow, trying to keep her head from swirling with thoughts of her death. Instead of being there in that cursed place, she was climbing down from the crow's nest of her ship. The sweet, yet salty, sea air whipping through her clothes. The sea churning on either side as the *Pursuer* cut through it. Men shouting down below. Sails whipping in the wind.

She wasn't afraid, because she was home. The only home she had left in this world. Those men down there were her family, and they trusted her to lead them.

A scream ripped her out of the daydream, bringing her back to that mountain. *Seraphina.*

She looked down and saw the nun frozen in place, screaming her head off. Mari blinked, and Seraphina's body jolted. The girl's wide eyes looked up, but not at her. At the vine.

It was breaking. Her bloody vine was breaking.

Mari started moving faster, her feet shuffling down the rock face. *Too slow. I won't get to her in time.*

Before she could talk herself out of it, she wrapped her legs around the vine, loosened her grip, and let herself slide. The wind whipped about her face, the world around her moving just too fast.

It felt too much like falling from Scarlet Mountains.

Snap the hell out of it, Mari. Your crew needs you, even if she is an annoying nun.

Seraphina drew closer, her vine hanging on by mere threads a foot or so above her.

Three feet.

Two feet.

Mari could see Seraphina's scared eyes looking right at her. A foot away. Seraphina stretched her hand, but she was still out of reach.

Seraphina's vine snapped.

The vine burned as it slid through Mari's hands, but she couldn't stop. She let her right hand go, stretching out to Seraphina. But she was falling too damn fast.

Dammit!

Mari let go. Nothing but free-falling air around her.

This was a stupid idea. Now they both would die, and there was no Redal out there to grant them favor.

Then Seraphina grabbed her hand, and a hope that Mari couldn't explain engulfed her. Did Seraphina have magic too?

Whatever it was, neither Mari nor Seraphina would die. Not that day.

Mari's hand found a vine and snatched it. They both jerked to a stop. Pain shot up Mari's arm and down her back, but she didn't let Seraphina go.

Though she couldn't hold her like that forever either.

"Grab the damn vine," Mari said through her teeth.

Mari's command finally registered, and Seraphina clawed for the vine with her free hand, taking a few tries before she grabbed hold.

"Thank you, Mari!" She moved to hug her but quickly got a hold of her senses. "I thought I was done for."

So did I.

"I just didn't want your sister to drown me for letting you die," Mari said, her voice shaking on the last words.

I need to get down from here.

They both hurried down the vine they now shared until the world went from clear blue sky to a cluttered jungle of green and stifling humidity. When she reached the bottom, she fought the urge to fall to her knees and kiss the ground—mud, leaves, and all.

Instead, she smoothed out the creases in her pants, affixing her face with the familiar scowl that masked her feelings of relief and anxiety. The captain rushed over to them, his face sweaty and concerned.

"You both all right?" He put his hands on his hips, his eyes darting to Seraphina and then to Mari. "For a moment, I thought—"

"Don't get your britches all in a bunch." Mari rolled up her sleeves. "We handled ourselves just fine."

Seraphina turned to her and smiled. All genuine, yet nervous, just like the day she asked to join Mari's crew back on Bluegate.

Seemed like a lifetime ago.

"Now that we're here on solid land," Luis said. "We need to decide here and now what we're going to do."

Seraphina stepped in between them. "Decide? There is only one choice— find the Secret Library, so we can help my sister save the world."

Mari's hands immediately went to her waist belt, the daggers still tucked in it.

The knives with my bloody name on them.

"All right, Seraphina," Mari said. "Before I take another step, and almost get my head knocked off by who knows what, I need answers."

I hope I don't regret this.

She pulled out a dagger, and Luis jumped back like a scared cat.

"I'm not gonna stab you." Mari rolled her eyes. "At least, not yet."

She presented it in her palms, making sure her last name was as clear as day to Seraphina.

"I found this hidden in a wall shaped like a compass. Now, how the hell can a bunch of ancient folks in a cave know my name?" Mari swallowed. "And how would they know that I would sell my left arm for daggers like these?"

Seraphina's eyes widened, inspecting every inch of the blade. "Zaltaire."

Luis frowned. "The God of Time?"

Seraphina nodded, looking into Mari's eyes.

"He predicted it. He told Macario that Bedros would return, and that was why the rest of Magia's magic had to be hidden away. Maybe he told the Sacred Sisters that you would come. That we all would come."

Her face lit up like a lighthouse on a foggy day. "It's proof that we are all supposed to be on this journey to the Secret Library."

They both turned to Luis, his lips tightening as if whatever he was hiding would slip out at any moment.

"Spill it," Mari ordered. "What did you find?"

He looked to Seraphina, who gave him a reassuring nod. The Order rat sighed and went into his back pocket. It took a minute for him to unfold a piece of paper, taking care to keep it out of Mari's reach.

But as soon as he opened it, she knew exactly what it was—a map of the Majestic Isles. He glanced at her, turning to Seraphina.

"I found this in one of the rooms. It isn't an old map." He pointed to the middle of the illustration. "Tradesman Harbor is gone." He pointed a little lower. "And that…." His voice shook. "I don't know what to make of that."

Seraphina held her hand out, batting those silly eyes. "You may not know, but Mari does."

He shoved the paper in her hands before crossing his arms and glaring at Mari. Seraphina handed it to her, taking care to point at the island of Bluegate in the lower half. Seeing those two ships drawn side by side, the serpent rearing its ugly head, brought back all the memories of that cursed night.

Swords clanging and bodies dropping as the crew stormed the Order ship.

The serpent shrieking and roaring into the night.

Smoke and fire engulfing the world all around them.

"What is that?" Luis pressed. "Is that what happened at Bluegate? Is that the ship where my brother—"

He caught himself, pressing his fist to his mouth, blood rushing to his face.

So that was it.

The reason he went through all this trouble to hunt them down. He wasn't a man seeking justice against some pirates. He was a man grieving over the death of a sibling.

If it were her brother, she would tear the world down trying to find out what happened.

"That's exactly how it happened," Mari said, handing the map back to him. "And there's no damn way anyone could've known that unless they were there."

Seraphina clasped her hands together, as if she was getting ready to spout more prayers.

"All of this was foretold, which means we have no choice but to keep going."

Luis turned around and stormed off, headed for a cluster of trees. Seraphina turned to Mari.

"Did you—I mean—his brother." She clawed for the right words to say.

"There's no way to know who killed who that night. It was every pirate for himself."

The plan was simple. Take over the ship. Use it to send that serpent back into the bloody ocean. If any Order men died, so be it.

"It doesn't matter now," Seraphina said. "What matters is that you two believe, just as I do."

Mari put her dagger back in her hip. *Damned if I do believe. Maybe even more damned if I don't.*

She didn't know what to believe anymore, but she'd come too far not to find out.

CHAPTER 28

SERAPHINA

Zaltaire foretold everything.

The serpent.

Samara and the scepter.

Seraphina, Mari, and even Luis going to that temple in the mountain to find what they needed to believe. Even when she began to doubt this entire quest, she stumbled upon the book in the sacred pool.

Macario, I'm forever your humble servant.

Seraphina opened her eyes, the full moon casting shadows through the trees.

She'd never meant to be out there that long, taking her leave from the awkward silence around the budding campfire to pray. Starting with the first prayer she ever memorized by heart, she only made it halfway through when the reality of their situation hit her like a stone wall.

This wasn't a time to doubt herself or question if she was up to the task. They were on the right track. She just had to keep the faith.

Twigs cracked behind her, and she scrambled to her feet.

"It's all right, it's just me."

Luis stepped into the stream of moonlight between them, holding his hands up in peace. Seraphina let out a breath of relief, willing her heart to beat normally as she grabbed her chest.

"You were gone a while," he said, "I wanted to make sure you were okay."

Hmm. He was worried about me. "I'm fine. I just needed to catch up on my prayers, that's all."

He nodded. "I've been doing my fair share of that myself." He took a seat on the large, fallen log behind him.

"It's been quite a day." She wrung her hands. *Should I sit next to him? Or should I just stand here?*

He sighed, running his hand through his beautiful black hair. He'd gotten so upset earlier. He lost his brother that night on Bluegate. She would've been a puddle of emotions if she lost her sister to that serpent.

On top of all of that, he'd also found out that the serpent and the prophecy were real. That would be too much for anyone to take. She walked over to the log, his eyes following her as she sat down next to him. Thank goodness he couldn't see the flush in her face.

"I'm so sorry about your brother."

"Me, too." His eyes turned to the floor. "I don't know what to believe anymore."

"This is all difficult to understand at first."

It was as if she were talking to Samara again. Trying to get her to believe she was worthy of being the hero she was destined to be. It wasn't until she surrendered herself and stopped fighting her demons that she was able to embrace her magic and her destiny.

Luis looked up. "How could you possibly understand all of this? This goes against everything we've ever known about our faith system."

"No. It goes against everything the Order taught us. They went to extraordinary lengths to hide all of this."

"Monsters? Magic? Predicting the future? It all sounds ridiculous."

"Yet, here we are, in a ridiculously cursed place."

The moonlight shone on his face, revealing the slight smile across his lips.

And this smile on my face must look ridiculous. She squirmed in her seat, looking out into the surrounding darkness.

"What happens when we find this library? How will we even get back home?"

You mean back to the part where you turn us in to be hanged for piracy?

"I wish I knew," was all she could manage to say.

"If anyone can figure that out, it's you."

She turned to face him, his dark eyes staring into hers. It was like he could see everything. What she wanted. What scared her. What made her heart do flips in her chest.

Just like it was doing now.

"I don't know about all of that," she mumbled.

"Of course you do. You carry enough knowledge and faith for all of us. And that is exactly what we need to find the library."

No. All they needed was the map Luis tore from that sacred book. All Seraphina did was find it.

She gave him a nervous smile. "I'm just following Macario's will, that's all."

His smile grew wider, and her heart skipped a beat. "You don't give yourself enough credit."

"What do you mean?" By Macario's grace, she was smiling too much.

"It takes a tremendous amount of courage to follow your heart and your faith, no matter the cost. Even if it meant joining a pirate crew and risking the Order's justice."

How could she not? She'd seen the magic of her god first-hand and gotten a taste of the battles to come.

"I've seen too much not to," she said.

She expected him to press further. Instead, he looked up into the sky, the moon brilliant.

"All I can believe is what is right in front of me." His eyes fell back to hers.

It took all her concentration not to fall off the log and utterly embarrass herself.

"Faith is much more than that."

"I know."

Now she couldn't breathe. *This is silly!* He was an Order officer. The man tasked with capturing her.

At least he was. Right?

"Why are you coming with us to the library? What made you change your mind?"

His eyes didn't waver.

"You."

***

An uneventful night's sleep didn't untangle the bundle of nerves in Seraphina's stomach. The way Luis looked at her the night before. His soft voice. Those dark, beautiful eyes.

Snap out of it, Seraphina!

She sat up, wiping the grass off her arms. The smell of burnt wood and ash from last night's fire filled her nostrils as she searched around for Mari and Luis. She jumped to her feet.

I know they didn't leave without me. She checked her back pocket and breathed a slight sigh of relief. The map was still there.

"That is the stupidest idea I've ever heard of!"

Seraphina walked toward Mari's voice, around the old campfire and into the little clearing where she prayed last night.

And that log where Luis gazed right into her soul.

"We'll starve before we ever get to that library!" Luis boomed and Seraphina picked up the pace. She squeezed through two tall, skinny trees to find them both standing over a pile of bright yellow bananas.

"I can't believe you spent your entire morning gathering up fruit like a bloody monkey!" Mari threw up her hands before noticing Seraphina.

"Look who decided to rise from her beauty sleep." Mari walked over to her, putting her hands into her pockets. Then, low enough for only Seraphina to hear, she said, "Do I have to find this place with the likes of him?"

Seraphina smiled. "We all have to go."

Mari glanced over her shoulder at Luis bending over to gather the fruit. "Fine, then he's carrying those stupid bananas."

Seraphina chuckled. "He isn't so bad."

He is charming, actually.

Mari scoffed. "Don't let down your guard just because we're all going on this little expedition with you." She leaned in closer. "When this is all over, he's going to be the same Order rat who was trying to hang us."

"People change. Even you are proof of that."

"A leopard doesn't change its spots no more than a pirate can change his scars."

Mari took a step backward, raising a brow to emphasize her point.

But she didn't see how he was last night. So sincere. So vulnerable. Not a captain doling out orders or demanding answers. If Mari saw that, she would understand.

Right?

"Well, I think it's high time we get a move on it, don't you think?" Mari said loud enough for half the jungle to hear. "Best if I have the map."

Seraphina reached into her back pocket as Luis started for them.

"Best you hand that to me," he said, holding out his hand. "I'm the best equipped to navigate our way there."

Mari spun around, stepping in front of him. "Be happy we don't tie you up and drag you along, Order rat. Now step back. The only one who is looking at that map is me."

"Unless you have a compass hidden in those fancy blades of yours, we won't be getting far with you in the lead, now will we?"

His eyes caught Seraphina's and she smiled. Handsome and clever.

"Hand it—"

"No."

"I have the mind to—"

"Is this the part where you threaten to stab me?" Luis walked around her, his face softening as he approached Seraphina.

"The map, please."

If he kept looking at her like that, it would be hard to see him as the mean Order captain Mari believed him to be.

And by Macario's grace, it would be a very good thing.

CHAPTER 29

LUIS

All I can believe is what is right in front of me. And yet, he couldn't quite make sense of that, either.

Following a pretty map through a forest was one thing. Unlike the overgrown flowers they survived a few days ago, this jungle was more familiar. Average-sized palm trees, their waxy green leaves trapping the humid air. The wild grasses grazed their ankles as they walked, normal-sized mosquitoes whizzing by.

According to the map, they would find a temple ruin in the middle of that jungle. He wouldn't mind coming across any structure, so long as it wasn't high on some godforsaken mountain. And, judging by the orange tint blanketing the sky, they would need shelter. Seraphina and Mari stayed at least a few steps behind him, trudging along.

If this were a few days ago, he wouldn't feel so confident having his back to them.

It wasn't that he trusted them. Well, he didn't trust Mari for sure. She still had that same violent fire in her eyes from the first day he captured her ship. As long as Seraphina wanted them all together, she would keep a handle on that temper.

And what of Seraphina?

Those wide and curious eyes.

That nervous, yet beautiful smile.

That soothing, yet confident voice.

It'd never felt so natural to talk to someone and just be Luis for a change. He'd forgotten he was supposed to keep his guard up. Listen for any cues that would let him know when she was lying.

I'm a terrible liar.

Seraphina was straightforward, brave, and full of conviction. There wasn't any doubt about where she stood on matters. Or how she felt. Not even a whiff of an ulterior motive. There weren't many people in the world like her.

Just like there wasn't anything like the temple ruin in front of them. White stone columns and slick staircases held and connected the various floors of the temple. But that was it. No walls or roofs, just the palm trees of the forest surrounding him.

But that wasn't the unexplainable part.

"Is this place glowing?" Seraphina said, holding her chest as if her heart would fall out.

The white stone glowed, the light pulsing like his heart beating in his chest. It was as if Macario had blessed this place himself, touching every stone with his magic.

"Looks like one giant lantern if you ask me," Mari said, appearing very unimpressed.

How could a pirate ever appreciate something as magical and as sacred as that place?

"This is incredible," Seraphina said, coming up beside him. Her eyes took in every inch, her face just as bright as the stone.

And maybe even more beautiful.

She started for the stone archway, the brightest part of it all.

"I'm waiting out here in case one of those columns tries to eat me," Mari said, taking a seat on a nearby tree stump. There was no way he was going to stay out there with her. Seraphina made for much better company, anyway.

She was already halfway up the first staircase when he made it to the archway, the light soft and warm against his skin.

Incredible.

He followed her to the first wall-less chamber in front of them, the ground barely visible through all that light.

"Isn't this amazing!" Seraphina glanced back at him, her smile contagious. "What does this mean?"

Something on the third column caught her eye and she walked over to it. Her fingers grazed the glowing stone. Before he could ask her what she found, the floor shook. He started for the stairs, but she wasn't following. She just stood there with the same giddy expression.

"What are you doing?" he called out.

"Just wait for it!" she called back, her eyes on the trembling floor below them. "Something great always happens!"

The surrounding light grew brighter, and Luis shielded his eyes with the crook of his arm. The light subsided, and Seraphina let out a cry of excitement.

"Yes!"

A pedestal with a sky-blue ball mounted on top of it had risen from the floor.

"Where in the world did that come from?" Luis stepped over to get a closer look.

"From the ground. Where else?" Seraphina's flushed face reflected at them both as she stared into the ball.

"If you both kill yourselves in there, I will not save you!" Mari called out.

I would expect nothing less.

Seraphina placed her hands on the ball, the color swirling like paint in water, then forming words. He and Seraphina gasped, turning to each other, their lips only a breath apart. Luis felt the blood rush to his face as they looked back at the sphere and he read the strange words aloud:

Sacra Immortals Sactum.

A gust of wind came from nowhere, swirling all about them. He held up his arm, trying to shield himself from the wind. His eyes teared as he tried to see the source of the sound. Indiscernible whispers rode the gale circling all around them. Female voices, so hurried they were hard to understand.

"Do you hear them?" Seraphina looked into his eyes.

He nodded, the tense knot in his stomach only tightening. The wind stopped, and Luis wiped his eyes dry as he struggled to open them.

He should've rubbed them harder.

Two transparent women moved about the shell of a room. The sun shone through their caftans, their hair flowing over their bare shoulders. Seraphina grabbed his arm, and he swallowed hard.

"You shouldn't have activated the crystal," said a tall apparition with a narrow nose and curly hair. The short, curvy girl in front of her glanced over to them before turning back to her companion.

"It should always be on," she said. "You won't know what may happen—"

The girls turned to the stairs as an older, heavier-set woman glided up the steps.

"Sister Ira," the girls said in unison.

"We must go to the library," the older woman pleaded, grabbing their hands.

"It's happening isn't it?" The short girl shook with every word.

The older woman nodded. "It was as we feared. We must meet the others there at once if we are to stand a chance."

"Will we have enough magic to stop it?"

"Let's pray to Macario that we do," the older woman said, hurrying for the stairs.

The tall girl followed on her heels, the two disappearing into the air when they reached the bottom step. The one left behind stormed toward Luis and Seraphina. He pushed the young woman behind him, not sure how he could protect her from a specter.

But the ghost girl's eyes weren't on them but the orb. She pressed her hands on its surface, mumbling words before looking up. His breath caught as her ghostly eyes looked into his.

"If you're watching this, we failed. Make sure you don't."

The girl faded away. It took him a moment to remember how to breathe, Seraphina's nails digging into his arm.

"What in the bloody hell?"

Mari stood halfway up the stairs, a dagger in each hand. She reached the top, scanning the room before making her way over to them. He took a deep breath, trying to act as if what he'd just witnessed didn't scare the soul out of him. Seraphina let go of him, stepping around him and the globe to approach Mari.

"Would you believe me if I told you there were ghosts up here?" Seraphina said with a nervous smile.

"I could've damn well told you that!" Mari sheathed her daggers in her waistband. "Couldn't go one full day without weird shit happening."

Luis cleared his throat, ignoring the weakness of his knees as he strode over to them.

"What was that girl talking about?"

Seraphina looked back at him, eyes wide and innocent. "I don't know."

"So, the ghosts were talking too?" Mari said. "Brilliant."

"Something bad happened to them, but they didn't say what," Seraphina said. "They looked so scared."

"And it's apparent they failed," Luis added.

Failed at *what* he didn't want to speculate.

The setting sun cast shadows in the wall-less room, just adding to the eeriness left behind by those ghostly figures.

"I never thought I'd say this, but I would feel most comfortable camping out in the forest tonight." Seraphina hugged her arms. Luis nodded in agreement.

Mari spun on her heel and headed toward the stairs. Seraphina and Luis followed close behind. They took the winding path around the haunted temple, not stopping until it was well behind them. Even with the full moon glowing in the cloudless sky above, it was still too dark to find wood for a fire.

So they stayed on the path, Mari taking a spot half a yard away from Luis and Seraphina.

"Takin' first watch," she said, turning her back to them before taking a seat on the grassy ground.

Luis waited until Seraphina found an acceptable spot on the ground, lying on her side to face the moon. He chose the spot across from her, to keep her in his line of sight without encroaching on her personal space.

To make sure she was safe.

Yeah. Keep telling yourself that.

"That was incredible," she said loud enough for him to hear.

Or frightening, as seeing ghosts would be.

"That seems to be the theme of this expedition," he said slowly, sitting down.

"I wish my sister were here to see all of this." Seraphina smiled. "For once, she's not the only one having adventures in cursed places."

How he wished his brother were alive to see that moon, let alone a ghost. His chest tightened.

But he's not. And it's not fair.

"She would have a hard time believing I was even in a place like this." She snorted under her breath.

"Why is that? You are a born adventurer."

Her face lit up brighter than the moon as she chuckled, tucking a loose strand of hair behind her ear. "I'm far from that."

The only thing she seemed to be far from was the pirate he was charged with bringing to justice. The way she smiled. The ease he felt whenever she was around. Never mind they were in a cursed jungle going after some ancient library. It was these quiet moments where they could just be themselves that made battling the magic and monsters worth it.

Would it be worth the heartbreak when they returned to the real world?

"I'm sure your sister would be proud," Luis said finally.

After a long pause, she sat up and looked right at him, her smile fading.

"What if there is something horrible waiting for us at the library? What if those ghosts were warning us?"

All of that was a big possibility.

If you're watching this, we failed. Make sure you don't.

He fought the urge to put his arms around her, sitting on his hands.

"If the Sacred Sisters foretold that we would be the ones to find the library," he said, "then Macario and all of his grace are with us."

Are you trying to reassure her? Or yourself?

Whatever might be waiting in that library, all he could do was pray it wasn't any worse than the monsters they'd survived thus far.

CHAPTER 30

MARI

No amount of bright sunshine or singing birds could convince Mari to put away the dagger in her hand. Sweat rolled down her back as she climbed over yet another boulder.

It was as if someone didn't want anybody on that bloody path to find a dusty building with books. If they weren't climbing over rocks, they were cutting through clusters of brush with thorny branches and smelly leaves. When they weren't gardening, they were jumping rotting logs or guessing what a pile of bones used to be.

At any moment, she expected Seraphina to beg them to stop, turn around, and find their way back home. But the nun and her little bodyguard kept pushing forward, staying on her heels as they whispered between themselves.

It was no use trying to warn her about that Order rat. She would learn soon enough when this was all over.

Some folks just gotta learn the hard way.

"Captain, you think we can stop for a moment?"

Seraphina struggled to catch up to her. Giving her aching legs a rest wasn't a bad idea. Mari gestured to the cluster of rocks as good a place as any to take a brief break. She sat down on a nearby rock, the flat surface just as warm as the day.

"I'm going to see if I can find something edible around here," Luis announced. Seraphina flashed him a smile before she took a seat by Mari.

Ugh, how pathetic.

"According to the map, we should be there any day now," Seraphina said, breaking the awkward silence.

"Good. The sooner we get there, the sooner we can get back to the crew."

"I can't wait to see my sister. Miss her more than ever."

"Well, I don't," Mari said, leaning back on the rock. "If she were here, we would all be snake food by now."

Seraphina laughed, and Mari fought back a smirk.

"She would've charged right at that monster without thinking twice." Seraphina sighed. "Not like me, where I overthink everything."

"Thinking things through isn't a bad thing." Mari let out a breath.

Now she sounded like Prisha back from the Enchanted Cape. When Mari found out she'd worked her way out of the whore house and into a tavern, she'd asked how Prisha managed it.

"Patience," she had said. "Knowing when to strike and being willing to wait for that moment to do so."

Waiting a few days was patience. Five grueling years? That was just damn crazy.

And Mari had no intention of being a lunatic. They'd better get to that library by tomorrow.

"You don't strike me as an over-thinker," Seraphina said.

"Whatever gave you that impression, sister?" Mari picked up a nearby pebble and tossed it out onto the grassy ground in front of her.

"The way you threw those daggers at that Griffin Valeman back on Crystal Crest." Her body shuddered. "It didn't take you long to—you know."

"Nothing to think about. Bastard deserved it."

"And that doesn't bother you?"

Killing people would make village girl Mari vomit into her brother's shoes. Mari Adlam the pirate? It was just another day.

"You're honestly asking me this question?"

"Pirates are known to kill people. Are heartless, even. But you aren't any of those things."

Mari twirled the dagger in her hand before turning to Seraphina. "You don't know shit about me."

She expected Seraphina to look away, but the nun held her stare. Gave her a warm smile.

"I don't know much about you. But I know that you care. Even in your own grumpy kind of way."

Oh no. She wasn't going to have any of that mushy, sisterly kindness rubbing off on her. No matter how good it felt. Mari jumped up from the rock just as the Order rat reappeared. He held a cluster of vines in his hands, small purple berries hanging from them.

"Found these in the brush over there," he said, holding them up.

"Are they safe to eat?" Seraphina wrinkled her nose.

He nodded. "Tried them myself."

"And you're still living," Mari said. "I'm disappointed."

She gave him a scowl for good measure before grabbing a vine for herself, inspecting the berries before popping one in her mouth. Mari welcomed the sour taste, though she wished they were cold.

Mari ate three more as they moved past the rocks, dusting off her vine as a beautiful, winding river came into view. She hadn't seen water in days. She suppressed the sudden urge to strip naked and jump right in. *You've been out in nature too long.*

Seraphina and Luis whooped and ran for the river.

"Map, Fozo," Mari called out, dampening the smile on the Order man's face.

He slapped it into her palm and raced after Seraphina. In moments, those two were splashing around like idiots. Like they weren't in a cursed jungle with no idea how the hell to get out of there.

What pissed her off even more? She longed to be that carefree.

But that wasn't for people like her.

She opened the map, searching for the river. She traced it a few inches upstream, around the steep bend, and then straight to that damned library.

One more day of this cursed place.

She stomped over to the water's edge, keeping a safe distance from the budding lovebirds. Didn't need any of that coming her way. Amrit wouldn't be doing any of that nonsense. He would be helping her figure out how to get out of this mess.

And wisecracking and sassing me the entire time.

A slight chuckle escaped her lips. Who knew she would miss that?

For the first time since they left the haunted ruins, she sheathed her dagger, cupping the cool water in her hands. She drank until her stomach hurt. Then she splashed the water in her face and ran it through her dreads. The rest of her body was begging to be drenched, but traveling in soggy clothes was the worst.

And she made a vow that no one would ever see her naked. Not ever. It was the last words that bastard madame heard before she bled to death.

And I'm a pirate who keeps her promises.

She rose to her feet, striding over to Seraphina and Fozo. "You two lovebirds done?"

They splashed out of the water, their sopping wet shirts sticking to their bodies as they stood just inches away from each other.

Was that a smile on Fozo's face?

"We should get going, Captain," Seraphina stammered, blushing like a schoolgirl.

Mari rolled her eyes, brushing past them, and headed upstream. She was walking so fast it took her a moment to realize the sun was no longer beating down on her head. She closed her eyes, taking a moment to appreciate the break from the heat.

When she opened them again, a cloud of fog rolled off the river as they came around the bend. She came to an abrupt stop, pulling at her collar. Dammit, it was hard to breathe, the humidity so thick she could slice through it with the dagger in her hand.

But that didn't send icy shivers down her sweaty back.

There wasn't a tree, a bush, or a patch of bloody grass in the fifty yards between her and the creepy building. Columns lined each of the four stories, the fog swirling all around it making it hard to see just how far back it went. She also couldn't tell what color it was. Ink-black vines snaked around the rock like the serpent Samara drove into the bottom of the sea.

What was that smell?

It was like her old madame was sitting right there, burning that blasted incense right into her nose. She hugged herself to keep from shaking.

"That cannot be it."

Mari jumped at the sound of Seraphina's voice.

"This is not the glorious sanctuary I imagined." The nun planted her hands on her hips.

"You sure this is it?" Fozo raised an eyebrow.

Mari snapped her head around. "Of course it is!"

Every nerve felt like it was on fire. Since when was she afraid of a stupid building?

That ain't it.

It felt like she was back on the Misty Isle all over again. When she steered the Pursuer through that wall of fog, her body fought her every step of the way. They had no business being there, and the sea let them have it just for trespassing.

And I don't care what Seraphina says, we have no business being here either.

Yet, here they were. The only thing standing between staying alive and getting back to her crew was a creepy building.

I'm going to regret this.

CHAPTER 31

SERAPHINA

Seraphina thought she would've learned her lesson by now.

Nothing was ever how it seemed. Yet, as she stood there surrounded by thick gray air, staring at a building suffocated by black vines, her heart plummeted to her feet.

And the smell! It brought her back to that miserable nightmare, where everything smelled of soot and death.

By Macario's grace, this cannot be the Secret Library.

She took a shallow breath. "Let us pray it looks better inside."

Mari turned back to the library, her eyes scanning the barren ground in front of them.

"For some reason, I doubt that."

The pirate captain bit her lip and pressed forward, though not at the swift pace she'd set earlier. Seraphina stayed close, Luis in lockstep with her. He drew his sword, brows furrowed as he scanned the open land. There wasn't any place for anything to hide. The dirt cracked under their feet, not a speck of green anywhere in sight.

Just gray and silence.

What she wouldn't give for the tweeting of a bird or the squawking of a seagull. Anything to ease the dread swirling in her stomach.

This is the task Macario gave to you. He will put nothing upon you that you cannot handle.

A pair of fingers grazed her hand, and her heart skipped to see they belonged to Luis.

"That place isn't as bad as it looks," he said, a twinkle in those gorgeous eyes.

"Maybe not," she said. "But an extra prayer never hurt."

He nodded in agreement.

The ground trembled under their feet, and all three of them came to a stop. It shook harder.

Samara?

Could it be her sister using the scepter, finally back from the Griffin Vales to save her?

Seraphina fought to keep her balance as the trio inched closer to each other.

No, Seraphina. It's high time you save yourself.

"What was that?" Seraphina whispered.

Mari shushed her, the ground shaking harder. The cracks in the dirt widened under their feet as if it would swallow them whole.

Maybe it would. Nothing was too far-fetched after what they'd experienced.

"We should run!" Seraphina yelled, the quaking ground deafening.

The rift under their feet widened, and they spun on their heels and started running toward the library. The rumbling turned to a roar as Seraphina zigzagged across the plain.

Had this been the first time the jungle tried to kill them, she would've thought this was the work of her sister. The dry ground shot out into the sky, the same ground spikes her sister used to kill the Order guards back in Lucia.

Except now they are trying to kill us!

One rocketed out of the ground a few feet in front of her, and she skidded to the left to avoid running into it. Dust and dirt pelted her like rain, the ground unsteady under her feet.

Run, Seraphina!

Mari came into view, the pirate bouncy on her toes, unsure of where to run to next. A dagger was in her hand. Seraphina rolled her eyes. What did she plan to do? Stab the ground?

Mari's eyes widened as Seraphina rushed her. The ground convulsed again, and before Seraphina could talk herself out of it, she grabbed Mari's hand and dragged her forward.

More dirt.

More rocks.

More dust.

Her eyes stung, but she didn't slow down. The vine-covered entrance to the library drew closer, the palm-sized thorns threatening them to stay away. They stopped short of the door, and Mari yanked her wrist from Seraphina's hand. She expected the ex-navigator to say something rude and crass.

But she didn't say a word, turning around to survey the madness they just escaped.

And it was madness.

Spikes of rock rose through the dust clouds, turning the flat land into a sea of sharp stone and spikes. The ground stopped trembling, quiet settling into the air.

Where is Luis?

As if he read her mind, he burst through the fog, covered in dirt and dust.

Oh, how she wanted to jump up and hug him, then slap him for making her worry.

"Are you all right?"

"Right as rain," he said, attempting to brush the dirt off of himself.

"Or wrong as shit," Mari scoffed, turning to the door. It was sealed up tight, but that didn't stop Mari from driving her dagger into a thorny vine.

"That's one way to get in," Luis said, twirling his sword.

Seraphina took a step back as he approached the door. One swift swing and a piece of the vine fell to the ground. He turned to Mari, raising a brow.

"I mean, I don't want to be here all day."

Her eyes narrowed.

"Bloody show-off," she said through her teeth.

Mari took a deep breath before stepping back, giving him room to clear the door of the ominous plant life. With a free hand, he wiped away a section of dust, revealing symbols etched into the door.

The language of the gods.

Seraphina brushed past Mari to help him clean the door, not caring if centuries of dust and grime touched her hands.

"What's all that gibberish?" Mari took a step closer.

"A forbidden language."

Seraphina touched the symbol that looked like a book. It began to glow, its white light pulsing like a beating heart. Then, one by one, the symbols took on the same light, until it was so blinding they all had to shield their eyes.

"Curses, what have you done?" Mari cried.

Seraphina held out her grimy hand, halfway expecting to feel the door. She felt nothing but air. She took another step.

"The door is gone! I think we can get through!"

She didn't wait for them to answer, rushing through the light with a burst of courage that surprised even her. The light flashed away in an instant.

"Well, that wasn't so bad—" Her breath caught in her throat.

"Mari!" Her voice echoed off the walls of the dim room. "Luis!"

Didn't they follow her? She swore they were right behind her.

Seraphina spun around and rushed to the wall where the door should be. She rubbed away the dirt, praying there were symbols there, too. She could make them light up and it would magically open again.

Nothing but dirty stone. She rubbed until her palms hurt, choking back the sobs gurgling in her throat.

"Seraphina!" She turned, the voice too sweet to be Mari's. But familiar all the same. A stream of sunlight appeared at the far side of the room.

"Phina!"

Oh, praises to Macario from the highest mountain! She ran right for that sunlight as if the god himself were on the other side of it. She was running so fast she almost tripped as the stone floor turned to sand. A gray sky loomed overhead, a sea breeze caressing her sweaty face. A frigid chill ran up her spine, the treeless shore too reminiscent of the nightmares that plagued her dreams.

Except for the young woman standing with her back to her, the clear water lapping against her ankles. Her frizzy brown hair was a messy halo around her as if she hadn't combed it in weeks.

"Seraphina," she said, voice flat, half turning her head toward her. Samara. But how did she even get here? Did it matter?

"I wasn't sure I would ever see you again," Seraphina said, the sand heavy as she walked across it.

"It doesn't matter now, does it?" There was a bite to her tone, so much so it made Seraphina's skin crawl.

"Sam, are you all right?"

She tried to pick up the pace, run even, desperate to wrap her arms around her sister and melt away the sarcasm like she always did. But the sand! It was as if it wouldn't allow her to move any faster than a snail.

"No, Phina," her twin answered. "I'm not alright ."

Samara turned around. Streaks of dirt and blood marred her face, her white shirt ripped in too many places to count. But that wasn't what made Seraphina stop mid-step, falling backward onto the sand.

Black took over her twin's brown eyes, the same dark pitch that covered the walls of the library.

The library.

That was where she was, right?

"Sam—Sam, what happened to you?" Sobs were clawing up Seraphina's throat.

Samara had no trouble stomping across the sand. Tears streamed down Seraphina's eyes as she gazed at her sister up close.

"You failed!" Thunder ripped across the sky.

Seraphina shook her head. "No! I found it! I found the library. It was just—"

Just where? Behind her? Back on the mainland? She didn't know where she was anymore.

"You were too late!" Samara spat. "What made you think you could ever help me?"

"I'm your sister! I'm supposed to help."

"You're pathetic!"

It was like rocks were piled on her chest, it was that hard to breathe. Seraphina coughed up a lungful of dust.

"You can't do anything on your own! You should've stayed at the convent and kept your nose in those stupid books!"

Ominous clouds rolled in, darkening the already-gray sky.

"You find one book and you think you're brave?"

"Sam," Seraphina croaked. "Why are you saying such horrible things?"

Samara leaned over her, those inky black eyes tearing through her heart.

"Because I'm tired of having to baby you. The fate of the world is on the line, and you failed. It's all your fault."

The sky roared like the serpent that attacked their realm. Seraphina's body trembled in the sand. What if she was right? What if she found the library too late? It took her too long to convince Mari to take her to the mainland. Too long to convince Luis to let them go. Too long to find the book with the map.

But Samara wouldn't talk to her like that. Samara didn't have eyes like that.

Seraphina sat up on her hands, her face just inches away from the Samara lookalike.

"You may be right about being too late, but I don't have to take that from you."

The black-eyed woman tilted her head.

Her twin had been through so much and would have blamed her for much more.

Abandoning her for the convent after their mother died. Looking down on her, instead of trying to help her get over her heartbreak. Not loving her for all she was, instead of who Seraphina thought she should be.

Samara wouldn't have been angry at her for taking too long to enter the library.

And that was where she was. Not on this beach. And not with this Samara wannabe.

"You are not my sister!" The pride and bravery Seraphina felt in her heart cut short. The woman's grimy hand shot out and grabbed Seraphina by the throat.

Seraphina clawed at her hand, but the girl's grip was too strong.

This is not happening. This can't be real.

And it all flashed in her mind. The rocks shooting out of the ground. The glowing letters. Stepping through the light.

"Not real," she managed to say as the girl smiled at her.

"Don't struggle," she said. "It will all be over soon."

"Only Macario can tell me it's over," Seraphina said through her teeth, her head dizzy. "And He has not deemed it so!"

She would not be afraid. She would not die. Not by the hands of whatever evil had taken hold of this place.

Seraphina couldn't feel the girl's hands around her throat. The surrounding sand floated into the air. The evil girl's confident expression turned to one of surprise.

"I am the sister of Macario's light. I will never be led astray, especially not by the likes of you!"

The same blinding light that brought her inside the library filled every available space around her. She gasped for air, holding her throat, her eyes shut tight to protect them from the light. When it subsided, she opened them up again.

The beach, sand, and evil twin were gone. The floor was polished, reflecting off the soft twinkles of light from the chandeliers overhead. Thick white columns lined the wall of the rotunda, faded paintings of the ocean the only thing staring back at her.

"Now, this is much better." She rose to her feet, the pain from almost being strangled a distant memory already.

"Guillermo! Guillermo, no!"

Luis's voice boomed from the hallway on the far side of the room, and she ran toward his screams. *Macario, please don't let there be something else trying to kill me over there.*

Escaping death twice in one day was more than enough.

CHAPTER 32

LUIS

Wind and rain whipped all about Luis as he struggled across the crowded deck. The boat rocked under his feet, his arm tired from blocking blows from the pirates that swarmed the ship. He didn't have time to figure out how he even ended up there.

One minute he was running after Seraphina through a beam of light. The next, he ended up in the middle of a storm on a ship.

On a ship with his dead brother fighting for his life.

Maybe this library meant to send him back in time, just as the fall off the cliff sent him into that cursed jungle. There wasn't time to figure it all out. He just had to get to Guillermo.

His brother stood at the port side, locking swords with a tall and broad-shouldered pirate. His brother was an excellent swordsman, but the pirate proved better, striking his brother in the arm and leg. A pirate came right at Luis, and he wasted no time taking his sword and plunging it into the pirate's heart.

He pulled it out as the ship took a hard right, knocking him off his feet. His body slid across the deck, and he pounded the boards in frustration before getting back to his feet.

Where was his brother?

His eyes searched the deck. Just more bloody pirates, including two weather-worn ones coming straight for him. He cut down the first. Ran through the second.

He fought his way to where he last saw his brother. Rainwater drenched his clothes. His legs ached as he fought to maintain his balance on the sinking ship.

"You won't get away with this!"

Guillermo's voice rose above the crashing waves and screaming pirates. The crowd of bloodthirsty pirates thinned, giving Luis a clear path to the mainmast. His brother's back was up against it, a sword at his throat.

The pirate holding it was more slender than the ones he had been fighting, his tricorn hat hiding his face.

"Get your hands off him!" Luis roared, charging right at them.

This was his chance. His chance to save his brother.

Then he wouldn't have that hole in his heart. He wouldn't be alone.

Luis grabbed the pirate by the shoulder, spun him around, and plunged his sword into the man's gut. A burst of wind blew the pirate's hat away. Wavy brown hair tumbled down to the shoulders.

This was no man.

"Luis." Seraphina's beautiful brown eyes stared back at him, blood dripping down the side of her mouth.

"What are you doing here?"

He could barely speak, his hand still clutched around the handle of his sword. He pulled it out, tossing it to the ground and catching her as her legs gave way.

"Luis!" his brother yelled. "What are you doing? Let that pirate die!"

Luis shook his head, his lip quivering as he watched her gaze turn glassy. He stroked her hair, the way he'd wanted to since he first laid eyes on her. Soft and full of love. He didn't bother to wipe the tear falling from his eyes.

"She's not a pirate, brother," Luis said.

But what was she? A sister of the Order? The one Macario chose to carry out his will? By Macario's grace, he wanted to find out. Learn everything about her before and after he told her how he felt about her.

How special he thought she was. How beautiful she was.

And I will never know. And it's all my fault.

Her body went limp, her eyes staring into nothingness as they fell to the floor. He cradled her body, her blood all over him.

"You are pathetic!" Guillermo spat, standing over him. "Since when do you consort with the enemy?"

"It's not that simple," Luis said, closing her eyes, his heart crumbling in his chest.

"It is, brother! She's a pirate, the scourge of our realm. It is our duty to dispose of filth like her."

Luis shook his head again. "She is different."

Guillermo scoffed, something his brother had never done before. Luis looked up at him.

"Praise Macario our parents aren't alive to see you like this."

Luis laid Seraphina down on the deck. He rose to his feet, taking a few deep breaths to suppress the sobs gurgling in his throat.

"There is so much you don't know, brother," Luis started. "Everything is not what you think it is."

Guillermo took a step toward him, glaring at him in a way that made his skin crawl.

"Everything is quite clear. My baby brother is a traitor."

"I am no traitor!"

His brother shoved Luis. The man he loved, admired, and grieved for months did something he would never do.

"Things have changed!" Luis shoved him back.

"How?"

"Your letters about the serpent and magic—it's all true! Let me show you!"

The cursed jungle, the magical temple ruins, the library.

The Library. I mean, that's where we are—right?

He looked around. All the pirates he was fighting a moment ago were gone. The wind stilled. The rain stopped. He turned to his brother, his eyes narrowed.

"What is going on? Where am I?"

Guillermo's arm shot out and grabbed his neck with an unnatural strength. Luis clawed at him, but the grip was strong. The pupils of his brother's eyes turned the color of tar, flooding the whites of his eyes.

The devious creature tossed Luis across the deck of the empty ship. He landed hard on a stack of barrels, his back screaming in pain. He bit his lip to keep from crying out, staggering to his feet.

"Welcome to your reckoning, brother!" the man exclaimed, thunder rolling through the air. Luis sucked in a breath and stood straight.

"You've betrayed everything you swore you protect! The Order, the god we serve, all because you fell for the guiles of a pirate!"

Had he been there days ago, he would have agreed with this evil impersonator. But now, he'd seen the magic of Macario himself. Survived the evils that plagued their path to the Secret Library. The Library he was chosen to find.

"You were supposed to avenge me! Not consort with the enemy. Where is your loyalty, brother?"

Luis knew who this person was marching at him. A manifestation of what filled the void his brother's death left in his heart.

Hate.

Anger.

Ugly revenge.

If he didn't get rid of it all, it would grow into a destructive monster. A monster that would kill everything beautiful around him. *Remember how you felt when you rammed that sword through Seraphina.*

Luis charged at him, using everything he had in him to push the apparition to the ground. He straddled him, his right fist plowing into his nose, his left fist into his jaw, the bones cracking under his knuckles.

Was that relief he felt? Or some twisted joy running through him as his hands pummeled the evil creature's face. Instead of crying out in pain or begging him to stop, it just laughed.

Luis froze, his fist in the air.

"How does it feel, Captain Fozo?" it said through bloodied teeth. "To feel that anger. To lean into that hatred?"

The horrid look on Seraphina's face as he plunged the sword into her flashed in his mind. A flash of anger could cause a lifetime of pain.

I am not equipped to handle my demons. But I know who is.

Luis jumped to his feet, grabbing the man by his shirt. "I felt it. Everything that I tried to suppress since my brother died."

The demon smiled as Luis slipped towards the banister.

"It was so hard to keep it all in," Luis murmured.

"The easiest way is to end it," the creature said. "End it all. Give up this foolish quest."

The back of the banister hit Luis's back. "You're right. It's time to end all of this."

Macario, give me strength.

Luis yanked the creature off his feet and hauled him over the side. He leaned over to watch that imposter hit the pitch-black water.

"Let Macario deal with you."

An orb of light rose out of the water, whiting out everything around him. When it receded, a lone figure stood in front of him. He took a few steps back, his vision still blurred by that sudden burst of light.

"Luis, it's me." Seraphina's voice bounced off the walls of the empty room. His vision cleared, and she stood just a few feet in front of him. She looked just like she did when they arrived at this hopeless place. The same messy braid over her shoulder. Same dirty shirt and pants. Same beautiful brown eyes. He rushed to her.

"Were you hallucinating, too?"

That was no hallucination. That felt too real. Without thinking, he grabbed her hands, searching her eyes for any indication that this was another cursed nightmare.

"I thought I—I thought you were—"

He wouldn't dare finish that sentence. Seraphina smiled.

"I'm okay and so are you. None of it was real." Her eyes scanned the room. "And so far, it's just us in here."

Luis looked down at her hands in his, and warmth flushed his face. He took his time letting go, clearing his throat before speaking.

"There's no question that this place is cursed."

"Have you seen Mari?" Seraphina frowned.

"No." Just a wretched interpretation of his own failings. "One minute we were following you through the lighted door, and the next I ended up here."

Seraphina spun around, facing the hallway at the far end of the room. "If she's going through anything like I went through, she's going to need our help, whether she likes it or not."

CHAPTER 33

MARI

This is one bloody sick joke.

Mari stood smack-dab in the middle of a room she swore she would never return to.

Blood-red and vile purple rugs lined in gold fringe covered every inch of the floor. The lighted candles from the large chandelier flickered overhead. The shiny urns scattered all about the room reflected its light. The walls had those puke-green velvet panels embroidered with gold trim that scratched one's face up real good when slammed up against it.

Mari touched her face at the memory. There was nothing but darkness outside the crisscrossed window panes of the floor-to-ceiling windows on the far side of the room.

A golden tray with an elaborate teapot, a plate of sweet cookies, and a chipped teacup sat on a knee-high table. The gold and green floor pillows looked freshly fluffed, waiting to be laid on.

Her eyes found the dressing screen a foot away from the evening snack tray. A glittery orange cat was sewn into the black fabric, the cursed animal's long body stretched between the three panels.

I need to get out of here.

But her feet didn't move, glued to that stupid spot like nothing she went through in the last few years had ever happened.

"My flaming rose."

Madame Mirielle's voice almost purred like she wasn't the ferocious jungle cat of a woman the brothel girls feared. And now, after all this bloody time, it made Mari's hair stand on end. She found it hard to breathe, fighting for words.

"That's not my name," Mari squeaked, wanting to kick herself. She would have if her feet weren't glued to the damned floor.

"Yes, it is," Madame said, not missing a breath. "It's what you always are, no matter what you call yourself these days."

She sauntered out from behind the screen, the sleeveless black robe a mere decoration. Every inch of her caramel skin could be seen through it—her melon-sized breasts, wide hour-glass hips, and even her shaved lady parts. Her silvery-white hair was a mountain of curls around her plump face, falling well past her shoulders. Her emerald green eyes inspected every inch of Mari from the far side of that room, twisting her lips in disapproval.

"You look like shit," she said, strutting to the pillows. "At least you didn't get fat."

Again, the words just wouldn't come out of Mari's mouth.

This can't be happening. She couldn't be here.

Madame took her time lowering herself to those pillows, the table perfectly positioned over her breasts.

"Strip down and let's get a look at you."

"Hell no," Mari blurted out, proud she sounded like herself.

Madame cackled, snapping her fingers. Three men appeared out of nowhere, rushing Mari before she could even think about reaching for her daggers. Two grabbed each arm, the third coming up from behind and shoving her to the ground. The powerful scent of incense in the rug made Mari dry heave. One man pinned down each arm.

Then she heard the fabric rip. Her pants. Her shirt. The chilly air hit her bare skin, and her body shook. Tears streamed down her face. Tears she hadn't shed since Jules died.

"Leave her undergarments on," the madame said, waving her hand.

The men pulled her up to her feet and shoved her forward.

"I will kill you!" Mari said through sobs.

"You tried that before, don't you remember?" Madame sat up, not bothering to close the robe. "Stupid girl, you can't kill me." She tossed her mess of hair over her shoulder. "I made you."

"You tried to destroy me!" Mari's tears continued to flow, her body trembling with rage.

That brothel wench laughed. "No, sweetheart, I made you tough. I gave you grit. Purpose. You were nothing but a backwoods girl when you came to me."

"You stole me from my family! I was just a child!"

"Darling, you had potential. Potential to make me a lot of money, and that's what makes the world go round." Madame Mirielle poured herself a cup of tea. "I mean, you went from being a prostitute to a pirate. There isn't much difference, you know."

"You don't know anything about being a pirate."

"Oh, my little flaming rose. Just when I thought I had nothing left to teach you." Madame took a sip from the cup, setting it down before continuing. "Men screwed you to make money. Now you screw men over to make money, steal treasure or whatever the hell you pirates do. Either way, you do anything to make a coin."

Don't believe her, Mari. Don't let that wench get in your head again. It was not the same thing. Her pirate crew was her family.

And they stole as a family. Lied. Cheated. Broke the law.

"You know what I'm saying is the truth," Madame said, inspecting the cookies on her dish before picking one. "That's why you can't kill me. I will always live here." She pointed to her head.

Every time she stepped into a tavern, smelled incense, or changed clothes, her mind always went back to the Enchanted Cape. She should've been over it. Told herself as much. And yet she wasn't. How could she shake nine years of her life?

"Alas, you still disappoint me," Madame said, breaking Mari's thoughts. "You couldn't even do the pirate thing right."

Mari's eyes found the floor.

"Lost your crew and got yourself arrested." Madame dipped her cookie in her tea before taking a bite.

Mari's head shot up. "I'm going to get them back."

The madame scoffed. "You won't. But that's okay. Take this loss as a lesson." Her emerald eyes locked with Mari's.

"You are no pirate."

"And I am no tramp."

The madame smiled. "Keep telling yourself that, dear. Besides, you're letting all that beauty go to waste." The brothel master gave a slight nod, and those buffoons let her go.

Mari spun around and ran to what was left of her clothes. She knelt down on one knee, picking up the torn shirt. Those blasted tears welled up in her eyes again, and Mari bit her lip to keep it still.

"You were such a favorite," the madame crooned. "Especially in those silk robes I got for you. I mean, wearing those rags, you'll never be taken seriously by any man."

Baz's face flashed in her mind, his confident smirk the day he handed over his father's ship to her.

"The salty life is the only one that you ever wanted," he had said. "And you're too damn good to be a navigator for the rest of your life."

Then Amrit. No matter how much she barked at him, he always stood at her side.

We're going to need Adlam the navigator tonight.

She had to save all of them, and finding the Library was supposed to help.

The blasted library Seraphina raved about.

I followed her inside. I'm inside this cursed place, not the Enchanted Cape. None of this is bloody real!

"Did you hear a word I said?" The madame scowled.

Mari dropped her clothes, rising to her feet. "No."

She spun around and charged, knocking that stupid table over, the tea spilling over those blasted rugs.

"I'm not hearing anything you have to say, because you aren't real!"

Madame laughed. "Oh really?"

"Fire-breathing serpents, magic, ghosts, prophecies about the end of the world—all of that is real."

Mari grabbed the madame's throat; the woman's eyes turned black.

"You and this blasted place are not." She lifted the woman off the pillows, her face not flinching. "You may be a part of what made me. But you won't ruin what I'm gonna be. I'm done being scared of you!"

With a strength she couldn't even explain, she threw her straight across the room, her body crashing through the window. A bright light burst through the broken glass, and Mari shielded her eyes until it receded.

The brothel was gone. Mari looked down to make sure she wasn't still naked. *Thank the stars!*

It didn't take long to figure out what went on in the vast room where she found herself.

Rows of dusty pews stood on either side of her. Stone alcoves lined the walls, statues of men and women in each one. A trio of candle chandeliers hung at least two stories overhead, casting weird shadows on the domed ceilings.

Mari started up the aisle, the sound of her boots slapping against the polished floor. They could fit an entire person on that stone altar, its surface bare except for one unlit candle. Behind it was a domed alcove that stretched all the way to the ceiling.

Judging from the size of the enormous statue placed inside of it, it had to be of Macario. His robes folded around his outstretched arms, cascading down and covering his feet. A stone sash circled his waist, and he had some kind of crown on his head. In his right hand was a very accurate replica of the jeweled scepter that started all of this magic business in the first place.

Just couldn't come back to life and save the world yourself.

She was almost to the foot of the grand religious stage when the sound of footsteps stopped her in her tracks. Drawing a dagger in each hand, she spun around, eyes trained on the open door at the end of the aisle.

Seraphina came bursting in, almost slipping on the polished floor. Fozo came up right behind her, scanning the room before his eyes fell on her.

"Mari! Is that you?" Seraphina called out.

"Who else would it be?" Mari rolled her eyes as she put her daggers back in her waistband.

Seraphina rushed up to her, a ridiculous smile on her face. "I'm so glad I found you! Were you hallucinating, too?"

Not sure what the hell that was. "Something like that."

"Someone really doesn't want us to be here," Fozo commented, strolling up to them.

"As long as that someone doesn't show his face, we'll be fine," Mari said.

Seraphina's eyes caught the statues along the left wall.

"A very evil someone."

Mari didn't want to acknowledge the shivers going down her spine, but they were hard to ignore.

"Just spit it out. What's going on here?"

Seraphina's eyes met hers. "The only one with magic strong enough to curse this place is Bedros."

CHAPTER 34

SERAPHINA

Just saying the evil god's name sent goosebumps down Seraphina's arms. Luis stepped into her line of sight.

"You mean the god of Life and Death?" Luis rubbed his brow. "That doesn't make any sense."

"Out of all the things we've gone through since we got here, that's the part that doesn't make sense to you?" Mari threw up her hands. "One minute, I'm standing outside a thorny building, and the next I'm—"

Mari swallowed hard, looking away without finishing her thought.

"I found myself on a beach with someone who was supposed to be Samara," Seraphina offered. "She said the most awful things, suggesting I end my life." She choked on that painful memory. Her mind knew it wasn't real. but that ghost's words still left a nasty mark on her soul.

"Mine was with my brother on his ship," Luis said, looking down on the floor. "He more or less told me to do the same thing."

Mari spun around, hugging her arms, and looked up at the altar. "I was back in the brothel."

Seraphina laid a reassuring hand on Mari's shoulder, and the pirate captain didn't shrink away. Seraphina gave it a gentle squeeze before stepping back.

"During the War of the Gods, Bedros was notorious for exposing people's worst fears," Seraphina said. "Part of his magic was looking into the souls of men. The deepest and darkest parts that we wouldn't dare share."

"Was that what the ghost women back at that temple were worried about?"

Luis straightened. "Why they were afraid of coming to the library?"

"It could be. Macario was the god he hated the most."

All of those lessons and classes at the seminary were flooding back to her. Macario discovered Bedros's betrayal and alerted his brethren to his indiscretions. This library seemed to be a very important place. Why not curse it for all of eternity?

"So, how are we supposed to fight some pissed-off immortal god?" Mari spun around to face them.

Seraphina turned back to the statues. Those whispers again. Soft, passing by her ears like a breeze. Seraphina started down the row of pews, the wood benches covered in layers of dust and cobwebs.

The whispers grew louder, going silent when she stood in front of the first statue. She recognized who it was right away. The man stood tall and proud, with short-cropped hair and a neatly trimmed beard. His robes hugged his slender body, and he clutched a book to his chest. There was no mistaking the griffin engraved on the cover.

Hammadi. God of Wisdom and patron protector of the Griffin Vales.

The realm where Samara went to find the Spell Keeper. The second piece of the prophecy puzzle her sister needed to help save the world. Seraphina wiped away the dust to read the inscription under him.

The Book.

She moved onto the next statue. This man had a long beard and a full head of hair.

A fur-lined cloak covered his burly body. A crown set with three jewels rested on his forehead, his eyes closed in thought. Inscribed on the bottom of his pedestal were the words *The Crown.*

The Crown of Time. Zaltaire, the one who foretold the prophecy and had the remaining gods hide away their magic in sacred items.

Like the Scepter.

Maybe Hammadi's magic was in the book. And Zaltaire's in his crown.

"You'll want to come see this!" Luis called out.

Seraphina turned to find him and Mari on the altar, leaning on the wide stone table. She hurried by the statue of Redal, the fur of a mountain cat draped over his shoulders. She joined the two captains, ready to tell them all that she discovered, but stopped short at the sight of the altar. Etched into that table were sentences in their language.

"It looks like a prayer," Luis commented.

"So your priests won't forget the words during service?" Mari chimed in. Seraphina shot her a glance before returning to it.

Prayer was a superpower. Mother Madeira taught her that, and Samara more than proved it with how she wielded the scepter. Maybe this one would grant them a little magic.

Praises to Macario, my light in the darkness, maker of land and sea. I ask for your light and your aid in this time of darkness. Guide my hand so I might guide others in your name. I seek this of you as your devout follower, Sister of the Sacred Order, and protector of your word. I pray I am worthy to be your chosen servant.

The altar glowed. Seraphina grabbed both Luis and Mari, just in case that light took them into another nightmare. But as quickly as the light came, it went, the loud clank behind them making her jump out of her skin.

They all whirled around, the majestic statue of Macario already in mid-motion. It spun outward like a door, shuddering to a stop once the dark hallway behind it came into view.

"I've had enough of dark hallways," Mari commented.

"Well, it was a prayer that opened it," Seraphina said, swallowing down the lump of fear in her throat. "Can't be that bad."

She let go of her companions' arms and shuffled to the passageway.

Praise to Macario. My light in all of this very scary darkness.

The dim light at the end of that narrow hallway shone on the thick layer of cobwebs on the wall. Mari's grumpy steps were right behind her, giving her the extra confidence she needed to press on. After fifteen minutes of sweeping cobwebs, she stepped out on the other side into a room just as vast as the temple.

But that was the only thing it had in common.

Out of the thirty bookcases in that room, only two were still standing. She took care not to step on any of the books, parchment, and bottles of ink strewn about.

"What in the blazes happened here?" Mari kicked one of the overturned desks.

Luis drew his sword, making his way down the center of the room. Seraphina put her hands on her hips.

Where there are books, there are answers.

She started with the stack of books in the far corner, trying to shake off the eeriness of the scene. After picking up the fourth book with nothing but blank pages, she sighed more than she spoke.

She was about to stand up and stretch her cramping legs when a yellow book caught her eye. Its faded cloth cover stood out among the other navy-blue tomes. It also had a title.

Etched in black letters were the words "The Vault". She knelt down and cracked it open, skimming its frayed pages.

Zaltaire's prophecy is locked away in this magical chamber, where only the chosen sister may enter.

Her mark is a mirror of that borne by the one chosen to wield the scepter.

Look for where the land and sea meet, and the vault will be revealed.

Seraphina swallowed, fear and excitement crawling up her back. They were close. Oh, so very close.

The stack of books fell over, revealing a golden arrowhead. She set the book down and cleared away all the parchment and books. A shiny, gold-colored bow.

A leather quiver full of golden-tipped arrows.

How beautiful.

"Wonder what this means?" Mari's voice cut through her thoughts, and Seraphina rose to look in her direction. The pirate captain pointed to the ink-stained wall behind her, words scrawled there in white chalk.

Protect the Vault.

"What is the vault?" Luis edged near them. "And protect it from what?"

"Well, we've already faced down giant snakes, man-eating plants, and an angry patch of rocks," Mari said, counting each of those dangerous encounters on her fingers. "Your guess is as good as mine."

An ear-piercing screech ripped through the air, and all of them put their hands to their ears.

"Spoke too bloody soon," Mari said, her eyes scanning the room for the sound.

Seraphina grabbed the bow and quiver, joining Luis and Mari, who huddled close by the room entrance.

"Well, that's fancy." Mari glanced at Seraphina's new weapon. "Hope you know how to use it."

"You and I both," Seraphina said, slinging the quiver over her shoulder.

Praises to Macario, my light in the darkness, maker of land and sea. I ask for your light and your aid in this time of darkness.

The bow grew warm, feeling less awkward in her hand. She hoped by some miracle she would become an expert archer.

A black creature crept along the ceiling, claws digging into the stone.

It looked like they would need all the miracles Macario could muster.

CHAPTER 35

LUIS

Just how many of my brother's stories are going to come true today?

Large black, bat-like wings extended out on each side of the slender creature's body. Its claws dug into the ceiling stone as it approached. Stringy gray hair hung from its head, its hollow yellow eyes trained on Luis and his companions.

It stopped in the center of the room, a few yards too close to them. It opened its mouth, and a screech roared out of the blackness inside its mouth.

"Bloody harpies," Mari hissed, twirling the daggers in her hand.

"It's only one," Seraphina said. "I'm sure we can take it."

Two more of those cursed creatures crawled into the room, hanging from the ceiling, flanking the first on either side.

"You were saying?" Luis said, leaning into his defensive stance. The only way to get any sort of cover was to run back into the main temple. A large clanking sound boomed behind them.

"The passageway!" Seraphina cried. Luis looked over his shoulder, the light streaming in from the temple snuffed out as the statue swung back into place.

"This day just gets better and better," Mari said.

"When they fly, we need to take cover," Luis said, watching one creature release its hold on the ceiling. Its wings caught the air and it hovered, its bone-like legs dangling under it. Light gleamed over both sets of claws.

"Cover where?" Seraphina said.

"Under a book? Where else?" Mari snorted.

He chose to ignore her annoying sarcasm for now. There were more pressing matters.

"The bookcases," he said. "It's the only way we can make it through that doorway on the other side. On my mark, we split up."

Out of the corner of his eye, he saw Seraphina nod. Mari huffed in agreement. The other two harpies also dislodged from the ceiling, baring their sharp teeth.

Now or never.

"Go!" Luis bolted right, pushing Seraphina against the bookcase leaning against the wall. The harpies shrieked and swooped after them. One flew in between him and Seraphina, its claws snapping after him.

He swung his sword, the wretched creature flying out of its way. It dove at him and he backed away, tripping over a book and landing on his back. The harpy smiled, diving in for a piece of his flesh. It chomped down on his blade instead as he brought his sword up just in time.

Despite looking frail, it was strong; his arms shook under the weight of the monster trying to eat him. A dagger struck it in the side of its head, and Luis caught a glimpse of the familiar handle.

Huh. Mari didn't want him to die. *That's new.*

The harpy screamed and flew up, its hand grasping at the dagger lodged in its skull. Luis shot to his feet and ran after Seraphina, who'd already taken cover under the bookcase. A second harpy was already clawing at the wood, screeching in frustration that it couldn't get to her. It saw Luis and charged at him.

He didn't miss this time, his blade swiping at its wing. It drew back. This was his chance to slay it. Luis climbed onto the bookcase, swinging his sword, but that thing was nimble, dodging every blow. It took to the ceiling again, joining the one with the dagger in its head. It pulled out the weapon and tossed it to the ground.

It wasn't dead. It was just angry.

Luis jumped down from the bookcase. "Run for the door! Now!"

Mari cursed, throwing her last dagger at the third creature that hovered over her hiding place behind an overturned desk. It struck the creature in the chest. The weapon stunned it a little, before the harpy pulled it out and threw the dagger on the ground.

Luis ducked under the bookcase, Seraphina already gone. The harpy came back, hovering over his only opening to the other side. He aimed for its legs, his sword hitting raw bone. Its talons sliced the forearm of his sword hand, forcing him to retreat behind the bookcase.

The cut wasn't deep, but it hurt like hell. He would give himself a minute to recover, then keep the creatures busy so Seraphina and Mari could get out.

"Leave them alone, you ugly creatures!" Seraphina's voice boomed over the flapping and screeching.

No! What is she doing?

The creature flew away, and he ducked out from behind the bookcase. All three harpies flew to the center of the room, facing the only way out. Luis climbed on top of the fallen bookcase, ready to call their attention, until he saw what they were snarling at.

Seraphina stood, tall and determined, in the black, stained archway. The bow in her hand glowed, a golden arrow nocked and pointed at the monsters. She pulled back the arrow and let it fly.

It soared straight into the heart of the harpy in the middle of the pack. It looked down at the arrow in horror before it shuddered and turned into dust. She'd already nocked another arrow, aiming for the second harpy before letting it soar.

But she didn't see the third one heading straight for her. Luis leaped off the bookcase, running to the center of the room to get a clear path to her. Her arrow struck true, turning the second harpy to ash, but the other one was already on her.

Reaching out with its talons, it knocked her to the ground. Her glowing bow was the only thing standing between the creature's teeth and Seraphina's face. He jumped on the monster's back, instantly regretting the decision as it took off to the sky. The smell of rotting flesh filled his nose as he hung on to its wretched neck.

"Kill it!" he called out.

"Even if it means killing you?" Mari remarked.

I swear, if I wasn't a gentleman!

An arrow flew, clipping its wing, sending it sailing to the ground. Luis put all his weight against it, forcing it to fall face-first on the ground. Though the intent was to have the creature break his fall, falling on bone seemed to hurt just as bad. He rolled off, Mari right there with a hand outstretched.

"Don't dawdle, Fozo!" she said, and he grabbed her hand.

He pulled himself to his feet in time to see Seraphina scramble back up, nocked an arrow, and sent it straight into the beast's head.

Luis let out a sigh as it turned to ash. For a few moments, no one dared to utter a sound.

He and Mari stared at the former seminary sister, who lowered her glowing weapon. The light dimmed until it was nothing more than a regular bow. She stared, wide-eyed, at the piles of dust about the room, then back at Luis and Mari.

"So, are there any other skills you picked up since we've been in this study?" Mari said, breaking the awkward silence.

Seraphina gave them a weak smile. "Not that I know of."

Luis took care to walk around the dust piles to meet her in the doorway. Mari scoured the room, picking up her fallen daggers before returning to them.

"How did you do that?" He didn't bother to downplay the astonishment in his voice.

She looked down at the bow and then at him, scrunching her eyebrows. "I don't know. I just prayed and fired."

He ran his fingers through his hair. "So, you mean you've never shot a bow before?"

Seraphina shook her head. Mari stood there with the same look of indifference.

"When you hang around her and her sister long enough, you just stop trying to break your brain to figure it all out." She turned to Seraphina. "Let's find this vault."

"Yes." Seraphina adjusted the quiver over her shoulder. "I'm sure the answers we're looking for are there."

Answers. That was something Luis needed before his head exploded.

Mari gestured to the door. "Since you're the one with the magic bow and arrow, you go first."

CHAPTER 36

MARI

Mari's heart slowed down as they walked the long stone hallway away from that study. No longer did she hear harpy screams in her ears. Not even the sea serpent's roar gave her such shivers.

Jules told stories about those monsters way back in the days before Samara and her scepter were ever a thought. The late boatswain claimed his father battled one back in the Griffin Vales. She thought it was bullshit, but it didn't make his story any less entertaining for the crew.

The only part of that fable that piqued her interest was how harpies came to be.

"Those winged beasts used to be women," he had said, the lantern swinging from the rigging casting light and shadow on his face. "That's the problem with bein' bitter. It's the right amount of fodder for cursed magic to take hold and transform you into the ugly hauntin' of your soul."

That part gave her pause back then. It had only been a few months since she escaped the Enchanted Cape. She still had nightmares about that hell hole, waking up grumpier than she did the day before.

No matter how much she wanted to laugh at Jules's jokes or enjoy those tavern songs whenever they docked on shore, she couldn't shake those dreams. Shake that hate for everything that happened to her. She could've easily become a harpy, had magic been real, screaming and clawing at anything that moved.

Now she'd faced two nightmares in one damn day, and she'd be a liar if she denied she wasn't on edge. Judging by how Luis held his sword at the ready, his eyes darting all around, she wasn't the only one. And Seraphina with her magic bow? She'd been praying under her breath the entire time.

Hope she throws in a couple of those for me.

The hallway opened up into a massive cavern, almost double the size of the one that crumbled down in that mountain with the rickety bridge. Stone extended several stories up. The wall lanterns were already lit, unable to cast their light more than a few feet up. While the space got bigger, the floor did not. It turned into a narrow walkway that went in between two things that just couldn't be safe.

A pit of grainy white sand on the left.

A still pool of murky water on the right.

"This would've been an ideal place for my sister to train with her scepter," Seraphina commented, tightening her grip on the bow.

"Crab Cove was a much better location," Mari countered. What she wouldn't give to be back on that island. *Shouldn't have been in such a rush to leave.*

"The quicker we can get across, the quicker we can find this vault," Luis said, scanning the room.

"And get out of here." Mari looked over at him. "I'll take the lead."

He nodded. "I'll take the flank."

Mari looked to Seraphina. "Get an arrow ready."

She nodded, and Mari not moving forward until the nun had an arrow nocked in that magical bow of hers.

Giving her daggers a twirl for good luck, Mari started for the bridge. She glanced between the sand and water, ready to throw her blade at the slightest movement.

Not a grain moved.

Not a ripple of water.

A quick glance over her shoulder—her companions were at the ready.

So far, so good.

They were halfway across when Seraphina's voice cut through the silence. "Luis! Luis, what's wrong?"

Mari spun around. Seraphina had paused beside the Order captain, who stood like a statue, looking at the water.

"What do you see, Fozo?" Mari strode over to them, her eyes on the water. She hated that she couldn't see to the bottom, but the water was still. She didn't see a fang or a scale anywhere.

But Fozo didn't say a word, standing there like an idiot with his eyes on the water.

"What is happening to him, Mari?" Seraphina looked Luis up and down. "It's like he can't hear us."

Mari's mind went back to Jules and the first day she came aboard the *Pursuer*.

"Be glad you're a woman," he had said.

"On a boat full of men?" Mari snapped, hiding her hair under her hat. "That's the worst thing to be."

Jules had furiously shaken his head. "No, lass. If those sea sirens ever show themselves and start singing, you'll be the only one to save us all."

Son of a sea monkey!

"Seraphina, get that arrow aimed at the water." Mari pointed at the murky pool. "You see so much as a ripple, you shoot it."

For once, the ex-seminary sister didn't ask questions and did what she was told. Mari gritted her teeth, using her dagger to tear away two slivers of fabric from her long sleeves. She balled them up and stuck one in each of Fozo's ears. It took a split second before his eyes blinked, and he turned to her, his face annoyed.

"What are you doing?" He raised his hands to snatch the makeshift earplugs out of his ears. Mari slapped his hands away.

"There's a siren down there," she whispered. "Had you standing there like an idiot for five minutes."

His eyes widened, looking back at the water.

That was when they saw it. A black outline of a wide tail. Mari tugged Fozo's arm and pushed Seraphina. Water splashed behind them, but Mari kept running.

"Luis!" Seraphina screamed, and Mari skidded to a stop.

By the time she spun around, Luis was halfway in the water.

"It's a woman! No! A fish! Praise Macario, I don't know what that was, but it pulled him in!" Seraphina fumbled around with another arrow as Luis slipped beneath the surface.

How many times am I going to have to save this idiot?

Mari sucked in a deep breath and dove into the water. The water was cold, the murkiness making it hard to see. But she glimpsed Luis's white shirt a yard below.

Ignoring the aches in her arms and legs from all that running and ducking earlier, she swam downward. It seemed like forever until she got to him. When she saw the siren cradling his body in her wiry arms, she came to a full stop.

The creature didn't even notice Mari, her misshapen hands caressing Fozo's frozen face. Her hair was a strange golden color, floating all about her, conveniently covering her bare chest. Her scaly green tail sauntered back and forth under her.

You're going to be mighty ticked off when I relieve you of your new toy.

Mari took careful strokes around her, approaching her from behind. It was bloody hard to see the base of her skull with all that hair. But Mari's chest was burning from the lack of air. No time to waste.

She darted after it, and the blasted siren whirled around. Her eyes glowed as green as the water around them, but there was no time to gawk at her. Mari sank her dagger into the siren's eye.

The creature's mouth widened in a silent scream, and she released the Order captain. Mari pulled out her dagger and stabbed the siren again in the throat, green goo spurting out. Pushing the body out of the way, she grabbed Fozo before he sank into the deep.

She hooked her arm around his neck and swam upward. Her head broke the surface, and she sucked in the fresh air. Seraphina abandoned her bow on the walkway and ran to them, taking Fozo under the arms to lift him out. He was still unconscious. Mari braced to lift herself out when a hand clamped around her wrist and yanked her down into the water.

The blonde one has friends.

This one had fiery red hair and a snarky smile. *She'll die all the same.* Mari twisted and swiped the siren's hand with her dagger. Her face twisted in pain, her other arm shooting up and grabbing Mari's wrist. Mari bit down on the bony wrist.

Dirty, bitter water filled her mouth, but the siren let go. She opened her mouth in a silent scream, showing off her stark white fangs.

Like that's supposed to scare me.

It just pissed her off.

The beast charged at her, and Mari dodged out of the way. The siren's stringy hair grazed Mari's face, and she grabbed a fistful, wrapped it around her wrist, and yanked. The siren's arms flailed, leaving her neck exposed.

Using her free hand, Mari stabbed it in the throat just long enough to see the beast convulse. She snatched it out and pushed the siren away. With all the energy she could muster Mari swam to the top, gasping for air when her head broke the surface.

She lifted her body out of the water before any more could yank her under, hugging that blasted stone, water dripping from her dreads.

Another splash. A third siren slipped above the water, which covered her tail. Her skin was stained green, jet black hair sticking to her human-like face. Narrow nose and chin, head cocked to the side as she eyed them. Then those yellow eyes fell on Fozo, who sat upright. The siren bared her jagged teeth like an animal.

Seraphina's eyes widened, an arrow already nocked in her bow. The siren's arms were outstretched, and Seraphina took aim, the bow glowing. She pulled the bowstring back and let it fly, sinking her arrow into the siren's chest. The creature shuddered before turning to dust, the black ashes sinking into the water.

Mari let out a sigh of relief, rising to her feet at the same time as Fozo.

"I swear I am done saving your ass," Mari said, squeezing the water out of her hair.

The Order captain cracked a smile, wringing out the edges of his shirt. "Thank you."

Mari was about to say something smart about Seraphina's archery skills, but Seraphina just stood there, eyeing the water where the siren had disintegrated. Her face was sad, too sad for someone who'd just killed another beast.

"Are you all right?" Fozo drew closer to her.

"She was a Sacred Sister," Seraphina breathed, turning her glassy gaze to him. "I recognized her as one of the ghosts from the temple in the jungle."

Fozo's brows furrowed, and Mari looked back at the water. What were these god-fearing women up against?

And how will we fare any better?

"Looks like we better find that vault and fast," Mari said. "Don't want to end up like those wretched things."

CHAPTER 37

SERAPHINA

The library wasn't the only cursed thing here.

Seraphina bowed her head again as she walked the curved corridor that led them away from the sirens' chamber. Mari and Luis walked on either side of her, on alert for any other monster that might show itself.

Macario, I ask for love and light for the Sacred Sisters who were damned trying to defend this library. Give them a place in your heavens when this is all over. Give them peace, so they will no longer suffer and be in pain.

She wiped a tear with the back of her hand as the trio came to a slow stop at the end of the hallway. Two thick double doors shut tight, a large S carved on each panel. Luis and Mari moved to each side of the entryway.

"Stand ready," Luis said, and, for once, Seraphina knew what to do.

Praises to Macario, my light in the darkness, maker of land and sea. I ask for your light and your aid in this time of darkness.

She nocked the arrow, the bow glowing as she aimed it at the door. Mari grabbed one of the rusted handles, Luis the other. They took a collective breath and pulled the doors open.

Now this is a library.

Sunlight streamed through three sets of oblong windows set in the intricate archways at the far end of the vast room. Roots and leaves in various shades of green grew along the stone rafters of the domed ceiling.

This room oddly reminded her of the one back in her seminary. The long, wide aisle. Seven-foot-tall bookshelves perfectly spaced on either side of the walkway. A statue of Macario holding out his scepter at the back of the library, right under those windows.

"About time this place looked like an actual library," Mari said, tip-toeing into the room.

Indeed it did, its shelves filled to the brim with books. How many centuries of lost knowledge did these books contain? Things that the Order didn't want them to know.

I could learn about it all!

She lowered her glowing bow, following Mari inside. Luis took one more glance around before joining them.

"Since I don't see any obvious way out, the vault must be somewhere in here."

Sure, but let me at least glance at this book.

A thick blue book caught her eye. Putting the arrow back in the quiver, she reached for it; the book was light for such a thick tome. She cradled it in her arm, slinging the bow over her shoulder to free up her hand. Her fingers grazed the blank cover. It was as if it were caught in a flame, curling and turning to black before disintegrating into dust.

What in the world?

She pulled out another book, then another, each one turning to ash before she could open the cover.

"I'm sure that's not supposed to happen," Mari said, peering over her shoulder.

It shouldn't have been that much of a surprise. *This place is cursed, remember?*

"Let's just hope whatever is in this vault doesn't do the same thing."

Luis was halfway up the aisle, sword at the ready as he peered down each row of bookshelves before moving on to the next.

"So where is it?" Mari peered around the room.

"The book I read back in the study said it was where the land and sea meet," Seraphina replied.

"You mean, it could be back in that siren-infested chamber?"

Seraphina shook her head. "No. It's here."

Seraphina didn't know how, but her gut told her as much. Just as it told her to pick up that bow and recite that prayer. Three dead harpies and a siren later, she needed to trust it more often.

All right, intuition. Lead the way.

She proceeded down the main aisle, each row of shelves darker and creepier than the next. Luis made it as far as the statue, waiting for her there. The gray stone was green with age, only a foot taller than Luis.

"From the way you're furrowing your brows," he said with a slight smile, "it looks like you know where this vault is."

She looked away, finding a random spot on the statue to study instead of his handsome face.

"I hope so," she said.

"You've gotten us this far," he said, moving in closer. "I'm sure you will find it."

She gazed at the wall behind the statue, one long sentence written on it.

Praise be to Macario, god and creator of the land and sea. I pray for light, so I see the path before me. I pray for the sea to wash away the hurt and pain, so I can let in love and belief.

The prayer Samara recited to unlock the power of the Scepter. She followed the words along the wall.

I pray for your mercy, so I can forgive myself. I pray for courage, so I can surrender my pride.

The shadows the bookshelf cast on that part of the wall made it hard to see. But she kept following, finding comfort in the familiar words.

I pray for your blessing, so I can have the strength to wield the scepter and all of its mighty power.

She was on the far side of the room, yards away from Luis, the statue, and a stream of sunlight.

I pray that I am worthy to be Chosen.

There, in the dimly lit corner, was a diamond-shaped stone the size of her palm. The sea was painted on the top half. Waves of sand were painted on the bottom.

This is it. Praise Macario, this is it!

She pressed the diamond, and the floor began to rise. She turned, Luis calling after her, as she held her arms out for balance.

Only the chosen sister may enter.

Her mark is a mirror of that borne by the one chosen to wield the scepter.

They were chosen to find the library together, but this part she had to do alone. Seraphina pulled the bow off her shoulder, grabbing it tight as the stone floor came to a stop.

She wouldn't dare look down. The wall in front of her pulled apart, revealing a golden hallway. She was tempted to pass her hand over the shiny brick walls to see if it was paint or actual gold. But the fear of triggering something else kept her hands at her sides.

It seemed like she walked forever to reach the polished wooden door at the end of the hallway. Seraphina took a breath before reaching for the brass handle. Before she could touch the knob, the door flew open, a blast of wind washing over her. She moved to shield her face, but her limbs wouldn't cooperate. She couldn't even blink her eyes as the windowless room came into focus.

All she could see was the small hearth, a cozy and crackling fire inside. She tried to look around the room, but her eyes wouldn't move, her feet grounded to the floor.

What type of cursed magic is this?

"This is no cursed magic."

The woman's voice shook with age as she walked into Seraphina's line of sight. Long, white robes hung off her frail body, her sandals shuffling along the floor. Stark white curls almost buried her narrow face, her slanted brown eyes trained on Seraphina. The woman took in every inch of her before speaking again.

"You look like you may be her," she said. "But I will be the judge of that."

The woman held up a slim wooden staff before hitting the floor with it, sending another blast of wind at her. Seraphina's muscles tightened, and a tear of pain escaped her eyes. The woman didn't seem to care, her scowl fiercer than Mari's as she shuffled over to her.

She yanked the bow out of Seraphina's hand, sliding the quiver off her shoulder. She dropped them both away in a part of the room Seraphina couldn't see. The lady stood in front of her again. She cut the air with her staff, and Seraphina tumbled to the ground.

She breathed through the wave of pain before it subsided and allowed her to stand.

"I mean you no harm," Seraphina said, holding up her hands in surrender.

"Who are you?" The woman raised a brow.

The mark. Show her the mark.

Seraphina lifted her left sleeve, revealing the circular mark she and her sister shared. The woman shuffled over, grabbing Seraphina's arm with a strength she didn't expect.

"My sister has one on her right shoulder," Seraphina said. "She's the one Macario chose to wield the scepter."

The woman huffed, taking a full five minutes to inspect the birthmark before releasing her arm. "Can't be too careful. Bedros's followers can be tricky."

"I can only imagine," Seraphina said, fixing her sleeve.

"So, what do you want?" The old woman made her way to the small cot by the fireplace.

"I've come to find the book where I can learn more about the prophecy. I have to help my sister."

The old woman chuckled, lowering herself down on the thick mattress with the help of her staff. She rested her wrinkled hands on top of it.

"You silly girl. There is no book." She tapped her forehead. "Everything about how our world ends is right up here."

CHAPTER 38

LUIS

Luis didn't know what button Seraphina pushed or what lever she pulled. One minute she was following words on a wall. The next she was soaring up into the air with the floor underneath her.

Yet there was no time to figure that out. The statue of Macario sank into the floor, and the bookshelves were moving on their own. It was as if they were cogs in a clock, moving to their own inner workings.

He ran to the center aisle, but the bookcases on either end slid together to block his path. The shelves folded back on themselves to create a slick surface. He darted left, but the shelves swooped around, blocking him in.

I can make it out the other side.

He took three steps before the other shelves boxed him in against the back wall by the statue. He ran over to it, searching for a device to stop the room from changing.

"You seem to be in quite a predicament, Captain Luis Armand Fozo."

A cold chill ran down his back, but he spun around anyway. A cloaked figure stood a few feet in front of him.

"I'm tired of the fear-induced hallucinations," he said, though his skin ran cold.

"This is no hallucination."

"Then show yourself."

He swallowed hard, steadying himself to see his brother's face again, but when the figure removed its hood, it revealed a man not much older than himself. His slick black hair was cut close, his beard shaved against his tan skin. His eyes were light brown and very normal.

"Who are you?"

The man held up his hands in surrender. "I mean no harm, Captain. I was sent here to help you."

"Sent by whom?" Luis wouldn't dare lower his sword.

The man smiled. "The one true ruler of this world."

Dark robes. Creepy smile. During this entire journey Macario never once sent anyone to help them. Just glowing books and apparitions.

"I'm not clear who that is."

The man lowered his hands. "You know soon enough. The question is, when that time comes, where will your allegiances lie?" He held out his left hand. "With man?" He held out his right, a ball of black and white light swirling in his palm. "Or magic?"

Bedros.

"You already know a war is coming, Captain," the man continued. "Otherwise you wouldn't be here. Luckily, I was sent just in time to save your life."

"Since when is Bedros in the business of saving lives?" The god had created an army of twisted men and monsters. Magia would've crumbled if it hadn't been for Macario and the others.

The sphere of light jumped off the man's hand onto the floor beside him, growing until it was as tall as he was.

"Bedros is the guardian of life and the afterlife. The keeper of souls and men's deepest desires. He wants nothing more than for man to reach his fullest potential."

"You mean give everyone magic. Didn't work well the first time."

The man still kept his smile and his gaze on Luis. "But this time there is no other powerful enough to stand in his way. Man alone cannot defeat him, so his reign is inevitable."

"What is that inevitability?"

"The restoration of magic. The unification of all realms. That would mean the end of wars and poverty. We would all be one people under one powerful ruler."

A noble intention. "But at what cost?"

The man twisted a finger. The smell of soot and blood filled his nose. He closed his eyes, and the horrible dream he had back on the mainland flashed in his mind. The mounds of dead soldiers on the desolate beach. Gray skies. Despair tugging at his heart. A loud voice booming from the heavens.

"You've all had a glimpse of what's to come if you refuse," the man said. Luis's eyes flew open again.

"You are a good man, Captain Fozo," the man said. "You have strength, conviction, and fierce passion for family."

The sphere opened, revealing the silhouette of a man inside. Narrow black eyes like his mother's. A stark nose like his father's. The same dark hair. He still wore his uniform, sullied and tattered from the battle that claimed his life. He turned and looked straight into Luis's soul.

"We could use a man like you in our new world," the man continued. "And as a reward for joining us, we will grant you your deepest desire."

Luis's heart dropped to his feet.

"We can give you your brother back, Captain," the man hissed.

He lowered his sword, grief and elation churning in his stomach and chest at the same time.

That was his brother. The man who taught him everything he knew. The one responsible for the man he became. Who gave him the grit to rise out of poverty. Who strengthened his faith.

Say your prayers, never betray your values, and always do what's right.

The harpies, the sirens, the frightened looks on the faces of those sisters' ghosts in the temple flooded Luis's mind. The destruction of Tradesman Harbor. A sea serpent that ravaged their islands.

That was not the work of a savior. That was the work of evil.

Yes, he could have his brother back, but at what cost? His life? His values? His heart?

It was as if the soul of Guillermo could hear his thoughts. He gave Luis that same reassuring smile as the day Luis started his first day as an Order officer.

"You were made in Macario's light," his brother had said. "You were meant for this."

Was being an Order captain still the right path? He wasn't sure. What he did know was that being a soldier in the army of the most evil god his world had ever seen was the absolute wrong one.

I love you, brother, and miss you terribly. But we will meet again when Macario decides.

His brother's soul nodded and closed his eyes. Luis raised his sword.

"I'll pass."

The man's smile faded, darkness flooding the whites of his eyes as he snapped his fingers, the sphere disappearing.

"Very well, then. Prepare to die."

In a flash, the man disappeared and the library began to convulse. The windows overhead shattered, and Luis darted out of the way of the falling glass.

"Mari!" he called out, but his voice was lost in the tumbling of rock and stone.

I will not die here.

He lowered to his knees, bowing his head, and swallowing back the shame of not doing this sooner.

Praise to Macario. I ask for your light, your strength, and your love to do your will.

And just as he opened his eyes, the walls began to crumble.

CHAPTER 39

MARI

Mari banged on the last bookcase that boxed her in the middle of that bloody library. *Unbelievable!*

Dust and leaves sprinkled down from the high ceiling, signaling that it was no doubt getting ready to collapse. That's what all secret libraries did, wasn't it? Goosebumps ran down her arms, and she spun around, a dagger in each hand.

Great. More creepy ghosts. Or some other monster.

Whatever it was, it wore a deep red cloak that flowed to the floor, the oversized hood hiding its face. She twirled her dagger, warming up her right wrist. She had the best aim with that hand. In a moment, she would fling her blade into that thing's heart.

It stepped within range, and Mari sent the dagger sailing. The stranger raised a slender white hand, bringing the blade to a halt in midair. Mari's dagger shook before it clanked to the floor.

"You've changed, Flaming Rose," a smooth female voice said. "Or should I say, Captain Adlam?"

She removed her hood, Instead of some creepy apparition, a snarling monster, or a figment of fear, it was a woman. Her skin was as white as the Winter Tide shores. Her dirty blonde hair braided away from her face, just as slick and perfect as the last time Mari saw her.

"Under normal circumstances, I'd buy you a drink, Gyrid," Mari said, pulling her second dagger from her waistband. "Ask you how you survived and all. But none of this is normal."

She chuckled, her ice-blue eyes sparkling. "No, it's not, but the god I serve saw it fit to send me to help you."

Bedros. She didn't have to say it. Just the way she referred to him sent goosebumps down Mari's arms. And judging from that display of magic, her old brothel sister had gotten herself so far down the trouble hole there was no hope to save her.

"You'd be the last one I'd expect to be tangled in this mess," Mari said.

Gyrid's face lit up like a lighthouse.

"He saved me, Mari. I was trekking through that wasteland, ready to throw myself off a cliff into the cold Arctic Sea. I hadn't eaten in days. I was delirious without water. Then one of his faithful warriors appeared and gave me a new lease on life."

"And some magic, from what I can tell."

She nodded. "That's just a small part of it."

"Let's just skip to the part where you're supposed to help me."

Gyrid straightened her shoulders. "You're on the wrong side. It's pointless to fight a war you can't win." She waved a hand, and a ring of light appeared beside her.

"So, trying not to get killed by magical monsters is a bad idea?" Mari raised a brow, her eyes darting between Gyrid and that display of magic growing beside her.

"Change can be rough, but necessary," Gyrid said. "Nothing worth fighting for ever comes easy." Her eyes dimmed a little. "But when our one true ruler ascends his world throne, there will be no more war. No more division, and no more places like the Enchanted Cape."

A beach appeared in that ring of light, a group of men cutting stone and hacking wood. Out of all the men in the line, the one with the stringy black hair and slender arms caught her attention. His brown skin was marred with scars and bruises. *Amrit.*

"Join me, Mari," Gyrid said. "We can save your crew right now and supply you with all the gold you need to set up your ship."

It looked so real. It took everything in her to keep her feet planted to the spot and not run through it like an idiot.

"And what do I have to give up in exchange for this generous gift?" Mari set her hands on her hips.

"You only stand to gain much more than what this quest could ever give you. You'll be a captain. But not of one ship, but a fleet, maintaining order throughout our one realm."

Mari could almost see it. An evil magical fleet.

She would be dressed in the finest captain's outfit, have the most pristine-looking ship, nicer than the *Pursuer* ever was. She would be respected, maybe even feared, as soon as other ships saw her flag flying.

All of that sounded pretty damn good. But then there was the part about destroying towns, killing innocent people, all because they believed differently. They wouldn't be fighting to defend themselves or to survive. They would fight to show off, like their numbers weren't enough.

Just like the Order navy and every other realm navy who thought themselves gods.

I'll be damned if they turn me into an Order rat.

She looked into the portal once more, taking note of the dunes and the shacks in the background. She would need to remember it when she got out of this cursed place and had the chance to free her crew.

"As tempting as that offer is, Gyrid, I'm more than capable of getting back my crew. I have these." Mari held up her dagger.

"You're making a big mistake."

The sphere and the hope in Gyrid's face faded away. Her eyes that were once blue were flooded with blackness, showing the evil lurking behind that fake smile all along.

Mari flung her second dagger, but Gyrid's dark magic stopped it in midair. Before Mari could even think to move, Gyrid flipped it around and launched it back at her. It struck her shoulder, just short of the bone. A wave of pain stole her breath, sending Mari to the floor.

Gyrid cocked her head to the side. "Don't worry, Mari. I won't kill you now. There are worse ways to die."

"Mari!"

Gyrid disappeared, and Fozo showed up, looking over the top of the bookcase behind her.

"I take it you didn't accept her offer to become evil."

"Hell no," Mari said, pulling the dagger out of her shoulder. "I'm evil enough on my own." She winced in pain, blood gushing through her fingers as she held her shoulder.

"If you have any ideas on how to get me out of here, now is a bloody good time!" she yelled over the rumbling of the room.

More dust and stone fell from the ceiling, some of it getting into Mari's mouth, forcing her to cough. Luis lay flat on his belly, shimmying forward and extending his arms a clear two feet over her. She breathed through the burning pain shooting down her injured arm and back as she got to her feet.

Parts of the grassy ceiling were coming apart, large stones landing in the place where Gyrid had stood. Mari grabbed her last dagger off the ground. This place wasn't going to take any of her precious blades.

"Stop dawdling and give me your hands!" the Order captain shouted at her, and she shot him a mean look.

I'm the only one allowed to be grumpy here.

She turned to him, clutching her shoulder, his two dirty hands the only thing that could get her out of this mess.

I'm more than capable of getting back my crew.

She jumped up and grabbed Fozo's hands. He pulled and she screamed.

Screamed about being captured in the first place. For being so hard on herself. For not giving herself enough bloody credit.

She'd escaped one of the most notorious brothels in Magia. Become the best damn navigator on the Magian Sea. She'd found a magical object, battled a sea serpent, survived this cursed jungle, and dammit she'd killed two sirens.

Why was she always doubting herself? Why didn't she follow her gut at the very beginning?

By the time she stopped screaming and cursing, they were both on the ground on the other side of the bookcase. Her hand flew to her shoulder again, a little blood flowing through her fingers. It wasn't enough to justify the searing hot pain encasing her entire arm.

Rocks and stone fell all around them, the library unrecognizable. Dust swirled through the air, making it hard to breathe.

But there was something else.

Sunlight beamed down the cracking aisle, streaming through a giant hole in the back wall. A way out. Luis was staring at it, too.

"We can't— "

"I know."

The wall that Seraphina had disappeared into was still intact. Wherever she was, she was still alive. At least, Mari hoped so. There was only one way to find out. Mounds of ceiling rock piled high around that wall, providing a bloody difficult way to get up there.

"You up for that climb?" he said, jerking his head in that direction.

"I killed two bloody sirens—underwater," Mari said with a smirk.

He nodded. "Fair enough."

CHAPTER 40

SERAPHINA

The small room rumbled again, and Seraphina glanced back at the door.

"What's happening?"

The woman, who had just introduced herself as Valentina, kept the same look of indifference on her wrinkled face.

"Either your companions took Bedros's offer and left you, so his magic is destroying this place. Or, they declined, are probably dead, and the library is still getting destroyed."

She took a breath. "No matter what happened out there, you are safe in here."

"It doesn't matter whether I'm safe!" Seraphina's voice rose higher than she intended. "I have to go out there and help them."

"There's nothing you can do." Valentina waved a hand.

We'll see about that. Seraphina crossed the room to grab her bow and quiver, then headed for the door. Her hand touched the knob when Valentina spoke.

"Once you leave here, you can never return."

Seraphina lowered her hand.

"You have a choice, Seraphina. Leave to save your friends or stay here. Hear everything I know about the time magic roamed our world and the prophecy that may doom it all."

That is not a choice. One could not choose between saving her friends and saving the world. The room rocked again, and she turned around.

"Macario chose them and me to find this place. I won't let them die."

Valentina smiled, looking warm. Endearing even. "You don't have much time, Chosen One. What do you want to know?"

A million questions whirled in her mind. How did magic come to be? What happened to the Sacred Sisters? Why did the Order not want the world to know about them? But all of that wasn't important.

Beating Bedros is the most important.

"How can my sister defeat Bedros?"

Valentina chuckled. "Defeating a god is not that simple. It's not Bedros you have to defeat. It's the man who inherited his magic."

The room shook so hard, Seraphina almost lost her balance.

Stay focused, Seraphina! This is your only chance.

"Tell me more."

"Samara cannot do it alone. She must find the others gifted with magic of the gods, just as she was."

"There are others besides the Spell Keeper?"

Valentina nodded. "The Crown of Time in the Winter Tide. The Feline's Eye in the Godswood. Your sister and the three other wielders of magic must come together before Bedros raises his evil army."

Find three complete magic-wielding strangers. Not difficult at all.

"You know as well as anyone that mastering one's magic is a challenge," Valentina continued. "But trying to take that magic and have its wielders work together is a monumental task. And frankly, my dear, you are running out of time."

Seraphina heard a scream. A scream laced with curse words.

Mari.

Valentina's face grew somber. "The man who has Bedros's dark power has already unleashed his monsters on our realms and is corrupting people with magic as we speak. All of Magia is in danger."

She remembered the monsters from her studies at the seminary. And the armies of men with magic. *Evil people with magic.*

Seraphina shook away the thought. There would be time to be afraid later.

"How much time do we have? When will Bedros attack?"

"I don't know exactly when, but the prophecy has already been set into motion. The war that will determine the fate of our world is approaching. You already know what will happen next."

"The Griffin Vales." The next realm to fall under the heels of Bedros's army during the War of the Gods.

Valentina nodded. "The Chosen Ones will find their magical objects, just as your sister did."

How? And when? Would there be more magical books? Self-drawing maps? Temple ruins buried by the Order?

"Do not worry or be afraid, Seraphina," Valentina said, breaking through the spiral of worried thoughts. "You were chosen by Macario, too".

"For what?"

"To be the Sacred Sister that will guide all the Chosen Ones. They will need you more than you could ever know."

Seraphina smiled at her. "Thank you. May Macario continue to keep you."

Valentina nodded, lying back down in her bed. Seraphina swung open the door, charging down the hallway. The golden lights flittered as the walls shuddered. The wall in front of her pulled apart, flooding the hallway with the roars and rumbles of destruction happening on the other side.

And, by Macario's light, it was destructive.

She reached the wall's edge and gasped. The vast room was just a sea of rock and dust, the bookshelves gone. Sunlight streamed through the large holes in the back wall.

"Seraphina!"

Luis was just as handsome and alive as when she'd left him, albeit covered in dirt, climbing the pile of rocks toward her. Mari was struggling behind him, holding her shoulder.

She's hurt, but alive. I wasn't too late.

Seraphina jumped down, almost slipping on the rubble. While Luis seemed to glide from rock to rock, she felt like a child, taking more time to steady herself before climbing down the next stone. So, he made it to her first, grabbing her arms to keep her from falling.

They were a breath away from each other. His eyes searched hers, and she could feel herself blushing.

"Are you all right?" He spoke just loud enough for her to hear.

"I'm more than okay." She grinned, and his smile was as bright as hers. She took his arm, and he guided her the rest of the way to Mari. Seraphina gasped at the pirate's blood-soaked shoulder.

"I'm fine," Mari said. "Just tell me you found what we needed, and I didn't get stabbed for nothing."

Stabbed? "Yes, but it was not what I ever expected."

The room roared louder, the back ceiling of the library caving in. Seraphina hooked her arm around Mari's. Luis led the way to the opening in the back wall. She kept her focus on the blinding sunlight, ignoring the shards of stone scraping her ankles or the throbbing in her knees from trying to hold her balance. They reached the opening and they picked up the pace. Seraphina's foot caught on a stone, and they all tumbled into the light.

She landed on her stomach, the roaring of the library stifled. The blades of grass felt soft and comforting against her face. The song of birds and roaring water prompted her eyes to flutter open. She pushed herself up.

Mari lay next to her, rolling over on her back, pain taking over her face. Luis was already on his feet, staring out at the waterfall a few feet ahead.

The waterfall!

The scent of palm fruit filled her nose as she rose to her feet. She extended a hand to Mari, and she took it, yelling in pain as Seraphina pulled her up.

"We're right back where we started," Luis said.

Mari turned at the sound of his voice.

Yes, we are. They were back at the place where they all should've died when they fell off that cliff. Where the library opening was supposed to be, there was now a winding path of grass, lined by a few sparse trees and thick bushes.

They were back on the main island. Seraphina and Mari were back to being wanted fugitives. Luis was back to being the Order captain who was to bring them in. Would what they just experienced, witnessed, and survived be enough? Enough to change the tide, change Luis's mind?

He turned away from the waterfall and walked over to them.

"What did you find in the vault?"

Seraphina skipped the part where the immortal Sacred Sister tried to kill her when she entered, and just got to the important pieces of information. As she recounted it, Luis's face didn't twitch. Mari kept her same steely look, wincing occasionally at her shoulder.

When she was done, the awkward silence between all three of them was stifling. Mari didn't even break it with a sarcastic remark.

The distant sound of hooves coming from the path snapped them out of their thoughts. Luis looked down the path before turning back to them.

"We've got to hide," Luis said, jerking his head to the nearby undergrowth.

"We?" Mari's eyes narrowed.

"Yes." He glanced down at Seraphina. "All of us."

CHAPTER 41

LUIS

Sharp twigs poked at Luis's dirty shirt as he crouched behind the bushes with Mari and Seraphina. He heard horses and was positive they were his men scouring the forests for the bodies of the women next to him.

Or his.

That's what he would do. He was also certain that he didn't want to be found. Not yet. Not until he sorted out all the feelings of guilt and loyalty twisting around in his gut.

Through the small gaps in the bushes, he made out three horses, the dark black boots of their riders gleaming in the sun. They came to a slow stop, a mere foot away from their hiding spot.

"Sir, our men have scoured these forests for the last three days," a man with a deep voice said. "The other search party went downstream and found nothing."

"One of the most prestigious captains of our Order deserves a proper burial."

Jaime Ruiz's voice quivered on that last word. Luis's stomach lurched.

They think I'm dead.

And why wouldn't they? No one could survive that fall. Not without magic anyway.

But only he and the two pirates at his side knew that. If Luis told his first mate what had happened, he would brand him crazy. Turned. Manipulated by the wiles of pirates.

The same thing you thought about Seraphina.

And then what? This prestigious Order captain would become a criminal rotting in a cell as more monsters and evil armies ravaged their shores. He would die a coward because he did nothing to stop it.

Would that be worse than donning a uniform and pretending nothing happened? Claim the two pirates were dead and he miraculously survived with nothing more than a few scratches.

How would he explain it? The truth would always find a way out. The image of himself shuddering in a dark cell flashed back in his mind.

"Sir, the Pontiff—" a third man insisted, breaking Luis's thoughts.

"I know," Ruiz snapped. "But he can't have just vanished!"

A horse neighed in the distance.

"Send one more party downstream, as far as the river goes. The rest will return to Saranzas with me."

Luis crouched, frozen in place, long after the sound of their horses faded away. Seraphina knelt over Mari, tying a cloth around the pirate captain's injured arm to stop the bleeding. She helped her to her feet.

"We need to get that cleaned," she said.

Mari's eyes narrowed at him. "And we need to have a conversation."

Yes, we do. Luis nodded and the three of them walked over the river. Mari was barely seated on the ground before she launched into her interrogation.

"You didn't turn us in. Why?"

For the sake of sparing them his rambling thoughts and possible scenarios, he gave the simple answer.

"It wasn't the right thing to do."

Seraphina fought a smile, dipping a ripped rag in the water. "I would've been concerned if you didn't believe me after everything."

He more than believed her, but that wasn't a conversation for Mari's ears. "I wish there had been an easier way to convince me."

"But it makes it easy, since they think you're dead." Mari shrugged. "Hard to explain why you're not without sounding crazy."

No matter how much the pirate captain grew on him, he wasn't going to give her the satisfaction of telling her she was right.

"So, what happens now?" Seraphina said, swiping the rag over the pirate captain's injury.

"I get my crew back," Mari said, wincing and speaking through her teeth.

"I'll help you." Luis cleared his throat. "And whatever else I can do to stop this evil army from coming here."

Mari raised a brow, nodding.

He was planning to help the very people he'd intended to hang.

I'm not an Order soldier anymore. The idea stung his heart so much he had to look away, focusing on the awe and splendor of the waterfall.

What would his brother have thought of him? What would he say if he saw him throwing away everything he'd worked so hard for?

Being a captain was everything he'd ever wanted.

Until Guillermo died.

Then, all he'd wanted was to find the person who killed his brother. To this day he didn't know who it was, but in the scheme of things it was unimportant. A war for the very heart and fabric of their world was coming. Seraphina, Samara, and all the others chosen by Macario would need all the help they could get.

The uniform doesn't make the man.

It was like his brother was standing right next to him. Luis knew how to free Mari's crew and the safest route to escape to the Griffin Vales. He'd been to that realm quite a few times as a sailor. Plus, he knew how to plan, and he knew how to fight.

In the end, he had sworn to protect the Majestic Isles with his life. He didn't need an Order uniform or a ship to do that.

He spun around, watching Seraphina helping Mari to her feet. Her wound looked better but still needed care to ward off infection.

I can help with that, too.

"You finished lounging around?"

Seraphina chuckled. "Are you done trying to talk yourself out of helping me?"

He nodded at Mari's injury. "She won't get anywhere with that open wound. We'll find a place to hide until nightfall. Get that wound sealed up and move out at dusk. Jaime should be on the move with the others by then."

"Sounds like a plan, Captain," Mari smirked.

"Of course it does, Captain."

***

Mari bit down on the leather strap of Seraphina's quiver so hard Luis thought it would break. Luis pressed the hot blade of Mari's dagger into her shoulder, searing her flesh, the frayed edges of skin around the wound blistering. Seraphina sat close to her, the campfire casting glows on her worried face as Luis pulled the dagger away.

Mari tore the strap from her mouth. She threw it to the ground with her good hand before wiping a tear from the corner of her eye.

"How do you feel?" Seraphina asked.

"Like I've been seared with a bloody hot dagger." Mari struggled to her feet, turning her back to them. He'd seen men scream and cry out in pain, but Mari did neither. This couldn't be her first time.

"I need to walk," she said. "Get my mind off this bloody shoulder."

Mari strolled away from the light of the fire and into the shadowy trees that surrounded their hiding spot. Seraphina wrung her hands, her face still worried.

"She's a tough one," Luis said. "She'll be all right."

Seraphina's face softened, and she gave him a beautiful smile. "You're right."

He returned the smile, and her eyes went to the fire, her skin flushed. This was the first time he didn't feel guilty for feeling something other than remorse, hurt, or grief since his brother died.

As he stared at her across the fire, he allowed himself to see her for what she truly was. A strong, brave, and faithful woman who wasn't afraid to fight for what she believed in, no matter what others thought. How wonderful it must be, to be one's true, authentic self, outside of what others expected.

"So, did you mean what you said?" She looked up, her eyes peeking over the flames. "That you'll help us defeat the man who now has Bedros's magic?"

"Of course. I'm a man of my word."

He had no idea what that would entail, what he would have to face or fight, or where that journey would take him. But, as he looked at Seraphina, a woman who had grabbed his heart before he even realized it, he knew he could face whatever came his way.

"That would mean becoming a pirate, so to speak." An amused smile crossed her lips.

Oh, brother, would you ever have believed I would have to become a pirate to save the world?

"If this is the path Macario has set out for me, then who am I to question it?"

She laughed, pushing a few loose strands of hair behind her ear. "That is easier said than done. Trust me, I would know."

"As long as you're around to help me, I'm pretty sure I can manage."

Manage being on a crew he chained up and sent to work on Tradesman Harbor?

That was a hurdle she knew nothing about. *And I'm not going to worry about that tonight.*

For now, he would enjoy the company of the wonderful woman sitting across from him.

"So, tell me, what was it like at the seminary?"

Her eyes twinkled. "What do you want to know?"

He couldn't help but smile. "Everything."

CHAPTER 42

MARI

The salt in the air and the sound of crashing waves didn't ease Mari's nerves. They approached the familiar shores just a few clicks south of Lucïa. The same shore where Fozo's ship had docked when he captured her and her crew.

Donning drab hats and bandanas, they blended in with the flurry of sailors scurrying around like boat mice. Hauling ropes. Rolling barrels. Carrying packages. Rowing their boats back to shore.

Things her men would do if they weren't prisoners.

She looked out toward the sea, ships of all sizes clustered together, making it hard to see the setting sun on the horizon.

Was her ship one of them? Did they tear her down for parts? Sink her to the bottom of the sea? Her stomach knotted at the thought, but she dropped her eyes and pulled down the brim of the hat.

The last of the sun's rays faded away. The stars had started to pop into the sky when they reached the edge of what was left of Tradesman Harbor. A wide wooden pier went halfway up the miles-long shoreline.

The moon broke from the clouds, shining on the tall mounds of rock that dotted the sandy beach. They darted behind one, then another, making their way closer to the line of torches further up the beach.

The wall that separated the town of Aridia from the harbor used to be there. A slight smile came across Mari's face at the memory of the last time she was there.

They'd just gotten the last piece of the map to the scepter. Baz put together the right ruse to get them through, which included putting Samara in a fish barrel. *She was pretty pissed.*

They were almost there, ducking behind the last mound just a few yards ahead of a winding dirt path.

"Where are they?" Mari whispered, wincing as she held her sore shoulder.

Luis nodded to the line of torches. "The worker houses are just beyond there. That's where they'll be."

Mari gestured at the dunes. "How many workhouses?"

"At least twenty."

"Guards?"

"Two on the path, and three posted at each guardhouse."

Seraphina scrunched her nose. "Those are too many guards and too many houses to check."

Luis shook his head, a look of confidence on his face. "Your crew would be the farthest one down the beach, by the Sima bluff."

Mari shook her head. "I'm not scaling a cliff."

"Then I hope your knife skills are as good as your sarcasm," Luis said. "Because we're going to have to go the long way." He drew his sword, and Mari pulled a dagger from her waist belt.

At least I get to fight people this time

Seraphina pulled the cloth from her shoulder, revealing her bow and quiver. She readied an arrow, mumbling a prayer, and it glowed.

"Lead the way, Captain Fozo," she said, and they started for the path.

No matter how careful their footsteps, the sand still crunched under their feet. The two guards posted at the top of the path spun around toward them. Mari flung her dagger, and by the time it lodged in the first guard's throat, she launched the other.

It hit the second guard in the chest, and his body fell to the ground. Mari's shoulder screamed in protest, but she couldn't let it stop her. She retrieved her daggers before following behind Luis, who was already heading down the side path.

The rotting wood barely held the massive houses together. The image of her men penned up in one of those like animals made Mari bite her lip. But they stayed in the shadows of the wooden cells, sliding from one to the other.

They had almost cleared the fifth one when a guard stepped out onto the side path. He gaped at Seraphina's glowing bow. Before he could utter a sound, Luis swooped in, pulling the guard into the shadows. He slammed the guard against the wall, using the butt of his sword to knock the guard unconscious.

They stepped over the guard's body, picking up the pace. A few unconscious guards later, plus a handful of dead ones thanks to Mari, they reached the last house. It sat a few feet away from the bluff in a makeshift clearing. Instead of three guards, there were four, two posted on each side of the massive double doors.

"I can take out the first two," Luis whispered.

"I'm not taking my chances with you clubbing them to sleep," Mari snapped. "I can take the closest two. Seraphina, you take out the others. And please, don't miss."

Seraphina swallowed hard as Luis stepped aside to let Mari get closer. Before she could let the anger burning in her gut cloud her aim, she launched her daggers. By the time the second soldier fell, the other two had raised their swords.

Seraphina stepped out into the lantern light, her bow glowing with fierce magic. She let an arrow fly, catching one guard in his thigh. He fell forward, screaming in pain. She nocked another and let it go, hitting the fourth guard in his shoulder.

Luis rushed out from behind her, rendering them both unconscious.

"I told you not to miss!" Mari hissed. Seraphina turned and looked her dead in the eye.

"I didn't. This bow is a gift, and I won't kill anyone with it."

You may feel differently when that army of evil magic people is coming at you.

Mari left her to join Luis, who was fumbling around in the guards' pockets. He pulled out a set of keys, and Mari snatched it out of his hand. She plunged it into the giant padlock on the door. It opened with a loud click, and Seraphina threw open the doors.

Damn Order rats.

The hard floor was covered with men, rags hanging off their frail bodies. Chains rattled as some turned to look at the door.

"Amrit! Brody! Ghad!" Mari grabbed the lantern off the wall to illuminate her face.

After the most uncomfortable minute of silence, a voice said, "It's about bloody time you got here, Captain!"

Amrit stood in the middle of the sea of men. What was left of his shirt hung off his body, his stringy black hair a horrible mess. But he was alive, and dammit that was all that mattered.

"Captain!" Brody rose to his feet in the far corner of the room.

"Awaiting orders, Captain." Ghad struggled to stand at the other side of the room.

Luis stepped inside as Mari used a key to undo the lock on the ground. Once it clicked open, Luis pulled out the long chain. That was when everyone else was able to stand, about forty men in all.

Amrit pushed his way to the front, stopping mere inches from her.

"It's great to see you, Captain."

"You're a sight for sore eyes, boatswain," was all she could say without sounding like an idiot. His eyes met Seraphina's, and he gave her a friendly nod. Then he found Luis, and that carpenter's fury burned in his eyes.

"Save that energy for those soldiers out there," Mari said, placing her hand on his chest. "He's one of us now."

He gave Luis one more death glare before looking back at Mari. "Aye, Captain. So how are we getting out of here?"

CHAPTER 43

SERAPHINA

Seraphina fought the nervousness tightening up her chest. Mari's plan sounded great, in theory. But if she'd learned anything in her time with them, plans always had a nasty way of going wrong.

But Mari was confident and stubborn. Nothing was going to change her mind about it. Frankly, with everything coming their way, they would need all the confidence they could get.

So, I will do my part.

The chains that once kept them prisoner were lifelines, the ropes that would get them away from the camp and on the beach. Brody and two other men got to work, using rocks to pound the pins that would hold their chains in place.

"Fancy bow and arrow you got there, sister," he mentioned before another powerful hammer blow pushed the pin into place. "Looks like all that prayin' paid off for you."

He gave her a smile, the bruise over his right eye purple and swollen.

"In more ways than one," she said. "I prayed that you all would be safe, and you are."

Brody gave her shoulder a light squeeze before giving a faint whistle. The men left in the workhouse began to pour out in a single file. Like ants on sugar cane bark, they marched to the chain link and worked their way down.

"Hey! Stop!"

A guard was running down the side path, sword raised.

Praise Macario, I only mean to wound him.

She nocked an arrow and it soared through the air, grazing the man on his side. He flew backward, hitting the ground hard. Another guard was coming up behind him. Her next arrow landed in his shoulder.

Mari and Luis freed another house, but when Seraphina saw them both running towards her, she knew this plan was unraveling.

"Brody, get down to the beach. Now." Seraphina sent another arrow sailing into a guard's knee, sending him tumbling down with the others.

He nodded and disappeared over the cliff, while Seraphina's eyes remained trained on the trio of guards coming at her now. *They will not stop coming!*

The soldiers pushed past the lanterns to get around the Order soldiers moaning in pain on top of each other.

The lanterns!

She set her aim on the torches and let the arrows fly. One by one, the standing lanterns fell to the ground, their flames landing on the rotting wood of the nearby workhouse. The flames danced on the side of the building and down the torch itself, creating a wall of fire. It deterred those men from running any further, but she wasn't sure how long that would last. Another group of men was running toward the bluff, Luis coming up behind them. He stopped when he saw the fire.

"I'm impressed," he said, turning back.

"Eh, lucky shot," Mari countered with a smirk.

Seraphina smiled and shouldered her bow. The chain link was warm against her hands as she lowered herself down over the bluff. It was just as high as she'd thought.

But you survived a rickety bridge over a sea of absolute death. You can handle this.

She shimmied her way down, relief washing over her as her feet hit the sandy beach below. Luis and Mari were right behind her, the full moonlight shining on the sea of men heading down the shore.

"Let's go!" Luis cried, and they all took off running.

The sea breeze blowing through her hair, the sand under her feet, the crashing of the waves. It felt oddly soothing. Could it be that they were running from actual men and not monsters? Or that they were closer to getting to Samara? They rounded the cluster of trees and the cove where the *Pursuer* came into view.

And so did the soldiers guarding it. Seraphina came to a stop, taking the bow off her shoulder.

Praises to Macario, my light in the darkness…

The bow shone as if she held the sun. The soldiers were beating the freed men to the ground, swarming like locusts in a field.

Guide my hand so I might guide others in your name.

With her feet planted in the ground, she let the arrows go, one after another after another.

A guard fell.

Then another.

A few more, until they realized it was her from fifty yards away. The rest turned and ran. Luis stood next to her, wide-eyed, as Seraphina lowered her bow.

"You never cease to amaze me," he said, taking her hand.

They ran down to the beach, their rowboats already onshore, ready for whatever trouble came their way.

And that trouble arrived precisely on time.

Order men on horses emerged from the tree line, moonlight gleaming on their swords. Luis saw it too. When they turned to each other, they didn't have to say a word.

They knew what they had to do.

CHAPTER 44

LUIS

Seraphina didn't waste time, shooting her arrows at the oncoming soldiers bursting through the tree line to swarm the beach. Luis pulled his sword out of his makeshift sheath.

They may have been your comrades once, but you have to do what must be done to survive.

The fate of the world was at stake, and the only ones that could help save it were on that beach. There was no time to explain. Only to fight.

Mari and her pirate companion came up alongside him.

"Fancy seeing you here, Fozo," Mari said with a slight smirk.

"Someone has to save your ass," he said. Seraphina aimed at the horses, forcing the men to dismount.

Clever girl.

His heart ached as he fought the first one, their swords clashing twice before he rammed his blade into the soldier's gut.

"May you find peace, brother," he said, pulling it out. The brown-skinned pirate was right behind him, swiping the soldier's fallen sword for his own.

A part of Luis wished these officers weren't so ill-trained. The second one he killed barely lifted his sword before Luis ran him through. The third put up a bit of a fight, but when he left his right rib cage exposed, Luis had to make the best of it. He surprised the fourth man, stabbing him in the back before he could kill Seraphina.

The way she looked at him, eyes soft and full of understanding, his guilt gnawed at him even more. Two more men charged forward. One of her arrows struck one in the shoulder, knocking him backward. The second Luis took care of with two swings of his sword.

But it wasn't enough. There were just too many to fight on their own.

Mari fought off a man with her good arm, but she staggered. Luis ran in, going in with the final blow to the throat. The soldier's body sank to the sand, joining the twelve other bodies on the beach. Seraphina and the brown-skinned pirate ran to them, the air rank with humidity and death. The second line of soldiers was already hitting the dunes, and Luis shook his head.

"It's too many. We have to go."

"We can take on those bastards!" the brown-skinned pirate cried, and Mari laid a hand on his arm.

"Luis is right," she said. "We live to fight another day."

Seraphina took his arm. "Let's go before anyone else here has to die tonight."

He nodded, and they hurried to the rowboat. As they rowed back to the ship, the men in the boat cursed and jeered, high off the energy of the fight. Mari gave Luis and Seraphina a nod of approval. Her companion, however, just glared at him.

Luis knew he deserved every bit of it.

"What are we going to do with him?"

The pirate's question brought all conversation on the small boat to an abrupt halt.

"Nothing, Amrit," Seraphina said. "None of us would be here right now if it weren't for him."

"We wouldn't even be here in the first place if it wasn't for him!" Amrit's eyes flared.

When he made the choice to help save the world, he had also made the choice to accept all the challenges that came along with it.

That didn't unnerve him. His stomach was already sick from the fight on the beach. He looked to Captain Mari, a woman he had learned to trust because how she operated was not that different from him.

She never betrayed her values.

She always did what was right, even if she didn't like it.

"Luis Fozo is a member of this crew," she declared. "Anyone who lays a hand on him will be swimming back to shore."

She turned back to her ship, the worn hull drawing closer. Amrit shot Luis a glance before doing the same. Seraphina gave his hand a squeeze. He wished it made his nerves still. Instead, his muscles tensed, his eyes scanning the boat for any sudden movements. The men were quiet until they docked with the pirate ship. Luis lingered back so he was one of the last men to board.

The cheers and shouts were deafening by the time he boarded, the men crowded together around the mainmast. He could barely hear the anchor coming up or the unfurled sails flapping in the wind. By the time Mari emerged from the crowd, they were already sailing west, away from the carnage in the cove.

She stood on the top stair of the upper deck, snatching off the hat she wore as a disguise back on the mainland. She raised her hand, and the crowd quieted.

"Well, you all look like shit," she said with a slight smile, and the crew erupted in laughter.

"I'm not big on speeches or saying things that will make you feel good about yourselves, so listen up. To my old crew, I'm bloody happy to see you lot are okay and held on. These newbies will need you for what we're facing next. If you thought sea serpents were bad, things are gonna get a whole lot worse."

She crossed her arms, her face stern and confident. Seraphina pushed her way to the front, locking eyes with Mari briefly.

"If you're not up for a high seas adventure, I want you off my ship when we dock. Everyone else? You'll await my further instruction. To your stations!"

The men scrambled. Luis had never felt more exposed. He pulled down the scarf around his head and kept his eyes low to the ground as he approached the upper deck. The captain was still there, speaking to a tall and rather broad-shouldered pirate. That pirate saw him first, and his brawny hand reached out to grab Luis by his shirt.

"Where do you think you're going—" The man's small, beady eyes narrowed. "Captain, it's the— "

Captain Mari raised a hand. "Don't touch him!" she barked.

She looked at Luis and then her crewman. "He's your new boatswain."

CHAPTER 45

MARI

Mari wished she could get a moment alone in her quarters before resuming her post as captain. Those Order rats had made a mess of things. Her desk was turned over, drawers smashed to bits. Parchment covered the ground with no rhyme or reason.

It would take her forever to clean this up.

And the bed, the one place she was looking forward to lying in after weeks of sleeping on hard ground, was bare. Those bastards took the bedding, leaving just a wood slab by the wall.

And all I wanted to do was lie down!

She held her head in her hands, her temples throbbing like it had ever since she made Luis her new boatswain. Surely Amrit would've found out by now, and he wouldn't be happy.

Still. She'd been expecting to lie in a comfortable bed while figuring out exactly what she would say.

The door flew open and Amrit came rushing in. Mari spun around as he closed it behind him and walked up to her. They were just inches apart. The closest he'd ever gotten to her that didn't involve sword fighting or setting fires to an Order work camp.

He had a faint scar over his left eye. Those notorious lined eyes were faint, like all that hard work and sweat had washed it away. But his bare arms had a lot more muscle, his skin a richer brown color. She raised her chin.

"What do you want, Amrit?" Her voice was softer than she intended.

"When was I going to be informed that an Order rat was taking over my job on this ship?"

Mari stepped back. "You have every right to be pissed off. Should've talked to you first."

He opened his mouth to speak but shut it again, his eyes searching the room a bit. He took a breath. "So what happens to me?"

Mari found her chair propped up against the cracked window at the far side of the room. She put it upright and sank into it.

"You will support your captain as her first mate." She dared to give him a smirk.

He opened up his mouth, probably to say something smart, but stopped, as if her words had finally caught up to his ears. He walked around the fallen desk and stood over her.

"No."

She jumped up. "What do you mean, no?"

"You won't make me first mate out of pity."

"Pity?"

"Or to ease your guilty conscience."

"Guilt has nothing to do with it."

"Then why? Why right now?"

"Because you're one of the few people I can trust."

"Never stopped you before."

"I was never trapped in a cursed jungle before." *Dammit!* Feelings. Captain Mari didn't do feelings. But they were there, all warm in her gut as the person she considered a dear friend stood before her getting what he always deserved.

"I need you if we're going to survive the end of the world."

He raised a brow. "Since you put in that way, I'll be your first mate." He took half a step back. "Only because it gives me license to ask why the Order captain that locked us away in the first place is our boatswain and not drowning in the ocean."

She sat back in her chair. She gestured to what was left of the bed, and he sat down. Except for the occasional twitch of his narrow jaw, his eyes remained steady on her.

Mari recounted what happened from the time they docked outside of Tradesman Harbor to escaping the collapsing library. Mari didn't spare any details about the giant snakes, plants, harpies, or sirens they battled along the way. She told him all the times Fozo could've killed her, but didn't, even after she told him it was their crew that killed his brother that night on Bluegate.

She ignored the fact that it still felt weird believing that Fozo was a big part of this prophecy thing, because she didn't understand it. But she didn't want to find out the hard way.

"I won't be Derklan," Amrit said when she finished. The image of the traitor that killed Jules sent fire through her veins. "Just because I'm not crazy about my captain's decision doesn't mean I won't abide by it. But if that Order rat is going to be on this ship, he has to prove himself to me before I can ever trust him."

Mari nodded. "Fair enough."

She'd expected nothing less.

"And I will deal with him on the ship my way."

"No shoving hammers down his throat."

"You're no fun."

They both smiled, and Mari leaned back in the chair, savoring this moment.

Amrit rose from the bed. "I have a lot of work to do, Captain."

"You sure do, first mate."

He made for the door, stopping short of reaching for the handle. "Before I go, there's something else you need to clear up for me."

She raised a brow as he turned around.

"You expect me to believe you killed two sirens—underwater?"

How I missed that sass. "Have you ever known me to exaggerate?"

He flashed a smile and pulled open the door.

"Just one more thing."

Amrit crossed his arms, raising his brow.

"Fozo knows how to run a ship and he knows how to keep men in line. Use that."

Amrit rolled his eyes. "You never make anything easy, do you?"

"Of course not. Pirates never do."

CHAPTER 46

LUIS

I'm the boatswain of the infamous pirate ship I was tasked with capturing.

Luis rubbed his temples as he sat across from Mari in her quarters. The modest chandelier above them swayed with the ship, the creaking of the rusted chain that held it up unnervingly loud. The pirate captain sat back in her chair, her worn boots propped up on the desk as she stared at the door behind him.

What he wouldn't give to shut his eyes for a few hours. Process exactly how his entire life was turned upside down since he fell into that cursed jungle. Get comfortable with the fact that he had to become a pirate in order to save the world from the dark and evil god his faith taught him to fear.

Yet here he was sitting in the captain's quarters his old crew tossed but a few weeks earlier.

"The hour is late," he said finally. "Can we just get started—"

"No. Not until everyone gets here. I hate having to repeat myself."

A breath later the door swung open, and Luis jumped to his feet. Amrit, the brown-skinned pirate who fought with them on the beach but a few hours ago, charged through the door. The silly smile on his face quickly soured.

"Why is he here?" The pirate's eyes narrowed as he took careful steps toward the far side of the room.

"I apologize for being late!" Seraphina rushed through the doorway, and Luis's shoulders softened.

She held up the leather pouch in her hand. "Unfortunately those secondary sails won't mend themselves." She shot Luis a nervous smile, and he suddenly didn't feel so tired.

"Shut the door," Mari commanded as she took her feet off her desk.

Seraphina quickly complied as the pirate captain rose from her chair. She shuffled through the mess of papers on her desk before settling on a long, rolled up piece of parchment. They all gathered around her desk, Seraphina's arm brushing up against his. He locked eyes with her for a glorious moment before returning his attention to Mari and the map rolled out before them. It had been a long while since he'd seen a full map of Magia and its five realms. The Griffin Vales to the north. The Godswood in the west. The Winter Tide in the northernmost edge of the world. The Crystal Savannah just as far west as its desolate sands were barren.

"We need to figure out how we find these chosen ones and stop the end of the world." Mari leaned on the desk, intentionally looking at everyone in the room as if waiting for one of them to speak.

Luis cleared his throat. "We can't sail anywhere with the ship in this condition."

Mari raised a brow. "So what's your plan, boatswain?"

"We can get the best supplies when we dock in the Griffin Vales. I know a former Order soldier stationed there who owes me a favor." It was more like a trunk full of Macarian coins. After his former comrade was caught sleeping on his post for the third time, Luis was able to get the man an honorable discharge and enough severance to start his life over.

"And I'm sure you'll make the proper assessments before we blow the little money we have on supplies?" Amrit glared at him from the other side of the desk.

"But of course," Luis replied.

"He can handle it, Amrit," Mari added, but his face remained taut.

"We can have the best supplies, but our crew is crap," Amrit countered. "It'll take me forever to train these new grunts."

"Luckily you won't have to do it alone." Mari glanced over at Luis. "And I'll need you to do some other things for me."

Amrit gritted his teeth. "Aye, Captain. Like what?"

Mari didn't flinch. "Charting our course to the Griffin Vales and the Winter Tide for a start." She pointed to the Griffin Vales. "Then I need you to captain this ship while the nun and I go after Samara and Blackwater."

Blackwater? The pirate who knew what happened to his brother on Bluegate? Did Luis even want to know? Run the risk of distracting himself from the bigger issue at hand?

Seraphina's voice broke through his thoughts. "How will we find them?"

"Fozo isn't the only one who has someone in the Griffin Vales who owes them a favor," Mari replied.

Amrit huffed. "Please don't tell me—"

Mari straightened. "We don't have a choice."

"Do I even want to know who this man is?" Seraphina looked from Amrit to Mari.

"No!" Mari and Amrit answered in unison.

Seraphina held up her hands in surrender.

"Last but not least." Mari turned to Seraphina. "By the time we reach the Griffin Vales, you will have taught me everything I need to know about the magic and monsters we're going to run into."

Seraphina clasped her hands, a bright smile across her face. Luis had to smile too. The thought of Mari, a crass pirate, becoming a student of his faith was just utterly ridiculous. But the pirate captain kept that stern stare, signaling that she would indeed take it seriously.

"It would be an honor ,Captain," Seraphina sang, and Mari gave her a nod.

"Now that you kiddies know what to do, clear out of my quarters so I can get some sleep." Mari waved them off as they filed out one by one. Luis was the last to leave, rushing to keep up with Amrit, who was already charging for the lower deck steps.

"Can I have a word, Amrit?"

The pirate stopped and slowly turned around, the lantern light illuminating his angry eyes.

"I can understand that working together can be difficult—"

Amrit held up his hand. "Difficult is having an Order rat infesting my ship."

Luis straightened his stance as Amrit took a step forward. "Out of respect for the captain, I'll let that crass remark slide. Whether you like it or not, we have to work together."

"Out of respect for the captain, I'm not throwing you overboard right now." Amrit crossed his arms. "Plus the fact I like a world without monsters."

"Then let's be civil."

"This is me being civil."

The creaking of the ship and the crashing of the dark waves filled the tense sliver of silence between them. Magia wasn't built in a day and getting this pirate to trust him would take a century from the looks of it.

But there was no time for that. The world was in danger. Seraphina and her sister needed all the help they could get.

"If you do your job and I do mine, we'll get along just fine." With that, Luis turned on his heel, opting to take the long way to his quarters below decks.

"We'll see about that!" Amrit called out, his voice getting lost in the furious flapping of the sails.

CHAPTER 47

SERAPHINA

Seraphina didn't need the banging of pots to get her up and out of her hammock that morning. She tiptoed past the groggy pirates and ran up the deck steps by twos.

The ship swayed under her feet, the morning sun feeling glorious on her skin. The air smelled more salty than sweet, the squawking of the gulls overhead the only other familiar thing besides the ship. She ducked by the few pirates scrubbing the decks to the port side of the ship.

Ocean.

Miles and miles of crystal blue water in every direction. It was official. This was the farthest away she'd traveled in her entire life. Her callused hands grabbed the banister, taking in the magnificent waters Macario had created.

No wonder her sister loved being out here.

She felt so important, yet so humbled at the same time. Blessed to be alive to breathe in this pure, untouched air, yet humbled that just as the sea could give life, it could take it away.

But not today. She could feel it. The sense of adventure. The excitement of the unknown. She took in another deep breath of the sea air, closing her eyes to feel the breeze on her face.

The loud clanging of pots ripped through the tranquility of the morning. Luis banged the metal spoon on a dented saucepan as he led a line of sleepy sailors up the stairs and onto the center deck.

"No time for sleeping! This ship needs to be in order!"

The men groaned, prompting Luis to bang even louder. She backed away from the railing, taking the long way to her station on the other side of the ship. She still had a secondary sail to sew, the material slashed to pieces from the storms that almost swallowed the ship all those weeks ago.

The material was right where she left it, bunched up in the corner between the water barrels and the banister.

"Good morning, sailor!"

Seraphina whirled around to see the handsome boatswain walking toward her. While his hair had grown a bit since they first met, it was neatly slicked behind his ears. His face was clean-shaven, though she could see the small sliver of pink skin where he nicked himself on his chin. Despite the dingy white shirt and loose brown pants, he still stood tall and proud like an Order soldier.

"You're up bright and early," he said, putting the pot and spoon down on the rickety deck.

"I prefer to wake up to the sound of the sea and not the banging of that dreaded pot!"

He matched her nervous laugh as he drew closer to her. He leaned on the banister.

"I can't argue with that. I was afraid I'd kept you up with all of the boring stories of my childhood in a Yaton orphanage."

Seraphina furiously shook her head. She hung on every minute detail of his childhood life. Just when they thought their nightly talks couldn't yield any more amazing information about him, she learned something wonderfully new about him.

"I love talking to you." She didn't even realize her hand was on his forearm until he placed his warm palm over it.

"I love spending time with you."

As much as her heart clanged in her chest, she couldn't look away from those beautiful eyes that searched hers. She wanted to say something. Tell him how she felt.

But what did she feel?

Infatuation? Love? A connection of the soul?

Well, just stand here and smile like an idiot until you figure it out, Seraphina.

"Rafti is making his famous stew tonight," Luis said, breaking the nerve-wracking silence. "Will you dine with me on the forecastle deck? We should have a beautiful view of the moon from there."

"Are you…I mean….is this a…" For the life of her she couldn't formulate a simple sentence.

His smile grew wider. "Is that the seminary way of saying yes?"

Seraphina laughed much too loudly before shaking her head. "Yes."

"Wonderful. I'll see you then." He took her hand, planting a gentle kiss on her knuckles. She was pretty sure she melted straight through the deck floor while grinning so hard her face hurt, even long after he left to tend to the crew. The sails she had to sew just looked like a fluffy cloud, her body feeling like it was floating over the ship. She touched her hand, not wanting the warm sensation to fade.

"Ahem!"

Seraphina spun around. Mari leaned on the wooden railing, her coppery red dreads tied away from her face. She shook her head, and Seraphina grabbed her cheeks to stop the blood from rushing to them.

"Good morning, Captain," Seraphina stammered.

Mari chuckled and gestured for her to join her.

"If you're acting like that from a peck on the hand, I hate to see what happens when he gets the nerve to kiss you," Mari said, staring out into the vast ocean.

I would float right off this ship. Seraphina leaned on the banister.

"When we arrive in the Griffin Vales, you need to have your wits about you."

When we reach the Griffin Vales. Seraphina nodded, the weight of going to a brand new realm bringing her crashing back down onto the ship.

"Knowing Baz, I have an idea of where he would go first," Mari continued. "But I need you to be on guard for whatever magical danger we may face when we get out there."

"You know I will, Captain," she said. "I just pray we won't have to face it alone."

Your sister and the scepter cannot do it alone. She must find the others gifted with the magic of the gods, just as she was.

The words Valentina had told her back in the secret library still haunted Seraphina. Every night since they left the main island, she prayed that her sister was all right.

The Majestic Isles weren't the only realm to face a monster during the War of the Gods. The Griffin Vales had its own demons. If it was anything like those she read about, they would need every ounce of magic and strength to face it.

But she kept that part to herself.

Mari already looked worried, her brows furrowing as the light outline of land came into view. She had to handle so much. A new crew. A mission she never planned on taking. Losing the crew members.

"We won't be doing anything alone," Mari said, a resilient strength in her voice. "Baz and Samara had enough time to gallivant all over the Vales."

Knowing Samara, she also had plenty of time to get into trouble. She missed her twin terribly.

Yet, Seraphina had changed so much. She wasn't the timid girl she left back in Bluegate. Not only did she learn to brave the world on her own, she could defend herself. Defend Mari and Luis, even.

She'd conquered her fear and did what Macario sent her to do. Her days at the seminary were a distant memory, but she had to draw on them, so they could be ready for what happened next.

The ship took a slight turn to the west, the wind fully catching its sails. Mari patted her on the shoulder and stood up straight.

"Let's go, Sacred Sister. We have work to do."

Acknowledgments

I started writing the Secret Library sitting in the hospital with my mom. She unexpectedly got sick and was in and out of the hospital for weeks at a time. Fear, anxiety, worry — all of those things were just zapping me and I needed a distraction. So sitting in that chair by her bed, I wrote a story with my favorite treasure-hunting nun braving a cursed jungle to find a secret library.

When I was feeling super frustrated with the contradicting reports from doctors, I let Mari be extra grumpy for me.

When I needed to be brave I leaned on my girl Seraphina to be that light in all the crazy.

And, especially when my mother passed and I needed to grieve, my loyal Order officer Luis was the one who could really voice what I was feeling.

This story holds a special place in my heart and I'm so happy you continued on this journey with me. And I want to thank Seraphina, Mari, and Luis for being the characters I need to get through a super tough time.

Thanks so much to my two little munchkins Aria and Maya. You two bring me so much joy and I get to bring that joy to the page. Mommy loves you two to pieces!

To my family Lidia, Pat and Annie, I'd be lost without our daily Facebook Messenger Group Chats! They give me so much life.

Katie, we did it again lady! You taught me it was okay to have fun with my stories and that you can never have too many monsters. You are forever my Editing Fairy (or the Uncle Iroh of Editing - your pick.)

To my beta readers Haylie, Kate, Brittany, and Sarah - your feedback gave this story the extra shine it needed. Plus you put a lot of my writer doubts to rest. I'm so grateful to you guys.

My Street Team - you ladies rock! Your support and excitement doesn't go unnoticed!

JOIN THE TRIBE!

To receive the latest news on Book Three of the Magian Series plus a free short story set in The Griffin Vales before the fated War of the Gods, click the link below and join the tribe!

https://dl.bookfunnel.com/smjb8s1h18

www.ingramcontent.com/pod-product-compliance
Lightning Source LLC
Chambersburg PA
CBHW050028180626
46810CB00002B/618